And the Devil Laughed

~

Carole Sutton

Published by New Generation Publishing
2009

*

And the Devil Laughed

Prologue

O ld Marty could have chosen a better day for his funeral. The gravedigger hawked and spat a gobbet of phlegm. He squatted against an old stone wall and sniffed the damp air. He turned his weary face upwards to check the progress of a threatening squall line. Fat drops of rain fell on his cheeks.

The warning on the radio that morning told of severe weather from the west approaching Sydney. It was coming in earlier than expected. He rolled his tobacco, lit up and let the weed dangle between his lips. He hoped to God they'd be finished in time. He shifted and sat, gangly arms looped around his legs – a bag of aching bones. Across the tombstones towards the church, he could see the funeral party on its way.

Reverend Timms led the procession along the narrow path, his balding head bowed to the wind, black and purple robes blown flat against his legs. The quartet of undertakers in maroon suits carried Old Marty in a coffin crowned with yellow roses. The widow, wrapped in a navy blue anorak, clutched the arm of her tall, angular sister. A few members of the Over 60s Club trailed along in their wake.

Large multi-coloured umbrellas mushroomed to shelter the mourners. The gravedigger sniffed again as the party stopped beside the hole he'd dug the night before. Brought up in an age when the predominant colour at funerals was black, the gaily-coloured golfing shades they used today struck a note of incongruity and turned his graveyard into a fairground. The billowing storm cloud burst. The

3

gravedigger lurched to his feet and stumbled to his shed.

Storm driven rain slanted in the wind, bounced off the ground. Ferocious gusts tore at the robust umbrellas, lifted the corners of the tarpaulin covering the loose earth and turned the soil into a running river of mud. Deep puddles formed at the base of the grave, shifting and resettling the dirt.

As the minister began his intonation, the first of the storm clouds passed. The sun found an avenue between the clouds. In the moment's respite, raindrops hung like splinters of glass from the surrounding bushes and trees. Freed from the umbrella's cover, the widow lifted her face to the sky to look at the expanding rainbow. Her tall sister took a step forward to peer into the waterlogged grave.

Her scream drove seagulls from the church roof into the air with raucous cries and brought the gravedigger back to the party. Reverend Timms jerked forward, his gaze following the agitated woman's pointed finger. Others bent to see.

There, in the dark wet pit, emerging from the muddied waters, they saw a human hand. Stark in its whiteness, washed by the rain, scarlet lacquer and bejewelled rings adorned the fingers. Runnels of water drained down the wrist and forearm as the water level dropped away. Only the tatty remnants of a thin blanket of soil remained to cover the naked, blue-tinged body of a young woman.

Straightening up, the minister met the gravedigger's eyes. Turning to the undertakers, he nodded for them to take up their burden once more. Then gently he shepherded the funeral party back to the church. The gravedigger returned to his shed. With someone else occupying his grave, Old Marty would have to wait awhile.

* * *

1

Monday lunchtime was busier than usual. Mac McKay, landlord of The Harbour Lights, felt his face burn as he ducked the questions thrown at him across the bar.

Brash young men and loud-mouthed women had invaded his old country pub. They filed in as though it was a city bar on Melbourne Cup day. Their media hype had caught him unprepared. He drew his breath in over his teeth as one thrust a microphone towards him and asked yet another question.

"Is it true Victoria Brown worked here as a barmaid?"

"I've nothing more to add," Mac said, waving their mikes away. He moved on without asking for their orders. The sooner they were gone the better.

The macabre details of the body found in the grave had drawn the media. It looked to Mac as though representatives from every TV channel and newspaper had descended on his pub to make a grab for the story.

Vicky Brown *had* been his barmaid. A young woman with a lively manner, whose friendly quips and earthy sense of humour ensured that most of the men adored her, while their women watched with narrowed eyes. Now, she lay on a slab in the mortuary, raped and dead. And some local bastard knew something about it.

On an average day, The Harbour Lights catered mainly for the locals and groups like the darts team, or the sailing club who partied in his old-fashioned dining room. Occasionally tourists found their way to Draper's Wharf, a small town on the banks of the Parramatta River, and stayed overnight. It wasn't rich pickings, as Mac knew well, but it got him by.

The overhead fans moved the blue, hazy air around in circles. Savoury smells of frying onions and grilling steak seeped in from the kitchen through the connecting door.

His eyes scanned the gathering, his actions robotic, as he served the customers pushing and jostling for position in front of the bar. Today, more residents than usual flowed in like a second tributary to mingle in a central pool. Did nobody care? The sound system lost its battle against the commotion. He turned it off; one less noise for his aching head.

The door opened yet again. A woman came in. She looked this way and that, as though not expecting such a crowd. Her eyes locked on his across the room and she made her way towards him. She held out a pair of dirty hands.

"I had a puncture, need to clean up," she explained. Her wet hair curled around her head like a nest of rats' tails. She raised a hand still further to scratch her scalp, seemingly oblivious to the black streaks she was leaving behind. Mac pointed the way to the Ladies, his face too stiff with sorrow to return much of a smile.

"Thanks. Got caught in that last downpour," she added, unnecessarily.

Another bloody reporter no doubt.

Short-staffed, he worked briskly, hard pushed to keep the beer flowing and the lunches taken to the tables in the dining area. The solid figure of Douglas McKay, in baggy jeans and casual shirt elbowed his way in.

Mac greeted his brother with relief. "Hey, Doug, what kept you?"

"Looks like you could use a hand around here mate." Douglas raised his eyebrows at the crush in front of the bar.

"The world's gone mad. Get in here and take over this end; I've got meals going cold!" A noisy group, laden with equipment, entered the lounge. Mac clenched his jaw to prevent his thoughts from taking to the air. Mrs Bates was so busy in the kitchen, trying to keep up with demand that she'd called her daughter in to help.

Doug lifted the counter flap and joined Mac behind the bar. A hefty six foot four, and built of well-worked muscle, Doug made his older brother, a lithe six-footer, appear slender by comparison. "Came over to see how you were doing, you know, after Vicky and everything, didn't reckon on this though. Where'd they all come from?"

"Don't ask me. Will you just listen to them; they can't get enough." Mac moved off to the far end of the bar, where the dining crowd bayed for attention, leaving his brother to cope with the public bar.

*

Doug slipped easily into the role of barman. He and Mac had grown up in this pub, and over the years, he'd spent a fair portion of his life on both sides of the bar. Trained as a diver he joined the water police in his early twenties. Now, at thirty-three, he led his own diving team. He loved the job and couldn't imagine doing anything else. However, helping Mac behind the bar on the odd occasion, came as naturally to him as helping his wife with the dishes.

Absorbing the clamour around him, he pulled a new jug of beer for his first customer. He paused, waiting for the foam to die down, before filling it further, acknowledging the regulars with a nod. There were even some faces from the nearby rival pub, The Crow's Nest. They normally only showed on a darts tournament night, like Friday – the night Vicky disappeared. Business had been humming that night, too, as Doug well knew. He'd covered for her when she supposedly went home sick.

"Is it always as busy as this?" A young reporter asked.

"Nah, I wouldn't say that," Doug replied. He pulled the man a beer and scooped his money off the bar-top. "I'd say there hasn't been so much interest in a death around here since the day Willie Draper hanged himself from the yardarm." He passed on the change, amused as the young man's head jerked up in anticipation.

Eventually the crowd thinned. Mac stood back and watched his pub empty as though someone had pulled the plug. Doug loaded the glass washer. A few of the regulars still banded together. Only one stranger lingered among the usual punters.

"Who's the blonde?" Doug asked Mac. She wasn't pretty in the conventional sense, but a handsome woman, their father would have called her. "Over there, the one hugging her drink like it was a teddy-bear."

"Thought she was one of them at first, but apart from ordering lunch, she hasn't said a word. She came in earlier looking for the loo. Went in looking like a drowned rat, came out freshly washed and dried, I hardly recognised her."

*

Hannah bristled. The glances of the two men behind the bar settled on her like bothersome flies. The tall, heavy one, smiled. Both had dark wavy hair, and she put them around their mid-thirties. They turned away, back to their duties. She bit her thumb in annoyance at herself. They were only being friendly and one of them was probably her contact. On the other hand, a rapist lurked in this town and in her view, every male was a potential rapist. Dark, good looks made no difference.

Over lunch, she weighed up the place prior to booking in. She had come to Draper's Wharf for a specific reason, and it had nothing to do with the rape and murder investigation she'd walked straight into. No doubt if she asked, her boss Peggy Dumas would pull her out. But there was no way she would ask to be relieved of this job. With her recent record, it would mean kissing her career goodbye. She had to prove to Peggy that she was fit to resume her duties.

As for the murder victim, Victoria Brown had been a distant relative. Not that she'd ever met the girl, but she had met her mother a couple of years back. She'd intended visiting Grace while she was here, but now that visit would become personal.

Hannah believed herself professional enough not to let it interfere with her work here.

Whilst appearing to concentrate on her newspaper, she let her mind wander and mentally tuned into the conversations of those around her. Two old codgers with grizzly chins, who she'd seen earlier, now sat behind her tucking into meat pies and beer.

"If it hadn't been for that rainstorm shiftin' the earth, they'd never've seen her."

"Yeah, just think on it. The coffin woulda come down on her, and Marty woulda been stretched out on top forever."

"And, you know what? Somehow, I don't think Old Marty woulda minded that one little bit." The first one chuckled.

"Whoever it was, must've worked all night..."

"Yeah, an' must've known about the empty grave being there. Who do ya think would've known that, Maggot?"

With no one knowing the answer and only sounds of sloppy eating to follow, Detective Sergeant Hannah Ford clicked into work mode and filed the information in her memory for future use. The old codgers' conversation turned to cricket.

Hannah stood, pulled her long, soft woollen top down to cover her thighs and straightened the stonewashed jeans that hugged the rest of her. Picking up her dishes, she walked towards the counter.

"You finished?" Mac greeted her politely. "Was your lunch all right?"

"Yeah, fine, thanks. Do you do rooms? I need accommodation for a few nights."

"No problem: double, single, with or without en-suite?" A smile started to crack through his craggy exterior, but faded. He reached under the counter for his booking-in register.

"Single – with – please. The name's Hannah Ford."

"Laclan McKay, better known as Mac," he said, holding out his hand for her to shake. The other man finished his stacking and sauntered over to stand beside Mac. He cocked his head to one side, as though waiting for Mac to make the introductions.

9

"Douglas, my brother, he's not here every day, but he comes over to help out on odd occasions." He turned to Doug. "Hannah Ford's booking in for a while."

Hannah held Doug McKay's eye a moment longer than was necessary. The pressure from his handshake and his steady gaze told her she'd met her liaison officer.

"Doug." He would recognise her name. But as this was an off-chance meeting, he would not acknowledge her as anyone but a stranger. She'd have to wait for him to make the first move. He could have done the job she was here to do, but the locals knew him as a cop and the investigators needed the observations of an officer working under-cover.

Mac McKay's voice broke her momentary pause. "Okay, Hannah, how long did you say?" Doug released her hand to let his brother complete the booking in details.

"Not sure yet, I'll see how it goes. I've come to see family," she said. She'd seen his reactions to the reporters earlier, and didn't feel ready to use journalism as her cover yet. "Grace Brown? You know her? Victoria's mother."

The look on Mac's face became wary. "Family, you say. Are you close? I ask because I do know Grace. I wasn't aware she had family outside the town."

"No, we're not close. We've only met a few times, but our mothers are cousins. When I realised the victim was her daughter, I thought I'd offer any support she might need in the next couple of days. How is she?"

"She's under sedation, today – the café's closed. It's not a good time to call."

"I'll leave it until tomorrow, then. If she doesn't want to see me, I'll just walk away – I'm not here to intrude, believe me."

Mac moved away to serve another a customer and Doug took over. "So, how come you haven't kept in touch over the years?" he asked.

"Our family originally came from Western Australia. Grace's family left there when she was a teenager and that was before my time. You know how it is when you're thousands of miles apart."

With the bustle of the bar now gone, the silence between them lengthened. She couldn't move off, as Mac hadn't come back with her room key. Doug gave no further hint towards establishing recognition. She hoped it wasn't a sign they were thinking of recalling her. The idea of going back to office duties in place of undercover work made her realise how much she had missed the real job. She looked up at Doug, now polishing a glass, watching her. Well, two could play the waiting game.

"So, tell me the story of the guy who hanged himself on the wharf," she said. "I heard little snatches of it earlier. Sounds intriguing."

He returned the glass to its rack. "It took their minds off Vicky for a bit, didn't it?"

"So, it's not true then?"

"Oh, it's true right enough. You really want to hear it?" Doug leaned across the bar, the laughter lines on his face creasing like a concertina.

"Yep, I'm all ears." Hannah pulled out a barstool, sat and leaned an elbow on the damp towel covering the bar top.

"You've been to Johnson's Cottage?" Hannah shook her head. "It's still in good nick; had a Heritage order slapped on it years back. That was the first house built here, around 1860 or so. It belonged to a retired sea captain by the name of Captain Johnson, and gradually a settlement grew up around it..."

Doug was a good storyteller and Hannah found herself drawn into the tale of the small town that grew up on the shores of this backwater, tucked away in a little known cove along the reaches of the Parramatta River, a place they called Johnson's Creek. Around forty years later, someone suggested they build a wharf for the fishermen to land their catches and tie up their boats. The idea split the town in two – those who wanted it and those who did not. The did-nots led by the vociferous Willie Draper felt it would ruin their quiet seclusion and eventually turn their little cove into a busy, smelly port, along with so many others of the time. The did-nots were outnumbered and the plan went ahead.

"On the very day the wharf was completed, old Willie Draper was found hanging from the yardarm on the jetty. To this day, the mystery of his death has never been resolved. Some say it was suicide, some say ..."

"And some say the ghost of Willie Draper still walks," Mac added as he returned to Doug's side. "Was he murdered or did he top himself? The cops of the day never found out. Some say he's still around, been seen wandering amongst the boats on the beach, and still the cops haven't managed to corner him."

Hannah smiled as Doug threw his brother a get-you-later look. "So, that's why the name was changed to Draper's Wharf?" she said, "I bet he must love that, wherever he is. Perhaps that's why his ghost still walks."

"Ah, that's the irony of the thing," Doug said. "The very construction Willie Draper had fought so hard against ultimately came to bear his name."

"Thanks guys; a bit of background history, just the sort of thing I'm looking for."

"I wonder how history will record what has happened here in the last couple of days," Mac brought them back to reality. "Here," he said, handing Hannah a key. "Number four, up the stairs and turn right. We can do all meals if you want. Just let Mrs Bates know about breakfast the night before. Okay, do you need a hand with bags?"

Hannah shook her head. "Haven't got much, thanks."

Douglas turned to his brother. "Well, if you don't need me anymore, Mac, I'll be off. Mara will be wondering where the hell I am."

"Okay, give her my love, and the kids. And thanks, Doug. Don't forget – if you hear anything, you'll keep me posted, won't you?" Mac tapped the side of his nose.

Hannah left them to it and went in search of her room. She opened the door to a plain, no-frills bedroom with a dark green carpet. The building was of the old colonial style, built cornerwise with a second-storey balcony running across the front and along two sides. Hannah opened the French windows and stepped outside. She glanced down the length of balcony, at all the closed windows and wondered how many other people shared her space.

She leaned on the balustrade and breathed in the faint tang of salt and seaweed that flavoured the air. The cry of gulls mingled with the hum of traffic. People scurried about their business on the street below. On the other side of the road to her left, in between the moving brightness of water, she saw the low-slung corrugated building of the local sailing club. The old wharf and its jetty stood directly opposite her. In a cold, dark corner of her imagination, she saw the shadow of Willie Draper swinging from the yardarm there. She rubbed the gooseflesh away from her arms.

Douglas emerged from the door beneath her and crossed the road to his utility parked along the opposite kerb. He appeared to be a genuine sort of bloke, a cop and obviously married. And Mac, with a touch of silver in his hair, looked a tad older than his brother. But only by a couple of years, probably hadn't made forty yet – a Scotsman without the brogue. A man who didn't like reporters, how would he react when he learned her cover story?

She returned to her room and shut the window carefully behind her. The lock turned with a satisfying clunk.

The van's double doors snapped shut.

The room tilted; she stumbled and fell to her knees. Noise filled her head. Her vision warped as though looking through a bull's-eye window.

Her legs are numb. An engine roars into life, tyres squeal. Time has no meaning. Then the motion stops and the doors fling wide. A dark periphery distorts her vision. Through its centre, she sees in the glare of a spotlight, the silhouette of a large man advancing on her. His hair, unkempt, long and curly surrounds his fat face, and against the light, it appears as a shaggy nimbus. Hair sticks out from the edges of his singlet and covers his arms like a wiry coat. The nearer he draws, the fatter his

13

face, the larger his open mouth and the obscene pink muscle waggling there. He releases the belt from his trousers. In the background, another man laughs. The sound is high and diabolical. Paralysed, she is unable to defend herself. The fat man's body finally blocks out the light.

Silence. Stillness. Hannah came to her senses gripping the baseboard of the bed in the hotel bedroom. Memory surged in like a king wave. It was over, all over. She reeled in the tatty remnants of her self-control and climbed to her feet.

It was five bloody months ago.

She thought of the barmaid. The coloured photograph in the newspaper showed a young woman with long, fair hair styled loosely around her face. Victoria Brown aged twenty-one: Hannah knew the horrors that she had been through were nothing to those that Victoria must have suffered. She also knew another thing for sure; the man who had raped and murdered Victoria Brown had not been her rapist. Her rapist was dead.

* * *

2

Hannah sat at a small table by the window in the dining room, toying with her toast and marmalade. April sunshine, slanting through the glass, brightened the blue and white willow pattern china and gleamed off the silverware. Hands encircling her warm coffee cup, she gazed out through the dusty pane without seeing what lay beyond.

In her mind's eye, she could see her boss, Peggy; short, tubby with a rough-cut mop of black hair as she leaned across her desk spelling out the parameters of the job. After so long in limbo, Hannah was thrilled to be back on the street. It meant they trusted her again.

"It's drugs – heroin, amphetamines. We need someone on the ground in Draper's Wharf," Peggy had told her. "We have a whisper of a regular supply coming in, though we don't know if it's by sea, or whether it's being manufactured there. Your job is to listen, observe and report, *not* to instigate any action. This is part of an ongoing investigation and we need our information verified. That is all. Understood?"

She understood. Her cover was one she'd used before, a journalist for *Piquant* magazine, this time doing an article on the history of the town.

Movement outside the window caught her attention. On the waterfront, a driver shunted back and forth trying to park the police caravan onto the wharf. He was not short of helpers waving their arms and shouting directions, like a sequence in a dream.

Mac came in from the kitchen balancing a tray of jugs. "Ready for a top up?" he asked.

"Mm, thanks," Hannah pushed her cup in his direction. "Going to join me, or are you too busy?"

"Not too busy I can't stop for a few minutes today. Taking a cup and saucer from a neighbouring table, he sat down with the courtesy of a host doing his guest's bidding.

"You've a great place here, Mac. It has a good atmosphere. Been here long?"

"Nearly all my life, I was raised here." Mac glanced around his warm, sunlit dining room, looking pleased at her compliment. She encouraged him to talk about the town he'd grown up in and soon gained his confidence. His smiles came more readily. Their conversation dropped to a comfortable silence while he refreshed the coffee cups. His mistrust of the press was an unfortunate turn-up. It meant that her cover story might result in resentment rather than placation. But, it was too late to change it now. She needed to find the right moment to tell him.

The way he sat, caught in a checkerboard of sunshine and shadows made by the heavy square-cut window frames, reminded her of her dad. The picnics under mottled shade of a giant gum tree down by the Swan River in WA when she was little. That was before her dad became ill, before the coughing started.

She tilted her head. "You talk about 'we' do this or that, like you have a wife or a partner hidden back there somewhere."

Mac treated her to a rueful grin. "No, the wife shot through. Found more congenial company." He fell silent and played with the breakfast cutlery, sending darts of light skimming across the walls and the smoke stained ceiling.

"Couldn't take the pub hours?"

"Wasn't that. I was a diver back then, same as Doug, only I worked on the oilrigs – better pay. Meant I was away a lot,

16

though."

"So, you gave it up?"

He let out a self-deprecating laugh. "More like it gave me up." He paused, and then catching her waiting expression, plunged on. "Accident. Meant I couldn't dive any more." The trace of bitterness in his voice was not lost on Hannah.

"Sorry to hear that," she murmured.

"Yes, funny that – the Old Man got his way; he'd always wanted one of his sons to take over the pub. That's where the "we" comes from. The business was always "our" business, not his. Too bad he had a heart attack and died the same year."

Hannah allowed the silence to linger awhile before she spoke again. "Vicky's murder must have come as a shock to you."

Mac's face sagged. "She was a lovely lass. Everyone loved her." He raised his hand to his face and squeezed the bridge of his nose between thumb and finger.

"Tell me about it."

"What's there to tell? One minute she's there, the next she's …"

"Who, other than a local, would have known about the empty grave?"

Mac frowned, collecting his thoughts. "Most of the locals would've known about Old Marty's funeral."

"What about outsiders, the reps, say? You said you get reps staying overnight."

Mac shook his head. "No reps on a Friday night. They're all rushing back to the missus or whatever."

Hannah sipped her coffee, watching him struggle with the subject. She knew about raw anger that coloured every moment's thought. He needed to talk it out.

After a pause, he continued. "The police have been around asking if I had any strangers staying overnight. Can't see it myself. It's too much of a coincidence for an outsider to have found a ready-made hole, just when he was looking for some place to bury a body. Who would do such a thing to Vicky?"

"Did she have boyfriend troubles or anything like that?"

17

He shook his head. "No troubles that I know, but if it wasn't a stranger, then it has to be one of us. Someone I know. The police have talked to everyone. They questioned Morgan for hours."

"I don't think I've met Morgan."

"Morgan Draper, he's the gravedigger. But he didn't know anything. It wasn't him; he was in here until nearly closing. He only left then because he had to take Billy home. Billy's his nephew. I expect you'll meet him around the place. He mightn't have two oars in the water, but he's the last of the Drapers and Morgan looks out for him. Though he made some fuss about it that night." He gazed out of the window and snorted.

"Something funny?"

"Not really. Well, better get back to work." He made no move to go.

Hannah looked down at the tablecloth, picked up a rind of marmalade she'd dropped and placed it on the side of her plate. She didn't want to appear over-curious. Sometimes it alienated those you were trying to get information from. And, she reminded herself, this was not her case.

Mac watched her, his face pinched. "I'll have to get someone else in, but I can't make myself do it just yet. You saw how busy we were yesterday – probably be the same again tonight with all this shenanigans going on."

"What about your brother? He covered for you yesterday."

"Yeah, salt of the earth is old Doug. Unfortunately, his free time doesn't always coincide with my busy times. He's both a cop and a family man." His mouth curved up one side in amusement, as though it was a well-known line between the brothers. "It's all right; I'll get on to the agency."

Hannah stared into the bottom of her cup, her mind sifting possibilities.

The outside door creaked open. Mac looked across the table at Hannah. "Someone's in early." He leaned back in his chair and looked across the room, through the bar opening, across the far counter to the public bar, waiting to see who would cross his line of vision.

"Inspector Steele," he called out. "Over here in the dining room, come and join us."

The inspector, tall and rangy, silver hair swept back over his head in waves, walked through the public bar and into the dining room.

"G'day to you, Mr McKay – no, I'm not stopping." He declined the chair Mac indicated. He acknowledged Hannah with a nod, before turning back to Mac. "There's something I need to check on your statement."

Puzzled, Mac stood and stepped away from the table. "What's the problem?"

Steele looked at his notebook. "You said, Victoria Brown was unwell and left the bar around 9.30 on Friday night?"

"That's right. She'd been sick, said she'd eaten something that hadn't agreed with her. I told her to go home. Doug was here; he gave me a hand for the rest of the night."

"Righty-ho, now, if she had gone straight home," Steele wagged a finger in the direction of the outside door he had just entered, "She would have gone out of that door, and turned right, correct?"

Mac hesitated, not sure where this was going, "Yeah that's right. She lived with her mum above the café down the road."

"We've had more than one witness say they saw Victoria come out of the bar door and turn *left*, not right. Any idea where she was going?"

"Left?" Mac shook his head, baffled. "No, she said she was going straight home."

"She was sick, but she was not too sick that you were happy enough to let her go home on her own?"

"Lennie Cooper was in the back bar. He could have taken her."

"That's right. He's her bloke, isn't he?" Steele flipped the pages of his notebook.

"I asked her if she wanted me to get him, but she said no. She was quite adamant; she didn't want Lennie taking her home. Said he was in the middle of his darts match, and she didn't want him disturbed. It seemed perfectly reasonable. She slipped out quietly and, as far as I know, no one in the bar even saw her go. Who said she went the other way?"

"Right, okay." The inspector ignored Mac's question and made some notation in his book. "We need more input from the public, someone who might have seen her on the road after she left here. As I mentioned yesterday, we'd like to do a re-enactment of her leaving here, Mr McKay. Tonight."

"Okay. What's the form?"

"One of our officers will play the part of the victim. She'll leave here at 9.30, same as Victoria did. She'll turn left and follow Victoria's supposed path towards the church. See if that jogs anyone's memory. We'll announce it through the town on the public address system of course, but if you would pass the word around your patrons, we'd like to see all those who were here on Friday night turn up again."

"You reckon it'll do any good?"

"Never can tell, sometimes we get useful information that way. Somebody must have seen something. Even if they think it's insignificant, it might turn out to be the vital link. Righty-ho, thanks for your time." He hesitated and stopped. "Oh, and if anybody has any questions before then, or information they can give us, we're setting up the mobile facility on the wharf." He raised a hand and started for the door.

Mac walked part way with him. "I'll pass the word."

He returned to Hannah's table to collect her breakfast dishes. Why would Vicky have turned away from home? Had she lied? She wasn't the devious kind, or at least, he didn't think so. In fact, she had a very forthright way of dealing with matters, as he knew to his cost. And, she'd been adamant that she didn't want Lennie taking her home. So, what had Vicky been up to?

"Think it'll help?" Hannah's voice probed his thoughts.

"You heard? About this re-enactment? If they don't even know where she was going, how can they follow her path?"

"Well, they know where she started and where she ended up

– the path could be somewhere between the two. Didn't she give you any clue where she might be going?"

He frowned. "She said she was going home."

"Where does turning left take you?"

"Up past the shopping centre, but no one that side of town would've been open, the deli's down the other end. Past Foster's garage, again shut. After that, going on up the main road, it's either the church, or the bus station. She couldn't have taken a bus, there were none going out at that time of night. The only other possibility would be to branch off right at the junction and follow the coastal track. There's nothing up there but a few derelict fishermen's huts, and miles of riverbank. There's no way she'd go that way, not in those fancy shoes of hers." He picked up the tray ready to take it out.

"Sounds like you had a busy night here on Friday," Hannah said.

"The usual sort of thing for a darts match night." He recalled the vibration of the music thudding against the walls. Vicky had turned the volume up to her level. The main bar was smoky and filled with the scent of spirits, ale, and women's perfumes. In the back bar, a couple of lads clicked the balls on the pool table.

The punters gathered around the dartboard. Occasional pauses of tense silence from the players exploded into ribaldry, or cries of congratulations, as the team member of the moment landed his dart. "We play *The Crows,*" he explained. "One month our lads go there, and the next theirs come here. Afterwards, the beer flows like Niagara; everybody forgets their petty quarrels and has a good time."

Hannah smiled as though she knew the routine. "Fighting over petty quarrels, it sounds like the old Willie Draper story. What's the modern quarrel about?"

"Should they renew the lighting on the wharf, or some such thing, but I don't get involved in town politics."

He added her empty cup to the tray noticing in this soft, morning-light, her eyes were the colour of amber. "Are you going to see Grace today?"

21

Hannah blew a long sigh and checked her watch. "First, I must get to a garage and get my tyre seen to. After that puncture, I have no spare. You mentioned a place up the road?"

"Izzy Foster's? Out here, turn left, he's up on the junction."

"Turn *left?*"

Mac smiled at her enquiring eyebrow and shook his head. "No way, Vicky wouldn't have gone there. But, watch out for Foster, he's a bit of a sleaze, if you know what I mean."

* * *

3

Hannah stood with her hands linked behind her back. The mechanic leaned forward to examine the rent in her tyre; long strings of red hair settled around his shoulders. He stood up, his pale green eyes on a level with hers. He scratched his chin where sparse gingery hairs masqueraded as a goatee beard.

"Well, you've trashed that one good and proper," Izzy Foster said, as though it were all Hannah's fault. "Lucky you didn't buckle the rim. Yeah, well, I haven't got one in. I'd have to get it for you. Might take coupla days," he added, eyes scrolling down her figure. Their touch made her flesh creep.

She took a step back and folded her arms across her chest. "Well, I'm not going anywhere for a few days, so that's no problem." When his glance finally met hers, he turned his head away, as though catching the venom in her look.

"Haven't seen you around here before. On holidays?" he asked.

She weighed her options, which story would be most likely to elicit information from him? There were drugs here somewhere in Draper's Wharf, and now there had been a murder. Could the two crimes be related? If so, she could not let sensitivity towards her relatives get in the way. She warmed up her smile. "I'm visiting family. I was in the area and thought I'd drop by. That's when I heard the news."

He looked at her with a different kind of interest. "You mean the body in the grave?"

"Bit of a shock coming here to find someone in your family has been murdered."

He turned his head away. "Vicky? Yeah, shame that. Place won't be the same."

"Mac was saying she was popular behind the bar."

"Yeah, but she wasn't her usual self that night. Took the orders and handed them over okay, but without the laughs, you know what I mean?"

Hannah raised an eyebrow and waited for him to continue. Rumour and innuendo were the seedlings of her job.

"She had a blue with Sebastian, when he teased her about it, you know, not laughing an' that. 'What's the matter Vic, cat got your tongue?' he said to her."

Hannah recalled the man named Sebastian. She could hardly miss him. He'd been in the bar over lunchtime the day before, a big fellow with a voice to match and he was using it for a sales pitch to one of the reporters.

"I know the bloke you mean. What was he saying to her?"

"I dunno, all sorts. Then she says to him, 'I'm not talking to you, Sebastian Peach,' Right up herself she was; could be when she wanted. 'Course, old Sebastian, he flashes his big grin all round, the others joke back at him and they pass it off."

"He was trying to interest someone into buying property when I heard him."

"Yeah, that's the man. Sebastian Peach runs the estate agent, smart bloke, always in a suit. Next thing I knew Doug was pouring the beers. Not as pretty as Vicky, but he pours them just as well." His Adam's apple bobbed up and down as his laughter crowed. He took another step forward, encroaching on her personal space. The ferret was actually trying to come on to her.

"Right," she said, taking a sideways step. "Hannah Ford's the name; I'm staying at The Harbour Lights. Would you give me a call when the tyre comes in?"

He jerked his head like a bantam cock and his eyes did another quick tour. "Yeah, anytime, I'm in there sometimes. See you around, maybe?"

As Hannah left the garage, she checked her rear view mirror. Izzie Foster remained standing on the forecourt, watching her.

Next job was to be acquainted with the place. Draper's Wharf, a small town shaped like a shallow horseshoe, curved around the bay, until at the far end, it swept away from the populated area and back inland to join the highway. Most of the shops and business premises lined the main road facing the water, with intersections between the buildings that led away to the school and houses built higher up on the sloping ground. With such a small population, it was difficult to see how anyone could conduct a large-scale drug operation without someone else stumbling over it. Once she'd covered the area by car, she returned her Honda to the hotel and set out on foot for a more detailed look. Mac had given her directions to Grace's café; it was time to pay her respects.

Sebastian Peach's estate agency occupied the opposite corner to The Harbour Lights. She crossed the road between them. Could the row between Victoria and her customer Sebastian have had anything to do with why Victoria left early? Although Vicky's murder was not her case, instinct wouldn't let her ignore it altogether.

On the quayside, the police mobile unit was open for business. Pedestrians stopped to read the notice preparing them for the night's re-enactment. A wide-eyed child stared at the trailer, while his dog lifted its leg against the back wheel. Dogs and kids ... she and Simon had made plans. That little nub of pain every time she thought of her husband of five years caught her off guard. This was not the time to reminisce.

The shops were a mixture of old and new. Some, shaded under a bull-nose veranda, displayed trinkets and modern antiques to attract the tourists, others sold ice creams and takeaways. Well maintained and painted in the traditional federation green and cream, they added a sense of affluence to Draper's Wharf, declaring that business was alive and well. She quickened her step.

Shoppers, predominantly women with young children, meandered along the pavement, heads turning, clearly bemused by the unaccustomed police presence. Gaggles formed where small groups stopped to talk. Hannah edged her way around them.

She found The Crow's Nest under a sign depicting a glossy image of its namesake. Much smaller than Mac's hotel, it had the appearance of a serious drinking man's bar, probably one of the last to let women through its door. It huddled in a terraced building, between a video store and the TAB, whose open door revealed punters filling their cards for the next horse race.

The road curved back to meet the sea. A row of old cottages, their gardens bright with autumn roses, followed the curvature and marked the end of the populated area. A large boatyard stood across the road. It stretched along the beach, above the high-water mark, where boats of every size and hue hugged the shore. Some on legs, some in cradles, and others sat on fin keels, crowding the small stony beach. A short wooden jetty with fuel pumps and lifting equipment jutted into the water.

If the drug traffickers smuggled their wares in, rather than manufactured them locally, then anywhere along the riverside could be their offloading spot. She thought of her conversation with Mac at breakfast. A list of those opposed to modern lighting planned for the wharf might be interesting.

Hannah stood for a moment, gazing in through the entrance to the boatyard. She could hear the sounds of electrical equipment at work, saws, sanding machines and the high-pitched whine of a metal cutter. From Mac she'd learned that Lennie Cooper, who was Victoria's boyfriend, owned the boatyard with a partner called Jed. This was where Victoria had worked her day job as Lennie's secretary.

She walked a short way inside then turning back, looked up the road trying to see the town through Victoria's eyes. She would have walked down this concrete ramp every day and seen this view. What was she like, this murdered girl, this distant relative of hers? That picture in the newspaper looked so much like the photograph Mother had framed of Hannah, taken ten years earlier, when she was Victoria's age. She had seen a certain family resemblance.

The sound of a car starting up somewhere out on the road broke her reverie. She watched it pass the open gateway, when its brakes suddenly squealed. The car came to a halt and rolled back level with the entrance. Its dark windows prevented her from seeing the driver. She took a step towards it, thinking someone wanted to attract her attention, when it accelerated away and headed for town. She looked back towards the boatshed to see what else might have caught the driver's interest, but could see nothing. For a moment, she wondered if she might have caused the incident, then dismissed the idea as absurd.

The Copper Kettle café stood across the road from the boatyard. That was where Victoria Brown had lived with her mother, Grace. Hannah knew all about the pain there must be under that roof with the family trying to cope. Would they see her visit as an intrusion, or a godsend? There was no way to know, but in all decency, she could put it off no longer.

* * *

4

Although the café was not the primary crime scene, the investigators would have examined it as the home of the deceased. No trace of police tape lingered now. The café's mullioned bay windows bellied out each side of the entrance. Hannah peered through the glass door.

A woman she thought was Grace stood behind the counter, with her back to the empty café, one hand on a hip the other holding her chin. Her head cocked apparently listening.

A bell pinged as Hannah opened the door and slipped inside. The woman turned her head and looked over her shoulder at Hannah.

"Hello Grace, it's only me. I heard the news."

Grace turned around to meet her face on, the distracted expression on her face cleared.

"Hannah. It's been a long time; what are you doing here?" There was no smile and little warmth in her eyes.

"I was on my way here when I heard about Vicky ... I am so sorry."

"Yes, well, you never really knew her, did you?" Grace closed her eyes for a moment and then looked again at Hannah. "It's been a long time since I've laid eyes on any of the family, apart from when you last called in a couple of years back."

"I'm surprised you remembered me at all."

"Never forget a face. And you look like your mum, like I remember her anyway. I was only a kid when my parents upped sticks and moved to Sydney," Grace said. Noises from above them caused Grace to glance at the ceiling.

Hannah raised her eyebrows. "Someone up there?"

"It's the cops. They're looking in her room again. They've done it once. Now they've come back and want to know if she kept a diary. I never saw any diary, why would they think that?"

"Did you ask them?"

"Yeah, and they said they wanted to know about Vicky's boyfriends. Well, I told them she only had the one, and that was Lennie Cooper. They said she was pregnant and they needed the name of the child's father." Taking a tissue from the pocket of her overalls, she blew her nose. "I saw the test kit in the bin the other day. I didn't say anything to her, just waited, but she never told me. Of course, the cops knew."

Hannah hoped the officers had been sensitive enough not to tell Grace how they found out. The sound of movement on the stairs indicated the police had finished their search. The female officer emerged from the back of the shop, followed by a spotty faced young constable. They both looked at Hannah.

Grace spoke up. "It's all right. You can say whatever you want to say in front of her. She's family and I want her to stay."

Hannah introduced herself. "And you are?"

"Constable Linda James, and Constable Ian Granger, we're looking for a diary, or an address book, something Victoria may well have kept hidden. Would you know of anything like that?" Linda asked her.

Before she could answer, Grace broke in, her voice strained. "I've already told you, Vicky didn't keep diaries."

In an obvious attempt to diffuse the tense atmosphere, Linda James gave Grace her full attention. "Mrs Brown, you do know about the re-enactment tonight, don't you."

"Yes, the other officers told me. They had to borrow some of Vicky's clothes."

"Were any of her clothes missing when you came to look?"

"Well, since then, I've noticed her running shoes have gone. She liked to go jogging some mornings. And one of her shoulder bags."

Linda made a note in her book. "Okay, got that." She paused a moment giving Grace a speculative look. "Mrs Brown, can you tell me if Vicky was on any medication?"

Alarm bells rang in Hannah's head. It was a familiar line, and she knew what it meant.

Grace frowned. "Not that I know of, why?"

Linda nodded to the constable and he held up a small plastic bag. "We found this in one of her drawers. Have you seen it before?"

Grace's eyes opened wide as she stared at the bag. "No, never, what are you saying?"

"All right, we'll take it with us and see what it contains," Linda said.

Hannah did a double take. The plastic bag contained what appeared to be two Ecstasy tablets. Her heart thumped against her chest. Two E's, if that is what they turned out to be, didn't constitute a drug ring. But, discovering who had supplied them was her job. She wondered just how well Grace knew her daughter.

Grace, bemused by the turn of events, followed the officers towards the door. She waited until it closed behind them. Then she turned on Hannah. "What are they saying? Are the saying my girl was doing drugs? I don't believe it!"

"Sit down a minute, Grace. Can I get you a cup of tea? You look a bit shaken."

Grace raised her hands. "Don't you go mothering me! I'm perfectly capable of getting a cup of tea. I suppose you want some lunch as well. The quiche is home-made and it doesn't look like anyone else is going to eat it."

Hannah mentally applauded her strength and took a table by the window. She watched the slim, neatly dressed woman with soft, light brown hair tied loosely at the nape of her neck walk briskly back to her place behind the counter.

Grace's hands shook as she placed the tea tray on the table and unloaded it. She sat with a deep sigh and poured the tea, she hadn't brought any lunch for herself.

Hannah inclined her head towards the quiche. "I hadn't expected you to be open, far less making quiches, today."

"I have to keep busy, need to occupy my mind. I'm going crazy thinking about it."

"I know what you mean about keeping busy."

Grace's eyes looked weighted with pain. "Do you have kids, Hannah?"

Hannah took a deep breath and held it a moment. "No, I don't."

"Then, how the bloody-hell do *you know* how I feel?"

Hannah's chest tightened. She'd walked right into that. She placed her cup down onto its saucer. "I do know about the need to keep busy, Grace. I lost my husband recently."

A shadow crossed Grace's face. "Oh, I'm sorry to hear that." She put her hand out and touched Hannah's arm, "How did it happen?"

Simon's death had not been her fault; she'd accepted that. Who could have predicted that such a healthy man would keel over from a deep vein thrombosis? Was it only six months ago? Some days it felt like yesterday, and others, years back. She'd been a thousand miles away chasing an elusive detail on a case when she missed her flight. Back home, Simon died in a stranger's arms. Eventually, she ran out of tears and went back to work. Briefly, she told Grace the bones of her story, but made no mention of the rape that came so shortly afterwards. Grace did not need to know that.

"So, what do you do to keep yourself busy?" Grace asked.

Hannah had no choice, she had to lie, but she didn't feel good about it. Using her new knowledge of old Willie Draper, the man who'd hanged himself from the yardarm, she told Grace about her research into the history of Draper's Wharf for a magazine article.

"You have another daughter," Hannah prompted, to change the subject.

"Elizabeth, she's nearly fourteen, I have to keep going for her. As for opening today, might as well have saved my breath, no one's been in. Usually had a few in for coffee and snacks by this time, but so far haven't seen anyone. It's like I've got the

31

plague."

"They don't want to worry you at a time like this." Hannah covered Grace's hand with one of her own and gave it a squeeze. She knew the syndrome. People didn't know how to react to another's trauma. What to say or do, so they said nothing, did nothing and stayed away. Far from helping, it had left her feeling like an outcast.

Grace sat quietly sipping her drink and the silence lengthened. At the sound of a braking car, their eyes locked. They both turned to look out of the window. A police car pulled onto the concrete apron in front of Lennie Cooper's boatshed and stopped.

Hannah remained seated and watched through the window, while Grace stood by the glass door and stared out. The two officers climbed out of their car and adjusted their caps. They each smiled at some comment that passed between them and walked into the workshop. Grace stood with her feet apart, one hand on her hip, the other against the wall as though for support. Minutes passed, until finally Lennie appeared between the two officers as they escorted him to their car.

"It's probably a routine matter," Hannah said. "It could be they want to ask him about Vicky's pregnancy, that's all. It doesn't mean he's done it, Grace."

Grace turned back, her face contorted. "It better not be. It can't be. Lennie's a good bloke. A hard worker and I like that in a man. Look at that place over there, a few years back it was an old fibro shed. He pulled it down and built that new one. Spent big bucks on it, I can tell you. He'd come here for his meals. That's when he and Vicky got together. Soon as she left school, she went to work for him."

The police car drove away. Two workers came out from the boatshed and stood talking together, looking aimless. Then one of them checked his watch, clapped the other on the shoulder and turned him in their direction.

"That's Billy Draper coming for the lunches. Here am I talking to you, and I haven't finished packing them, yet." Grace returned to the counter and picked up a list. She popped a container into the microwave, and loaded a cardboard box with pre-packed sandwiches and rolls from the cabinet.

A large figure dressed in paint-spattered overalls and a battered wide brim hat, crossed the road and came shambling towards her. Hannah stiffened, his shape, so close to that of the shadowy figure in the background of her life. The bell above the door rang as Billy Draper pushed his way in. Without looking at her, he trudged straight up to the counter.

"Hullo Billy," Grace greeted him, "bit early today, aren't you?"

"Hullo Missus B, Jed says I was to come early. The police came and they taken Lennie away. What they want with Lennie?" He shuffled his feet.

"What did they say? Did you hear any of it?" Grace asked.

"Jest, they wanted to ask him some questions. But I thought they done that the other day. Why they do it again?"

"Here, Billy, come and say hullo to Hannah." Grace brought out the cardboard box of lunches and placed it on a table near Hannah. "She's family, a cousin of mine."

Billy whirled around and stared at Hannah with large, round baby-blue eyes. His big face flushed crimson. He snatched the hat from his head and held it in front of his chest.

"Hullo," he mumbled, the look in his eyes darting around like those of a captive bear.

"G'day Billy. Do you come over for the lunches every day?" Hannah smiled, trying to ease his shyness.

"Yus, that's one of me jobs, that, an' painting an' getting the drinks, things like that." He lowered his eyes to his paint stained trainers, and circled the brim of his hat through his hands. "Well, I better be going. We're having an early lunch, see." He picked up the box, hefted it beneath his arm, slapped his hat on his curly head and left the shop.

"He's a bit slow, but he's a nice enough boy," Grace explained. "His mother's bedridden with arthritis now, but Billy looks after her. They live over there." Grace nodded towards the row of old cottages near the boatshed.

"The one with the roses?"

"Yes, Morgan Draper looks after their garden. He's Billy's uncle. He's the church sexton, or the gravedigger, as he calls himself." Grace's voice faltered. "He was there when they found her ..."

She sat down suddenly. "I can't believe it. I can't believe she's gone." Grace covered her face with her hands. Abruptly took them away. "That packet they found – she wasn't into drugs. I would've known, wouldn't I? I would've seen it?"

"Not necessarily, Grace. Did she go to parties, or clubbing?"

"Working at Mac's most evenings didn't give her much time. Occasionally she went to a late night rave with friends. She was twenty-one, I mean, it's not like she was a kid. Asking her where she was going and who with, and so on didn't wash with Vicky. Like she said, the odd night away was none of my business."

Hannah nodded sympathetically. "What about her local friends, are they likely to be involved in passing round the odd Ecstasy tablet?"

"Oh, I don't think so, but how do you tell? Anyway, why are we talking like this? We don't even know what they were. More than likely they're vitamin pills, seeing as how she was pregnant."

Hannah left Grace with a promise she'd call in again later. She crossed the road towards the boatyard. Billy was back at work, sanding down a clinker-built fishing boat on the hard forecourt. Another man, deeply tanned and well padded with muscle, wearing short, stained cut-offs, pulled a tarpaulin from one of the boats nearby. His fair hair swung around his shoulders in ringlets. Jed, Lennie's partner, she supposed.

Two jet-skis raced each other down the river, fountains of white water gushing up behind them. The whine of their motors filled the air like angry hornets.

Hannah leaned against the wall between the road and the shore, and cupping her hand against the breeze, lit a cigarette.

34

She drew in a deep, smoke-laden breath. It was ironic that the first inkling of illicit drugs should come from Vicky. It made her feel queasy. After a few more drags, she nipped the cigarette out and dropped it in a litterbin.

Following the wall to an opening, she turned down the couple of steps onto the beach. Away from the shelter of the boatshed, the wind blew in her short hair its salty tang clean and refreshing. Vicky had been pregnant, too.

Hannah kicked along a piece of seaweed until it disintegrated and the tide reclaimed its remains. Her pregnancy was history. In the aftermath, she had refused regular counselling in spite of Peggy's urging. Such was her guilt, she could tell no one. She scuffed the sand with her Reeboks and walked back along the edge of the water. A long, blue and white ferry passed by going down-river, its wash bringing gentle waves to lap the shore. She dodged back to keep her feet dry, and walked on with her eyes to the ground, hearing a distant bark of a dog and the purity of a child's laughter.

She listened for the mocking sound of a baby's cry, but today she heard none.

* * *

5

Mac looked up from his glass polishing when he heard the saloon door open. His latest guest breezed in like a canvassing politician, all geniality and bright-eyed hope.

"G'day, Hannah. How's Grace, did you get to see her?"

"She's bearing up better than I expected."

"Yeah, she's a tough one; made a good job of bringing the girls up since her husband upped sticks and left."

"This morning you said you were short handed. If you like, I could tide you over for a few days until you get someone in."

He gazed at her, unsure if he'd heard correctly. "Why would you want to do that?"

She shrugged as though it meant nothing to her either way. "I'm not going anywhere until after the funeral. I've time to spare and thought you might be glad of an extra pair of hands."

Returning the glass to its rack gave him time to think. He flung the cloth onto his shoulder and looked back at her. "You had any experience?" He hadn't phoned the agency yet, but he'd never get anyone in tonight at such short notice, anyway.

"I've done bar work before. It'd only be for a few days, I'm not planning on making it a career." A smile lit her face. She appeared genuine enough, but that worm of suspicion wriggled in his mind again. What if she *was* a reporter looking for the inside story?

"Where did you say you worked, now, I mean?"

"I'm with *Piquant; it's a* glossy magazine dealing with homes, gardens and suchlike."

He knew it. "A reporter!"

"Hey! Relax." Hannah held up a hand. "I'm not after the story of Vicky's murder. *Piquant* is not into hype. You can check with my editor, if you want. I'm a feature writer. Look, it's no big deal. If you don't like the idea, forget I mentioned it."

Now he felt bad. She'd offered to help and he'd thrown it in her face. "I'm sorry. My fault. I can't tell my arse from my elbow, I'm that wound up. Yes, if you could help out tonight it would be great." Tonight was going to be harrowing enough without the stress of working understaffed. All the same, a reporter is a reporter whatever fancy name they go under. At least, here, he could keep an eye on her.

*

Mac selected the *Tuesday Night Music Club* album and turned the sound system on. He adjusted the volume to a suitable low pitch. Placing the clean drip towels along the top of the counter, he glanced across to the back bar to see how his latest barmaid was going. She'd been getting to know her way around the bar before the place filled up.

He studied her as she crouched to check out the lower shelves of the cool drinks cabinet. Her long sleeved, red silk shirt and black pants clung to every curve. Her blond hair, brushed into a modern shaggy shape, curled enticingly around her ears. She looked gorgeous. Maybe she didn't have the glitz that Vicky had, but she was definitely more up-market. "How're you doing?" he asked, "found everything?"

Hannah stood up. "I know where to find most things. I'll be right. If not, I'll yell!"

"Doug said he'd come in to give us a hand tonight. That'll take the pressure off you."

"Uh-huh. What's happening, do you know?"

"You must've seen it done before. There was a spate of it over in Perth a few years back when girls went missing. Here, they're not so much interested in what happened inside. Everybody knows what everybody was doing – it's more a case of what happened after Vicky left the bar. Where did she go from there?"

*

Meg Henderson sat at her dressing table. She dabbed the excess blusher from her cheeks and paused, gently biting her lower lip. She took a sidelong glance at her husband's reflection in the mirror. In his early thirties, he was still a good-looking guy. With his dusky skin, and his dark brown curly hair, he had a touch of a young Ernie Dingo about him. He jerked on his cords and zipped them. Unaware of her scrutiny, he combed his hair with his fingers in a gesture she knew so well.

It was precisely because she knew him so well that she knew something was amiss. For some time now, she had suspected Zack had something, or someone, on his mind. She had been through his pockets, examined his wallet and his credit card statement. She did all the things doubting wives are prone to do, but so far had found nothing to confirm her suspicions.

In fact, she couldn't tie the feeling down to any particular thing. That dreamy look that crossed his face when he stared out of the window was hardly evidence. It wasn't as if the attention he paid her had dropped off, the very opposite in fact. His protestations that he loved her had increased and his lovemaking more ardent. He had even started to experiment – he talked about 'G' spots, and changed their routines. Nothing too radical, thank God, but little differences she'd noted and wondered about.

If Zack *was* having an affair, where would he find the time? A schoolteacher, he spent most of the week in a classroom. No, never a student, he wouldn't do that. Friday nights he played darts with the guys down the pub. On Wednesdays, he went to practice night for the amateur operatic society with Colin, the school music teacher, and sang his heart out.

With nothing at all to pin on him, she had put her worries to rest. But earlier today, he said he'd be going out for the evening.

No mention of her coming along, and her misgivings were re-ignited. She'd put her theory to the test and blandly, so as not to alert him to her suspicions, suggested she went with him.

"Why?" he'd asked, looking unusually perturbed. "I'm only going to the pub. You hate it in there, gives you a headache."

"But why on a Tuesday? You never go out on a Tuesday."

He'd shrugged. "It's this re-enactment business. You know the police are looking for Vicky Brown's killer. We're supposed to do tonight whatever we did on Friday night. I have to go – or, the next thing you'll know is they'll be pointing the bone at me. Come if you want, but I'll be playing darts"

"Will Colin be there?"

"What do you want to know that for?" He asked sharply.

"Just wondered."

*

Zack's guts squirmed as he pushed his way through the crowd. Meg trailed behind him. It was unlike Meg to come to the pub with him, especially when he was playing darts.

He ordered their drinks, a gin and tonic for her and a Coke for him. As a kid, he'd experimented with alcohol along with the boys on the station, but it made him so sick he never tried it again. Even the smell of it put him off.

Looking around, he did a mental roll call. He saw Sebastian Peach. Better still, Sebastian had brought Jane along, although like Meg, she'd not been here Friday either. The estate agent, looking smooth and polished as he always did, ushered his wife into the lounge bar. He guided her towards a corner table with the exaggerated courtesy of a showman. Sebastian put the tray down just as Zack caught up with him and clapped him on the shoulder.

"Hi, Sebastian, are you playing tonight?"

"Ah-ha, our esteemed professor, how are you? How are the little egg-heads up at the school treating you?" Sebastian held out his hand to shake. "Be there in a jiffy, just settling the lady-wife in." His mouth split open in a bright smile that showed a perfect set of dentures. Jane nodded to Meg, curving her lips into a hesitant smile.

"Hey, Jane! Good to see you." Zack pumped her hand. "I suppose you'll be on your own too? How about if Meg joins you for the duration of the darts match?" He winked at Meg, and giving her no opportunity to back out, he turned to Sebastian, who also looked pleased with this precipitate arrangement. "Right, that's settled. Let's go!"

That should keep her out of his hair, and away from Colin. There was no way Zack wanted those two getting into conversation.

*

At first, Hannah found herself too busy to get to know the names of those she was serving. But as she became more familiar with the routine, she had time to stop and converse with the customers. Mac had lost some of his earlier reserve. Occasionally, either he or Doug, if they were nearby, gave her a running commentary, fitting names to faces. She had recognised Sebastian Peach, as soon as she saw him. *Smart bloke, always wears a suit,* Izzy Foster from the garage, had said.

Jed, came in with a group from the *Crows* team and went straight through to the back bar and the dartboard. Hannah hardly recognised him from the man she'd seen working on the boats earlier in the day. Jed's crisp, pale blue open-neck shirt contrasted with his sun-browned arms. His designer jeans fitted as though made to measure.

"Can I help you?" she asked, as he approached the bar.

When he looked at her, his eyes flared in an expression she couldn't read. He wasn't the only one to have done a double take this evening. Her presence emphasised the absence of their usual barmaid. He ordered a jug of beer for his team. His appraisal lingered longer than most, his golden hair, shining under the lights, fanned out across his shoulders. His grin had too much of leer in it for her comfort. It showed strong uneven teeth with a small gap and a broken eyetooth that gave him a slightly lop-sided look. But, aware she was playing a role she smiled back.

"No Billy tonight?" Mac asked Jed, over Hannah's shoulder.

"Nah, looks after his mum on Tuesdays. Doug playing tonight?"

"Doubt it. He's helping on the bar. We're building up quite a crowd."

Jed took his tray and holding it aloft, edged away through a clump of customers.

"Billy follows that man like a stray dog," Mac said, "you rarely see one without the other. Don't know how Jed puts up with it sometimes. Billy's okay, but you don't want him on your heels all the time, do you?"

The outside door swung open and bounced against its rubber stop. A man in a hurry strode in. "That's Lennie, Vicky's boyfriend," Doug whispered in Hannah's ear.

"He doesn't look too happy – hardly surprising as he's lost his girlfriend."

"Not only that, Lennie's not a happy little Vegemite. He's been down the station nearly all day. It seems Vicky's pregnancy came as a shock. Says it's not his."

Lennie reached the bar, glanced along it looking for staff. "I'll have a whiskey chaser, if anyone's serving here tonight," he said, in a loud voice to combat the background music now turned up to the volume that Vicky liked to work with.

"I'll do this," Hannah stepped forward to make up Lennie's order.

"Hey, wasn't this one of Vicky's favourites?" shouted one of the punters.

"Yeah, that's why they're playing it, dickhead," answered another. She glanced sideways at Lennie as she poured his beer. He ignored the comments.

With his short black wavy hair, his light grey eyes framed in dark lashes, she could see why Vicky would be smitten. As she handed him the second glass, their eyes locked. Her budding smile congealed in the face of his cold, unfriendly stare. She backed away.

He pulled up a stool and sat, one elbow on the bar, his forehead resting in the heel of his hand. His posture did nothing to encourage conversation and people left him alone.

Other customers backed up behind him. "Yeah, I'll have two middies and a Bacardi and Coke, please," called one over Lennie's shoulder.

Bacardi and Coke. Hannah took a long glass from the rack above her head, and tonged in the ice cubes. That used to be her drink. She hadn't had one of those since *that* night. It had been the retirement party for Simon's boss. Only a month after Simon's death, a party was the last thing she wanted. But Simon's friends persuaded her a night out would do her good.

How wrong they were.

She turned her back on the customer to find the Bacardi bottle and began to mix the drink. The smell hit her nostrils. She pulled back ... too late ... the room darkened.

Amongst his friends, but without Simon, desperation drives her away from the celebrating crowd. She strolls outside to the shadowy light of the illuminated beer garden. Not thinking straight, she leaves her drink on a table while she visits the loo. She returns alone to pick up her glass. Other drinkers watch her from the shadows. She moves away from them, face aching, sick of socialising. The sound of running water attracts her and she wanders towards it. The gentle splash of water falling over rocks into a pond relaxes her, while in her glass the dark coloured liquid hides an added ingredient ...

"You all right with that?" Mac asked, as he brushed past her.

Hannah, startled, pulled away from him. "Yes, I'm fine," she snapped, and finished pouring the potent drink. She added lemon slices to the glass before turning around to face the customers. She pulled the middies to complete the order, the sweat on her upper lip growing cold.

*

In the lounge bar, light filtered through the red shades of the wall lamps creating the soft lighting. Meg struggled to find topics of conversation that might interest Jane, furious with Zack for dumping her like that. The slim waif of a girl sat opposite her with her long straight hair covering the sides of her face. Jane's comments, mainly monosyllables, offered nothing in return. It was heavy work. They'd been talking about the murdered barmaid. Who talked of anything else?

"I heard that Vicky and your Sebastian had a fight across the bar on Friday," she said, watching for a reaction. "Do you know what all that was about?"

Jane looked up, her eyes like those of a startled possum. Her mouth dropped open for a second before she took control. "Who told you that?"

"I heard someone talking about it in the newsagent's this morning.

"Some people have nothing better to do than gossip." Jane retreated into the shadowy corner of the seat and sipped the dregs from her glass. Meg sighed, another dead end. Her glass was almost empty, too. "Look, I'll go and get us another couple of drinks. Doesn't look like the guys will be back for a while, anything else you want?"

Jane shook her head and surrendered her glass, looking nervously around the dimly lit room, as if to see who was watching.

Meg returned with two long gin fizzes and a bag of prawn crackers. When she approached the table Jane sat a little more upright, adjusting her clothes as she did so. It must have been the shadows from the wall light. She hadn't noticed it before, but Meg could have sworn that above the cuff on her three-quarter-sleeve blouse, Jane was sporting a ring of black bruise.

* * *

6

At nine-thirty, after a nod from Steele at the back of the room, Mac rang a bell for the start of the re-enactment.

Someone turned the music off and conversation died. Hannah moved away into the lounge bar. A young woman came through the hotel's interior swing doors to a collective intake of breath from the waiting punters. She took Hannah's place alongside Mac behind the counter.

Constable Linda James wore a skimpy top, short black leather skirt, and high heels. She shook her head and ran her fingers through her blond wig, settling it over her shoulders. She looked up at Mac, her smile letting him know she understood his pain.

He nodded, swallowing hard. Victoria's look-alike moved around behind the bar as though she was working. After a couple of minutes, she gave Mac a small wave and quietly slipped away. She collected a jacket and the tote bag from a peg on the wall and walked out the door of The Harbour Lights.

Mac held his breath. In the silence she left behind, he could almost hear a number of heartbeats drum-roll the moment.

He cleared his throat and addressed his customers. "Okay, folks, that's as far as it goes inside. The police officers outside will be monitoring who goes where and when. If anyone has any queries, or notices anything different from Friday, sing out. All that is asked of us now, is that you leave here the same time as you did on Friday, and take the same route home, or to wherever you went afterwards. So anyone who may have left at this time should go, now. Okay?"

There were a few murmurs of dissent. One looked at his

watch and remained seated. Another gave his companions a self-conscious grin and headed for the door.

Mac changed the CD. Wendy Matthew's *"The Day You Went Away,"* took on a whole new meaning. He turned the music up to its former volume. Conversation resumed the battle against its decibels. Vicky would have liked that.

*

Back in her room at the end of the evening, Hannah's body ached with fatigue. She ignored the pain while she briefly wrote up her notes, a daily journal she could edit later and use as a basis for her report. Although tempted, she couldn't track every man's alibi for the night Vicky was murdered, that was not her job, but she could look at those closest to Vicky for her own satisfaction.

Only by becoming deeply involved in her work would she drown out the images in her head. There could be large-scale drugs in Draper's Wharf. And Vicky had two Es. She'd find out who Vicky's friends were and who supplied her. But there was also a rapist and a killer. If she could only find him, perhaps she could exorcise the demons in her own head.

She opened her laptop to the file she'd dubbed DW, checked previous entries and began to type. Re-enactment Tuesday:

Doug had arrived 7.30 – Arranged their routine contact times – evenings at Harbour Lights. Confirmed tablets taken from Vicky's drawer were Ecstasy and gave her a general run-down on persons of interest..

IZZY FOSTER: arrived 7.40 with partner, plump, pale face, plum coloured hair, not his wife. On Friday, the night of the murder, he played darts for Crows team. No one saw what time he left after match.

SEBASTIAN PEACH: Arrived 7.45 with wife Jane, a young timid looking blonde.

Friday: Left the pub around 9.30 went straight home, time

45

confirmed by wife.

ZACK HENDERSON: 7.45 and wife joined company with Sebastian Peach. The women stayed in lounge bar, while the men moved on to the darts game.

Friday: Claims he was there all evening. Confirmed sighting in car park at closing time.

JED MANNING: 7.50 with other members of the Crows. Began darts game at 8.00.

Friday: Went home after match 9.30. Wife Cassandra confirmed time he came in 'looking for nooky.' (Perhaps that's the only thing left to do in DW after dark!)

COLIN PRENTICE: (the music man) Arrived with Jed.

Friday: Stayed 'til closing. Played piano after the match. Confirmed.

LENNIE COOPER: 8.25 didn't join darts game. Sat at the bar most of the night.

Friday: Was there 'til closing, took part in the singing. Confirmed

MORGAN DRAPER: the town's backhoe worker and digger of graves came in at 8.00 ready for a game of darts...

Hannah fingers hovered over the keyboard and she recalled an incident involving Morgan in the pub earlier in the evening. She'd been behind the bar when she spotted a disturbance from the back of the saloon.

"Shit! What's that stink? Who's let one off?" A man yelled, getting to his feet, holding onto his nose and stomping around in a good imitation of a circus clown.

"Hey, Morgan!" a second voice joined in. "Isn't it time you took Billy home and changed his pants?" The speaker clapped his drunken mate on the back, and they both folded up with belly wrenching laughter. Hannah recognised the two old codgers she'd heard discussing Marty's funeral.

Morgan Draper, his face dark with a three-day stubble, looked fit to spit. He glared at the culprits like they were something that had crawled out of one of his graves.

"Shut your mouth, Maggot. Billy's not here and you know

it!" he said.

She'd asked Mac what it was all about.

"It's only old Ned and Maggot taking the piss," he said. "They're harmless really, but we could do without their sense of humour tonight."

The two troublemakers started a slow handclap. "Billy out, Billy out, Billy out!" The chant swelled as some of those nearest to the stomping pair, tired of the solemnity of the evening, followed suit, grinning at the two instigators.

"What's Billy got to do with it?" she whispered. "He's not even here."

"On Friday, he had the runs," Mac explained. "Shit his pants, big time. He was despatched out of here pretty damn quick. Morgan – as his uncle – had the job of taking him home. That lot were doing this then."

Morgan had left with bad grace and the old codgers settled down once more; no one could argue they weren't there until closing. Her fingers went back to work. Morgan and Billy adequately provided each other with alibis.

BILLY DRAPER: No show tonight. Friday night: Morgan left at 10.15 to take Billy home, time confirmed by Billy's mother.

Weary to the bone, and too tired even for a shower, she packed her work away. She undressed and fell into bed exhausted. But her mind wouldn't rest. Every time she closed her eyes, old images from her last flashback appeared and grew fat as though the memory needed to finish its progression through her head before allowing sleep to take over. Too drained to fight it off, she let the painful scene continue.

Alone by the waterfall, her glass slips from her hand. Her legs feel weak. She needs to get back to Simon's friends in the lounge bar. She stumbles onto wobbly feet. Two men appear out of the shadows. Too late she realises they haven't come to help. They slip their hands beneath her arms and lead her away from the safety of the crowd, out of the back gate to a waiting van. She hears the familiar sound of police sirens, but oh, so far away and not for her. They open the van's doors and throw her in.

Enough. She couldn't go any further tonight. Going to bed without washing her hair was a mistake. She dragged her body out of bed, put the light on and washed her face in cold water to wake up thoroughly.

Earlier in the day, she'd located the linen cupboard on the landing. She opened the bedroom door. Outside in the hallway a small security light burned. She crept out of her room along the passage to the cupboard. Apart from the roof timbers creaking, the house was silent. She checked over the banisters, nobody about. She opened one of the cupboard doors, found the pillowcases, quickly tucked one under her arm and closed the door. Back in her room, she stripped off her pillowcase and replaced it with the clean one. Taking the first into the shower with her, she washed it thoroughly and hung it over the rail to dry. She scrubbed and dried her hair before climbing back into bed.

The day had been so full. This morning's breakfast was a distant memory.

* * *

7

Hannah walked alongside Grace up the short path to the church. Young Elizabeth, Grace's younger daughter, walked on the other side of her mother, her face pale, her gaze brittle. The girl was trying so hard to be brave. Hannah wondered if she was even aware of the runnels of tears that slid down her cheeks.

As Hannah was her only relative this side of the Nullarbor, Grace had asked her to accompany them to Victoria's funeral. Her husband, Vicky's father, had not yet been traced.

To Grace's surprise most of the town turned out for the occasion. Newspaper stories had touched the hearts of strangers, too. People crowded into the church. Banks of floral offerings lined their route.

Grace had not yet managed to cry for her first-born. Instead, as she tried to explain to Hannah, the tears evaporated in the dry desert of her mind and caused her blinding headaches. Down the narrow aisle, Hannah walked a few steps behind mother and daughter. She followed them into the front pew, where the three of them sat in melancholy silence waiting for the service to begin. Victoria's coffin, draped with casket sprays, stood waiting between four burning candles in wrought iron holders.

Hannah turned to look over her shoulder at Mac sitting behind them, then on to Lennie, who looked unusually pale and sickly, and why wouldn't he? Vicky had been his girl. Would the killer have the nerve to attend his victim's funeral? Was *he* sitting among them? She knew police officers in plain clothes would be watching and making notes, looking for that one small oddity that didn't fit.

The TV cameras kept a discreet distance. Afterwards, the media packed their gear and went away. Draper's Wharf was yesterday's news.

*

The following day at The Harbour Lights, with the evening winding down, most of the patrons had gone home. Doug sat on the customer side of the bar in a despondent mood, his hands wrapped around a glass of iced orange.

He'd always prided himself he could take the rough with the smooth, but sometimes he reckoned his job was the arse end of the careers market. Today, he'd found a baby's body stuffed into a sports bag, lying at the bottom of the harbour. Not such a rare story – baby cries, de-facto whacks it, hides the body, then claims someone walked off with it. But this time they had him. The stupid bastard left his name and address inked in on the fabric inside the bag.

Doug hadn't wanted to come out tonight. It had been one distressing thing after another today. He kneaded his temples. He should've been home with Mara and the littlies, but they were away down at her sister's place. In the end, the empty house drove him out. He missed Mara. She could read him like a bush-tracker, and knew how to gentle him back to his usual humour after one of his bad days.

Hannah came alongside him carrying a tray laden with used glasses. "Cheer up Doug; you look like a wet weekend." She put the tray down on the bar top within reach of the glass-washer. "When does Mara get back?" she asked.

"After her sister's had the baby, I suppose. It's due any day. What, between my brother, and her sister, it's a wonder we ever get time together."

"Ach, stop your whingeing, man. You've got it made." Mac's voice held a tinge of envy, and it wasn't the first time Doug had heard it. Reminded of Mac's failed marriage, he hauled in his sinking morale. Sometimes, he forgot how lucky he was. As boys, he and Mac had fought a constant battle for supremacy. Mac had the years, but Doug had the weight. Now, of course, he no longer had to strive to beat his brother. They both knew that since Mac's diving accident, Doug was streets ahead. His career and his health intact, his marriage happy, and kids to top it off – no wonder Mac sounded cheesed.

"Anyway, how about you, Hannah, is he working you to death yet?" Doug dropped the lid on his bad day and tried to relax.

"Me? I'm his galley slave." She laughed as Mac's mouth dropped open. "Only kidding!"

"Watch it – I can always sack you. Tonight, you haven't even earned your keep."

Doug watched their inter-play relieved that Mac had taken a shine to Hannah. It made communication with Hannah that much easier for him. The last group of punters waved and cheered as they made for the door. Mac followed behind them ready to lock up.

"Don't suppose you've anything worth reporting yet?" Doug asked Hannah. "I'll be here most evenings. We can go into the back room while Mac's busy with the till."

"Nothing of substance yet. I'm taking it slowly; getting to know the place, the people and generally fitting in."

Mac headed towards them glasses and dishes piled on his tray. "Do we get to hear any results from the re-enactment, Doug?" he asked, passing his load to Hannah to deal with.

"Not much to tell, a number of inconsistencies showed up. You know, people turning up in places they shouldn't have been. The light that was on in the back of Foster's garage the night Vicky was murdered wasn't on the re-enactment night. The man seen running into the pub's car park around ten, didn't appear this night. And repeats of the stuff we already knew. Someone was having a domestic, others smooching in the school playground, someone loitering outside the toilets – a lot of chaff for the lads to work through, it becomes a slow old job when, so far, it's all hearsay and there's no hard evidence."

"Your search of the harbour was a waste of time," Mac said. "When are we going to get some real information?"

"Like the rest of us, you're gonna to have to wait." Doug answered shortly. He could understand Mac's impatience, but too often, the public had no idea of the amount of effort going into an investigation. Just because answers didn't drop off trees, they assumed the cops weren't doing anything.

Mac threw him a speculative look. "Want a nightcap?"

"Not for me, I'm driving. What about you Hannah?"

She beamed at him, and then turned to Mac. "Thanks, I'll have a brandy."

Mac took two glasses down from the rack, poured a neat whiskey for himself and gave Hannah a snifter.

"With no physical evidence left behind," Mac asked, "why did the police test all the men in Draper's Wharf? What was the point of that?"

Doug sighed. "A question of timing. They closed the town immediately, in the hope of catching their man before he left the area. It's easy enough to do a mass saliva swab in a small place like this. If the chances are high that the perp is a local, it can be helpful to test everyone fitting the profile." Doug said, and finished off his orange juice.

"I remember they did that a few years back." Hannah said. "In a small town up north, it was in all the papers at the time. They tried out the voluntary mass testing of every man between the ages of 16 and 60."

"Yep, and it worked. It would have looked a bit suss in such a tiny community if anyone had refused. Nobody did, and the investigators got their man. It also shows up the innocent, most guys are only too glad to be eliminated."

"Should we be talking about this?" Mac inclined his head slightly towards Hannah. "Walls have ears, and all that jazz."

"Lighten up, Mac." Doug sat back on his stool. "Hannah's not going to rush off to the papers with a scoop, and there's nothing here that isn't already on its way to the public arena, one way or another. You know me better than that."

Hannah raised her hands, "Okay, if you guys want to talk alone, I'll go and ..."

"There's no need," Doug said. "Stay. It's good to have the feminine input."

Mac pressed his lips together and shrugged. "Just thought I'd mention it."

Hannah looked from one to the other. "So, what if the murderer wasn't a local?"

Mac peered at her, as though looking over the top of half-moon spectacles. Doug knew the mannerism; Mac had picked it up from their father. In those days it meant, tread carefully, or you'll get a thick ear. He could understand Mac's reticence. Doug had told him often enough to mind his own business when it came to police work. Mac would resent a stranger listening in on their conversation. But then, Mac didn't *know*.

He rattled the remaining ice cubes around the bottom of his tumbler. "I will have that nightcap Mac, thanks. Make it a Scotch, will you." He turned to Hannah. "Yeah, the stranger theory, that's one line of enquiry still being followed, although no one really believes it. There's local knowledge. They reckon it's more like our man went ahead and took the DNA test, confident nothing would show."

"You mean he wore a condom," Hannah said.

"Not necessarily – that's the funny thing about it. Other than the soil from the grave, she was *too* clean, like she'd just come out of the shower. There was no sign of him on her anywhere, apart from the massive bruising, of course."

"Bastard!"

"Maybe she was clean because the grave was full of water," Hannah suggested.

"Forensic reckons it's more than that; inside her nails had been scraped, and even her own bodily fluids were absent." Doug took a long swallow of his drink. "Whoever cleaned her up took their time about it. Forensic say someone had physically washed her out before burying her. That cold-blooded shit had

53

used a hose on her."

*

Hannah took her cigarette onto the balcony for her nightly ritual. Down to three smokes a day, morning, noon and night. The solitary sojourn, standing in the dark gave her time to think, time to sort her disenfranchised mind, time to pick up the pieces and put them back in their rightful memory boxes – to become normal again.

At the far end of the balcony, light spilled through the curtained windows of Mac's room. At night he left his French windows open to the fresh air. He'd never attempted to join her on the balcony, thank heavens; she had come to regard this space as hers. She leant over the balustrade. The red glow of her cigarette performed aerobics in the air from her hand movements.

Before coming out she had completed her notes on the laptop. Mac was cagey about her presence. But when Doug shared his latest piece of news, mutual revulsion had united them. The murderer had washed his victim down, no, *hosed her out*, let's have it in plain English. Had there still been life in Vicky's body at the time? Had she felt the water cold on her face, streaming through her hair? Hannah's scalp prickled, her fists bunched in a conscious effort to prevent her scratching nails from reaching her head. She took a few deep breaths to stop the images before they started.

Slowly, she guided her thoughts back on track, back to the scene of the Draper's Wharf crime, trying to work out the mechanics of the burial. After cleaning his evidence away, Vicky's murderer still had to transport her to the graveyard without being seen. He must have lowered himself into the open grave in order to dig a niche for her at its base. Could he have reached out to pull her in while he was standing in the pit, or would he have had to climb out? After that, he had to cover her with the excess earth, and smooth it out so it was not obvious during the official burial the next day.

Like the old codger said, but for that rainstorm, he might have succeeded. The task must have taken him hours. Someone surely, would know who was out all night, and who came home with soiled clothes.

The moon looked high and lonely, the sky clear and brilliant with stars, some large enough to reflect in the gently moving water. Hannah's glance swept the navy blue canopy, pausing to locate the Southern Cross. Lower down, against the loom of the distant Sydney lights, she could make out the whole of the wharf, the cross trees of the yardarm on the jetty. The night felt eerily quiet, hardly a ruffle of wind to disturb the rigging on the moored boats; nor any sound of traffic on the river or on the road below.

It was as though the world was holding its breath, waiting for something to break.

* * *

8

At breakfast the next morning, Mac told Hannah Izzy Foster had phoned and left a message to say her tyre was ready for collection.

"Good, I'll go this morning." She needed an excuse to nose round his place. Going on looks alone, she'd put Foster among the traffickers – but she knew looks didn't count. There were untold legions of smart blokes in city suits pulling in dollars from the drug trade. What was more interesting was that he had a light burning in his back room on the night Vicky died. As he didn't live on the premises, what had he been up to in his back room at that time of night? Had he accidentally left it on, as he claimed? Was the date coincidental?

Mac said no way would Vicky have been visiting Foster. But Mac didn't know about the Ecstasy. Could Vicky have turned left in order to visit her supplier and possibly seen something she shouldn't have – is that why she died? On the other hand, why would she do that if she still had two tablets in the drawer back home in her bedroom?

Hannah pulled into the side of the forecourt and parked. Foster had a customer with him. The two of them looked busy, their heads bowed beneath the bonnet of a car. Her glance around Confirmed Foster's garage looked the same as any standard service station. The fuel pumps lined up in the front forecourt under a large metal canopy. The toilets on one side of the main building, shop in the middle and large workshop on the end.

She strolled towards the building, angling for the corner, intending to walk around the back. This side had a do-it-yourself car washing area. Two hosepipes connected to large brass taps, and coiled neatly around drums mounted on the wall. The sight sent prickles marching along her spine. She shook her head and moved on. It was perfectly standard equipment for an auto station.

The ground sloped downwards and what she supposed was the back room was an extension stuck out at a ninety-degree angle behind the main building. It had a window placed high up, and a low wall ran along the front of it. A light in there would be easily visible from the road. She turned back and retraced her steps. Foster and his customer were no longer on the forecourt. She entered the shop and browsed along the shelves offering a range of motor accessories. Foster stood behind the counter chatting with his customer. They appeared to be sharing an 'in-law' joke. She didn't catch the punch line.

"Yours cause you much grief?" The customer asked at the end of his chuckle.

"What, the Old Goat? Nah, I'm paying him off next week. After that, he can stuff his hassling where the sun don't shine." Foster's slightly nasal voice sounded whiny.

"Wish mine were that easy to get rid of. Right, seeya later, Izzy."

She moved back and waited while the customer pocketed his change and left.

"You looking for something?" Foster's voice hailed her.

"I've just come to collect my tyre. You phoned."

His grin, hampered by a piece of green stuff lodged between his teeth, widened as he recognised her. "Oh yeah, this way, it's in the workshop." He jerked his head for her to follow him.

Outside, a black Magna had pulled up at the pumps. Foster ambled ahead of her to the workshop, whilst constantly glancing towards his new customer. The man stood, with his back to them, filling his petrol tank.

Foster's former flirtatious manner had taken a hike as he hurried her through the bill paying process. He turned away leaving her to carry the spare wheel to her vehicle. With a few choice words about non-existent customer service, Hannah fixed the spare in place in the boot. She did a U-turn and checked her rear view mirror. Behind her, the driver of the black Magna and Foster stood side-by-side staring after her. She pulled out onto the road. Where had she seen that black car before?

Foster: what had he been doing in the backroom around ten o'clock last Friday? No one could positively pin him down in the pub after the darts match. His wife had been staying over with her parents that night and hadn't seen what time he came home, so Mac had said. On the other hand, being creepy and eyeballing the girls didn't make him a villain. And, everyone had access to water and hoses of one kind or another.

*

Grace's café buzzed with activity. Hannah stepped up to the counter as Grace was loading one tray, while another customer waited to pay and two others queued.

"Can I help you?" Hannah asked. "You look a bit busy."

"Oh, Hannah, if you would, I'm rushed off my feet today. You could take this order over to those two, if you like." She nodded to a couple of women sitting at a table in the corner.

"That's Betty and her sister Vi. They're the ones I said might help you with the history of the town, you know, for your article. Well, Vi has some story up her sleeve she's dying to tell someone."

Hannah smiled as she approached the two old ladies. She put the tray on the edge of the table. Violet, who sat tall and unbending, studied her critically. With deep-set eyes that looked out over a stern, angular face, she reminded Hannah of the women in old sepia photos her grandmother had on her sideboard years ago.

"Grace got herself a waitress now, has she?" Violet sniffed.

As sisters go, they were opposites. Betty, had light blue eyes a plump round face, her skin looked as soft and lined as old tissue paper. In a fleeting moment of fancy, Hannah wondered if each resembled a separate parent.

"Eat your cake, and don't be so bloody ungrateful." Betty tapped the table with her forefinger in front of her sister. She helped Hannah unload the tray and then nodded to the creamy Pavlova. "Look at her, skinny as a cricket, yet she stuffs herself silly with things like that. And me – I've only got to look at it for the weight to roll on."

"You're only jealous. I always did have a better figure than you." Violet preened. Betty waved a dry papery hand towards Hanna. "Sit down, come and join us. You're no waitress, you're Gracie's cousin, I hear. Didn't you bring yourself a coffee?"

"No, that's all right, I'll have mine later. Grace told me about your husband, Betty. I'm sorry to hear about your loss."

Betty's face clouded over. "Yes, poor old Marty, but it was a merciful release. He'd been ill for a long time and it never suited him. He was what you'd call an active man. I reckon he's better off where he is. So, don't you go wasting your sympathy on me." She nodded sagely towards the counter. "She's the one that needs it."

Hannah nodded. "Grace tells me you ladies have a story to tell?"

Violet snipped a piece off her delicacy with a fork and put it in her mouth. She glared across the room. Grace gave her a nod and an encouraging smile.

"Go on Vi, tell her about your ghosts," Betty said.

"It's all right for you to laugh. We don't all play possum with our heads in a book. Some of us take note of what goes on around us." Vi paused for another bite. "Shadows that's all. People moving around at night where they've no business being."

"Ooh, like where?" asked Hannah, instantly alert.

"In Betty's backyard for a start," Vi said, nodding her head towards her sister.

Hannah recalled that Betty and Vi lived in the cottages next door to the Drapers.

"No Vi, not him, that's only Lennie going to the shed." Betty turned to Hannah to explain. "Lennie rents our shed down the backyard. Marty arranged it, a couple of years back. Pays good money, too." She lowered her voice and cast her eyes around the room. "But don't go shouting the odds – all right? Don't want those nosy bods at Social Security getting wind of it, do we?"

Hannah shook her head quickly. "Won't breathe a word," she whispered. "But, I would've thought Lennie had enough shed room of his own, why does he want yours?"

"Too right!" Vi said, "you don't even know what's in it."

"Never looked, Marty said we weren't to. Any man paying over the odds was entitled to his privacy, he said. But then Marty was like that, help anybody, he would. And he didn't poke his nose in anyone's concern. Not like some I could name."

"But, you say he goes in and out *at night*?" asked Hannah.

"Well, can't say I've ever seen him," Betty continued. "There's a gate down the back he uses, so he doesn't have to come to the house or anything, but according to Miss Marple here ..."

"That'll do from you, Betty Martin! He might have that window boarded up, but I can still see the light around it some nights. Anyway, maybe that's not important, that's not all I've seen."

"Okay, Violet, tell us the rest," Hannah said, and gave Betty a warning look. She wanted to hear the story from Violet's lips.

"I see other lights."

"Where do you see these lights?" It was like pulling a donkey out of a pit.

"Oh, round about. Sometimes it's up around the wharf, and sometimes I see them across the water on the beach over there."

"Okay." Hannah drew on her mental picture of Draper's Wharf, how the coastline curved around like a shallow horseshoe, and could see that from the position of Violet's cottage she would be able to look straight across the little bay to the beach on the other side. "What about you Betty, you're right next door; do you see these lights?"

Before Betty could answer Violet interrupted, "No, you can't see the same bit from her place. Lennie's boats are in the way."

"So, that's what you were doing poking around my curtains the other night," Betty shook her head in mock exasperation. "She'll be telling you next that it's the ghost of old Willie Draper!"

"I will not! Look who's talking – won't come for a walk with me after dark. Anyway, that's the story, for what it's worth. Though, I don't know why Grace bothered to tell you. What do you know about it?" Violet sniffed again.

"Nothing Violet, but I'm trying to get a few stories together about the town for an article I'm doing for a magazine. I haven't been along that side of the beach. Mac McKay says there's nothing up there but a few shacks. Could it be a late night fisherman, do you think?"

Or, had she hit pay dirt? Could that be where the drugs were off-loaded?

Violet pursed her lips, the lines around her mouth cut trenches into her face. "S'pose it could be a fisherman," she said, doubtfully, as though not really wanting to believe it was something so mundane. "But if it is, he's a regular one. He's there most Wednesday nights. And, judging by the second flashlight, he has company."

"Have you told the police this?" Hannah asked, her pulse quickening.

"What, and have everyone laugh at me? No way, she's bad enough!" Vi nodded at her sister.

* * *

9

Hannah returned to the Harbour Lights for lunch. Most of the lunchtime drinkers had left. A few punters sauntered around the games room watching the horseracing on TV. The barely audible sound of taped music mingled with the rise and fall of the caller describing the latest race. She bit into one of Mrs Bates' prawn rolls and the homemade seafood sauce oozed out the sides of it and dropped onto her plate. No one watching, she rescued the escaping dollop with a finger and licked it clean.

Mac worked on the other side of the counter, wiping down the shelves and restocking them: routine jobs. His dark hair looked damp and curly where the last shower had caught him helping to unload a delivery truck. He wore grey T-shirt with a faded *Save the Bears* motif across the back and a large bear paw imprinted on his chest. It suited him. It made a change from the shirt with the rolled up sleeves and tie that he usually wore. She hadn't taken him for an animal lover, but the thought that he cared warmed her.

"What do you make of Violet's story, then?" she asked, the next time he was near enough. She'd told him about Vi's possible fisherman and asked about the shacks, but as usual, someone needed serving and the discussion had become disjointed. Customers were Mac's livelihood, but to her their constant interruption was a pain in the arse, especially when they broke her train of thought.

Mac stopped, dishcloth in hand. He leant against the back counter while he considered her question. "Ramblings of an old woman?" His dark eyes met hers, questioning. "How come she told you about it, anyway?"

"No special reason, it was more her sister egging her on."

Mac smiled. "Talk about the odd couple, like quarrelling chooks those two. I wonder you got any sense out of them."

"Once Vi got into her stride she was pretty sharp remembering what she saw, especially about the lights. Every Wednesday she said, and at least two of them."

"What about this week?"

"No, she looked out for him this week, but he didn't show."

"So, what's different about this week, apart from everything?"

"Do you think it's a coincidence? Thought I might take a walk up that side of the beach this afternoon, have a sticky-beak."

Mac gave her one of his granddad looks. "Feel like company?"

"Hey, that'd be good. What about ..." she indicated the bar.

"Mrs Bates, apart from being our greatest cook, also doubles as a counter hand in quiet times. She's glad of the overtime, just as long as I don't expect her to do the evening." He smiled. "She gets flustered if she has too many customers at once. She's booked in for today anyway, I was going to work on the boat for a couple of hours."

"I didn't know you had a boat."

"No reason why you should; it's an old fishing boat I'm converting. I don't plan on being behind this bar forever, you know."

"So, what are you going to do, go fishing?"

"Fishing for wrecks more like," Mac said, his smile crinkling the lines on his face. "It's a way to get back into diving. Since the accident, I can't deep-water dive any more, but there's no reason why I can't provide a boat for divers who can." He warmed to his subject. "I'll get a partner, one whose certificates are still intact. I know some blokes who'd like to get out of the commercial diving business and into something less stressful.

63

"Hey, Mac, that sounds really good." It was obviously a subject close to his heart; she had never seen him so animated. "I'd like to see your boat sometime."

*

The river, when they could see it between the low-slung branches of the mangrove trees, was the colour of molten lead, and choppy from a brisk southerly breeze. Occasionally, the bank opened out to a rocky beach where seabirds paddled and searched for titbits, and where small, determined waves offered up broken seaweed, driftwood, and aluminium cans to the mangrove roots. With the sun appearing between the showers, the ground gave out a warm, earthy smell.

In spite of Doug's assurances, Mac's fears that Hannah was more than the visiting relative, or the history article writer she claimed to be, still rankled. On the one hand, he felt a constant suspicion that they were under surveillance, but on the other, he enjoyed her company behind the bar. The path narrowed and they moved into single file. He followed her, watching the swing of her hips. She moved like a woman with purpose. He wondered what that purpose might be.

The mangroves ended and the track widened. It led down a slope onto a sandy beach bordered with grassy tussocks. He lengthened his stride to catch up with her, paused and gazed around the shore. Apart from the old shacks, it was empty. Above them the cloud was building again, he hoped the rain would hold off.

"We used to come here fishing when we were kids, but I haven't been out this way for years. Hasn't changed much," he told her. "We made camp over there, in that first shack. Not much left of it now."

"No doubt they were in better nick back then," she said, hands on her hips, feet apart, and hair ruffling in the breeze as she gazed around at the four derelict huts.

"Come on, let's take a look." She waved him on.

The old shacks stood spread across the beach above the high-water mark. Their broken timbers rose, weathered and stark, against the grey sky. The first two resembled little more than bonfires-in-waiting. The next, although minus a door, had part of its roof intact. The fourth, sheltered more from the elements by the nearby stand of tea-trees and banksias, appeared to be reasonably whole.

"Hey, look at this." Hannah whistled and pointed to a shiny padlock on its door.

"So, the old lady was right." Mac glanced across the bay to Violet's cottage. Trust nosy Vi to be the watch-keeper. He wondered how long she'd known about this. "Funny that she's never mentioned it before."

"I think her sister's been teasing her about seeing ghosts and things that go bump in the night. She didn't want to make a fool of herself."

Mac's frown deepened as he looked at the padlocked door. "Okay, so who uses this once a week? If it's a beach bum, you'd expect him to be here every night."

"I don't think beach bums would bother with padlocks," Hannah said, walking around behind the hut.

He peered through a narrow gap in the planking then heard her call.

"Mac! Back here." He hurried around to join her. "Look, I've found a loose plank. Think we can shift it and have a look inside?"

Not normally given to interfering in other people's business, Mac hesitated. This had to be a clandestine arrangement. If it were a legitimate enterprise, so near to home, he would have heard of it by now. He looked around uneasily, but could see no sign of anyone watching.

It didn't take much. Rot had eaten into the edges of the plank and it came away easily. Mac lowered it to the ground, and following Hannah's example, he leaned forward to look inside. His eyes adjusted to the gloom. Small pockets of light leaked in through the crooked planks, which made it possible to see most of the interior.

"He's even got lighting," he whispered, pointing to the candles in wine bottles. "What's that smell, perfume?"

"More like incense. Why are we whispering – there's no one here."

He cleared his throat. "Just because we can't see them ..."

A thin double-sized foam mattress, flanked by mats, took up most of the floor space. On top of the bed lay a brightly coloured comforter, cushions and throws. Beside the bed, a portable stereo CD system sat like a pregnant handbag, and above it all, an oil lamp hung from a central ceiling beam.

"I wish we had more light. I don't suppose you thought to bring a torch." Hannah reverted to her whispering.

"No more than you did, and this isn't someone's fishing shanty." Mac laughed softly. "It's not hard to imagine what goes on here – I wonder who's arranged this little lot." He fell silent as he peered further into the gloom, suspicion growing in his mind. He backed up suddenly. "Han, let's go. This is none of our business."

"Hey, what's up? You've seen something, haven't you?" She looked back into the tiny cabin as though trying to see it through his eyes. "What is it? Has this got something to do with Vicky?"

He couldn't be sure, but his uneasiness was growing. "See that shawl by the pillow? She had one just like that."

"Could this have been where she was coming to the night she died?"

He shook his head. "That was a Friday, not a Wednesday. You said the light showed only on Wednesdays."

"Maybe something cropped up and they had to change the timing."

"They?" His teeth ached. He unclenched his jaw.

"I know you don't like the idea, Mac, but think about it. Supposing, she wasn't sick at all, that she made an excuse to leave early to meet someone. Perhaps something had gone wrong, they had to change the arrangement, unexpectedly."

"She would've asked for time off." He couldn't believe she would have lied to him. In the past, he'd harboured a secret yearning for his barmaid, but she'd never shown the slightest interest in him, not in that way, anyway. She'd tease him sometimes; but underneath it all, her flirtation meant nothing. For him, Vicky was always the butterfly just out of grasp.

"If she was playing away from Lennie, she wouldn't tell you. She'd need to keep it secret, or maybe she had to protect her new lover's identity. Maybe he's married?"

"I can't see it. It doesn't make sense," he said.

"But, it does make sense. Look, outside your door she turned left, instead of right. That fact alone tells you she was lying. After the junction, no one saw her on the road. Maybe, that's because she took this track, and presumably no one but the person she'd come to meet would've seen her."

"Vicky couldn't have walked that distance in high heels, it's ludicrous." He clutched at straws.

"She didn't have to; she had her trainers with her. Grace said they were missing from her wardrobe. Come on, Mac. Think! She must have planned it all along."

"So why weren't her trainers found with her body?"

"Nor were her high-heels, or her jacket, bag or any of her clothes, come to that. They were too bulky to go in the grave with her. He probably disposed of them some other way." Mac stared back along the track. He frowned as an unpleasant thought struck him.

"What?" Hannah asked.

"If you're right, and she came this way, it would have made it easier for the killer to dispose of her. The bottom end of the graveyard backs on to this track. It's not far from the track to the empty grave."

"But the police searched that area, surely?"

"We had heavy rainstorms that day. It washed away any evidence of a struggle, or footprints long before the crime scene lads got there."

Hannah looked back at the hut. "I assume we're ruling out Lennie, you said he stayed in the bar until you closed."

"I don't think this has anything to do with Lennie. Not Wednesdays. He belongs to the local amateur operatic society. Colin Prentice runs it up at the school. Wednesday is their practise night. As you say, it looks like Vicky's been using that night for melodramas of her own. Wednesday is one of my quietest nights. That and Tuesday were Vicky's nights off."

"Okay, how about you call Steele? We have to tell the police investigators about this."

They moved away from the hut onto the beach as the first spattering of rain fell. Mac checked out the sky. Fat, grey storm clouds raced above them. The wind picked up, and small whirls of sand around his feet took to the air. He pulled his mobile from his belt and the inspector's card from his back pocket. He turned to Hannah and used the antenna to indicate the next hut along.

"That one still has a roof; we could shelter in there until they come."

*

Hannah left Mac to complete his call and walked towards the next hut. When she'd found that new padlock, her mind raced ahead imagining the shack being used as drop off point for drug dealers. Then, to discover it was only someone's private shaggery was a huge disappointment.

The cosy little set-up had nothing to do with the drug trade. Mac recognised a wrap of Vicky's. How it got there was anyone's guess, but it could be of vital importance to the murder investigators. It could answer the question of where Vicky had been heading the night of her death.

Approaching the doorway of the next hut, she hesitated. Its door lay flat on the ground. Gingerly, she stepped onto it. Inside, roof timbers angled down across the space, while others lay askew on the floor. A faint smell of decay dusted the air.

Overhead, an aeroplane climbed towards the heavy blanket of cloud; the rumble of its engines echoed back to earth, drowning out all other sound. Hannah paused as she felt its tremor in the loose planking. The whole thing looked like it could collapse around her. When nothing came adrift, she picked her way over the rubble and continued towards the clear space in the back corner.

She stooped to check the floor for rot under the debris. Without warning, a hand pressed down on her back. She let out a strangled squawk, and whirled around hands ready to strike.

"Get off me!"

He towered over her, his body a black silhouette against the light of the sky. She scrambled away, hissing like a cat.

The man took a backward step. He held both hands up level with his shoulders.

"Hey, I'm sorry. It's all right. It's only me. Tripped. Wasn't going to hurt you."

Only then did she recognise Mac. She didn't care. Trapped, she wanted out. She shoved a way past him and made for the opening.

"Hannah – please. Come back. It's only me."

His voice, calm and strong, penetrated her fear. She stopped and looked back at him. With the light on his face, instead of behind his head, she could make out his features.

Fool, stupid fool, she raged at herself for losing control. She covered her face with her hands. Once, she had been an outgoing, carefree woman. One party night had changed all that. Now, she saw peril lurking around every male, and it coloured her reactions to everything. When would it end?

"Hannah. It's pouring with rain out there. Wait here until it eases, all right?"

She hadn't even noticed the rain. Now, its drumming on the tin roof nearly deafened her as she watched it sheeting down through the open doorway. She looked back at Mac. He was holding a red plastic bucket which he turned upside down and put on the ground before stepping away from it.

He held his hand out and smiled. "Would madam care to take a seat?"

It was so incongruous that she laughed, and whatever threat she had seen in him, vanished. Mac lowered himself cautiously onto a fallen roof beam.

Hannah took the bucket from where he had placed it and moved it next to him.

"Oh, Mac! I'm sorry, I'm so sorry. I didn't mean to be shitty."

"Want to tell me about it?"

She didn't have to tell him. He didn't rank as one of those on the 'need-to-know' list. But after that fleeting moment of hurt surprise she'd seen on his face, she wanted him to know the reason for her irrational behaviour. She told him about her husband Simon, and about her rape, briefly with the barest possible details. She siphoned out every bit of emotion that tore into her gut every time she thought, or spoke about it. The only thing she left out was the nature of her real job and her role in Draper's Wharf. That was business.

He listened, squeezing her hand when she came to the more excruciating memories. The rain eased off, and the sun came out. Hannah fell silent.

"Oh, Han, what can I do, what can I say?"

"Nothing. Perhaps we could risk a hug, eh? Then forget all about it," she whispered.

Mac stood, held out a hand to help her up. He put his arms around her gently and held her against him. Strangely, she felt him relax as though she'd answered unspoken questions in his mind.

"I always thought there was more to you than you were letting on, but I never thought it would be anything like this," he said, eventually.

She stirred and extricated herself from his arms, hoping she hadn't said too much. A sympathetic ear and she bawled like a baby. Get up woman, and get on with it. Briskly, she brought her mind back to the business in hand. She brushed the dust off her jeans.   "Did you get hold of Steele?"

"No, the call kept breaking up. It's a bad spot around here for mobile phones."

"Then we'd better get moving. You fit?"

"Okay, let's go." He smiled as though understanding her abrupt change of tack.

On the way back, they passed a small clearing. Mac pointed out a trail that led in through the trees. "See that path? That's the one that leads back into the cemetery," he called out against the wind. The rain had begun again and neither of them wanted to stop.

Back at The Harbour Lights Mac tried once more to get hold of Steele.

"Shit, they've stuck me on hold. Where is the bloody man? How about you make us all a cup of tea, Mrs Bates. Suit you Hannah?"

Hannah scratched at her wet hair, pulling it away from the side of her head. "I have to wash my hair," she said distractedly. "I'll come back for the tea."

"Talking of police," Mrs Bates cut in before Hannah could move away. "Zoe's just back from school, says the police were up there lunchtime today. They wanted to talk to Mr Henderson, that's one of her teachers," she explained to Hannah. "She said they took him off in the police car."

"Zack Henderson!" Mac and Hannah said in unison.

*

Zack Henderson faltered at the doorway, staring into the cell. A green, vinyl-covered mattress on a narrow bunk provided colour in a flaking cream painted cell. The place reeked of old vomit and disinfectant.

A heavy hand landed between his shoulder blades and pushed him forward. Behind him, the steel door clanged shut. He jerked around in time to see the flap of the peephole open. An eye appeared before the swing-cover settled back into place.

71

Alone, for the first time in hours. He sat hunched on the edge of the bunk, disoriented. The walls crowded in on him. No one had ever locked him up before, and the speed at which it happened, he couldn't believe it. All those years of trying to better himself and he still ended up in jail.

Brought up on a cattle station, where his dad worked as a Pommy jackeroo, and his mum, a pretty girl from the local tribe worked as a teacher at the nearby mission. He'd even had the benefit of an education along with the boss's kids. He was the one who'd made it good, school, university, history teacher. He was going to make his mark on life. Who was he kidding? He looked around his cell. A primordial fear crept into his heart.

Only this morning he'd been safely ensconced in his classroom discussing the year 1901 and the history behind the Federation with his Year 12 students, when they called him out. At first, it had seemed like any other request from the police. Simply to help answer a few more questions. He had gone along with the officers in good faith. During the interview with Detective Inspector Steele and his sharp-faced sidekick Sergeant Pike, he received his first shock.

They knew about his affair with Vicky Brown.

"Why didn't you tell us this when we first questioned you?" the sergeant had asked.

"I didn't want my wife to know. It wasn't relevant. I thought I could keep it quiet." As an excuse, it sounded weak. If Meg found out, there'd be hell to pay. He still loved his wife and didn't want to lose her, but Vicky had been a passion that absorbed his every waking moment. He wanted desperately to keep them both.

"So, would it be true to say that you would do anything to prevent your wife getting to know of your affair?" Steele asked.

Spotting the obvious trap, Zack remained silent.

"Answer the question, please."

"Not anything – I wouldn't have harmed Vicky in any way. I did not kill her."

"I put it to you that you did kill your girlfriend to stop the news of her pregnancy getting out." The sergeant's cocky voice betrayed his smugness.

"What pregnancy?" Shocked for the second time, he looked at Steele for confirmation.

The Inspector studied him quietly for a moment. "You telling us you didn't know?"

"It's no good you denying it. We have a DNA match."

Zack ignored the bumptious little sergeant and waited for the Inspector's reply.

"Yes, it's true. The foetus was about ten weeks old. As Sergeant Pike says, the DNA in the sample you gave us voluntarily last week tells us that you are the daddy."

He should have asked for a solicitor there and then, but his mind was reeling. Could that have been why Vicky broke all the rules and called him at school to arrange an extra meeting? Was that the news she had to tell him?

And so the questioning had continued. How long had the affair been going on; when did she tell him she was pregnant; had it been the night she died; who knew, and so on? Then, someone had interrupted, and the officers stopped the interview. He asked if he could go, but they said they hadn't finished with him yet. At least it gave him a break to try to assimilate the information he'd learned. That time the two officers had left him in the interview room with a cup of tea, and a hefty officer guarding the door.

*

"Hannah? Steele's here," Mac's voice called through the door.

"Okay, coming," she put the dryer down, and fluffed up her hair. She slipped into her clean jeans, a blue shirt and ran down the stairs to join them.

Hannah nodded to the two officers and Mac guided them to the table where he had a pot of tea waiting. Steele declined, and Pike looked peeved but shook his head as he watched Mac pour his and Hannah's tea.

"Okay, McKay, you were saying, you walked up the beach to the fishing huts, then what?" Steele resumed his questioning.

Mac described as best he could what they had seen.

"You didn't touch anything, I hope," Pike said.

"We didn't go in, just looked in from the outside."

"Righty-ho. How do you connect it to Vicky Brown?" Steele asked.

"I recognised a shawl, or wrap or something there. It looked like hers."

"Good. And that's when you decided to call us." Steele paused and turned his head slightly to look at Hannah. "What made you go there in the first place?" He asked, eyes narrowed.

"I was talking to a lady in the café, and in the course of conversation she mentioned seeing lights over there at night. I had nothing better to do, so I thought I'd walk over and explore the place this afternoon. Mac came along for the exercise.

"It didn't occur to you to tell us about it first?"

"No, frankly it didn't. There was nothing to tell. At that time, nobody had connected it with Vicky's murder. I was just curious, that's all."

He looked straight into her eyes. The directness of it made her feel uneasy. She gave him a closed lipped smile and raised an eyebrow.

He sat back. "This lady in the café – she has a name?"

After they had gone, Hannah mulled over their conversation. Steele appeared to be uncomfortable around her, yet the local constabulary had been informed of her presence here, so he must be aware of her role. Was he playing it cool in front of others, or was he warning her to stick to her own case and keep out of his?

* * *

10

Hannah pushed the café door open. The Copper Kettle buzzed with muted conversation. The arrest of Zack Henderson had brought the media back in town. Unlike the locals, who stayed away and gossiped behind sheltering hands, the reporters had no such qualms. The police had a suspect for the graveyard murder, the victim's secret lover, the father of her unborn child. They'd found the padlock key to the love-nest on his key ring. The very stuff their editors slavered after.

Behind the counter, Grace was coping with the orders, her mouth a determined line. "Glad to see you, Hannah. Could you do something for me?"

"Just say the word."

Grace moved on to the coffee machine. "I've got Jane in the back room, she started to tell me something, then this lot came in and I haven't had time to get back to her. Can you take her this and sit with her a few minutes, 'til I've got through this lot. I don't want her slipping off before she's had time to say what's on her mind." She handed Hannah two cups of coffee.

Grace's back room felt comfortable and well lived in. Jane, Sebastian Peach's wife, sat at the table, her head resting on her folded arms. She sat up, her face pale, her straight blond hair reaching the table.

"Hi, I'm Hannah, Grace's cousin," she said, handing Jane a cup of black coffee. "Grace won't be long. Mind if I join you?"

"Can if you want," Jane said, as though nothing mattered any more.

Hannah took a chair to sit opposite Jane. "Unusual," she commented, nodding to a vase in the centre of the table, covered with cowry shells.

"She's had that for years. It's crap; I don't know why she keeps it. Vicky and I made it when we were kids." Jane wrapped her hands around her cup.

"Did you spend a lot of time here back then?" asked Hannah.

"Yes, I suppose I did. Grace was like a second mum to me." She indicated the framed photographs on the sideboard and the chintz armchairs. "Nothing's changed. We used to do our homework on this table." She put a hand on its polished surface, fingers tracing the grain as though it were Braille, her eyes filled with tears.

Grace came in and raised a questioning eyebrow. Hannah shook her head unsure if Jane was crying for the past, or the present.

Grace took a chair beside Jane. "Okay, spit it out, what's the problem?"

Jane hastily wiped her eyes with a tissue. "I think I've done something awful."

"Let's hear it, then."

"It's like the other night, with Meg Henderson. I didn't know what to do, what to say." She closed her eyes and covered her face with her hands.

"Meg? What has Meg to do with anything?" Grace wanted to know.

Hannah recalled seeing Jane and Meg together on the evening of the re-enactment. She'd wondered at the time what made a robust figure like Sebastian choose such a delicate creature as Jane for his wife. She was at least ten or twelve years his junior and slim as a wisp of straw.

Jane shook her head. "I don't know. I don't know what she knows."

"Okay," Grace said. "This is getting confusing. Just tell us what happened with Meg. Then we'll see what we can make of it together?"

Jane's face contorted. Thin blue veins showed through the white skin on the back of her hands, as they returned to the table and resumed their tracing. The shop doorbell rang. Grace and Hannah exchanged frustrated glances.

"I'll go. It might be something simple," Hannah said. In the circumstances, Grace might get more out of Jane without her there. It turned out that people had finished up and were leaving, rather than coming in. She waited for the café to empty before returning to the back room in time to hear Jane say:

"I knew Vicky and Zack were lovers. Vicky told me so herself. Then, on the night we went to the pub for the police thingy, there was Zack teaming me up with his wife while he went off to play darts. Meg was the last person I wanted to see. What was I supposed to say to her? And now they think Zack killed Vicky. But he didn't, I'm sure he didn't."

"How can you be so sure?" Grace asked a gruff edge to her voice.

"Well, you've only got to look at him. He's not exactly a big man, is he? She could've fought him off easily, but not just that, Zack's sweet, he's a gentle man. You should see him with the little kids at school. He wouldn't hurt anybody." She took another tissue from her sleeve and blew her nose. "When Vicky and I went to school, we all had a crush on him – Vicky in particular. She's always had a thing for him."

"When did Vicky tell you they were having an affair?" Grace asked. Her voice cracked a little at the mention of her dead daughter's name, but it was obvious to Hannah that Grace was determined to winkle out any grain of information that might help to explain Vicky's death.

"The day before she died. Anyway, Meg obviously suspected something and pumped me to see if I knew. I couldn't tell her, could I?"

"So, what happened?" Grace asked.

"Then, Meg tells me about an argument, between Sebastian and Vicky across the bar."

Jane went quiet and pressed her lips together, as if trying to make up her mind if she should go any further. Abruptly, she undid the cuff of her long sleeved, silk shirt, and avoiding Hannah's eyes, she slowly rolled it up. On her forearm, she wore a bracelet of dark purple and yellow bruises.

Hannah's mind leapfrogged with possibilities. She studied the waif-like face, beautifully sculpted with high cheekbones, flawless skin, and large oval shaped eyes. Jane could be a photographer's dream, but for the shadows beneath those eyes.

"Who did this to you?" Hannah whispered. Jane covered her face with her hands.

"Did *he* do this? Your *husband*?" Grace asked, harshly.

Hannah's thoughts raced ahead. "What you're saying is that Vicky told you her secret about her and Zack, and you reciprocated by telling her yours." She pointed to the bruising. "Am I right?"

Jane nodded.

"And that's what the argument was about between Vicky and Sebastian. She said something to Sebastian that made him realise she knew?" Again, Jane nodded her head. "Did he take it out on you again?" This time Jane shook her head.

"Well, that's something. But that's not it, is it? There is something more?" Hannah asked.

"You don't understand!" Jane took her hands away, and her eyes were bright with fear. "You don't know Sebastian. If he thought Vicky was going to tell, maybe ..."

"Maybe what, Jane?" Grace demanded.

"If he was in a rage, he could've done it. Sebastian could've killed Vicky, don't you see? It makes much more sense than Zack Henderson."

"But you said Sebastian came home at the usual time on the night of the murder," Hannah said, all her senses firing now.

"Yes, that's right. He was home just on 9.30 – he was real ratty when he got in. He wanted to watch some film on TV. But the footy went on over time and all the programs were running late. It made him even madder."

"Well, there you are; you saw him at home. So, he couldn't have done it, could he?" Grace sat back, sighing heavily.

"That's the trouble. I don't know. I went on to bed. Didn't want to stay around and cop any more flak. He could have gone out again. I just can't be sure."

Hannah pursed her lips. The little she knew of Peach indicated he was a social climber. Grace had told her the newly wed couple socialised with 'all the best people,' and Jane had dropped her friends in favour of those of her husband. Could the threat of a wife-bashing charge be enough for Peach to kill in order to keep it quiet? Was this the missing motive?

"Have you told Inspector Steele this?" she asked.

"No! I can't!" Jane yelped. "Look ..." she opened the front of her shirt to show mottled coloured skin attesting to prolonged abuse. "What do you think he'll do to me if I break his alibi? Don't tell them what I said. Honest to God, he'd kill me!"

"It's okay, Jane," Grace put her arm around the girl. "But you have to do something. You can't go on like this. I'll help you if you like. We can do it together."

"No, I can't. You've got to promise."

Grace thumped the table. "Good God, Jane, if you're not going to do anything, why the hell did you tell us?"

"I don't know what to do."

"Grace is right," Hannah said. "You're only twenty-one; you have a whole life ahead of you. You don't need this."

"He's a good husband most times." She paused and wiped her eyes with the crumpled tissue. "He has this great dream for us. We're going to make it big time, but I have to play by his rules. I can't leave him. Ever. If I try that, he says he'll come after me and kill me. He would, too. Look, I think I made a mistake coming here." She pushed her chair back and got up to go. "Come to think of it, he couldn't have gone out that night, or I would have heard his car. Yes, that's it. I would have heard his car, and I didn't. I'm sorry I troubled you Grace, I shouldn't have done that, especially ..." She grabbed her handbag from the back of the chair and stumbled from the room. At the last

79

moment, Jane's courage had failed her. Even though she believed her husband capable of murder, she couldn't go through with the idea of denouncing him.

"Well, what do you make of that?" Grace asked as silence fell again.

"She's in denial. Part of her knows something is terribly wrong, but the other part won't accept it. Did you know Peach knocked her about?"

"Never. When they're out, they always look such a happy couple. But Vicky knew, and she never said."

"Vicky only learned it the day before she died, Grace."

* * *

11

Hannah cleared the tables while Grace completed the take-out lunches. She could see Jane's story was weighing on her mind. But, when Grace next spoke, it was on a different subject. "Did you hear, they confirmed those tablets of Vicky's were Ecstasy?"

Hannah did know, but didn't want to let on she had prior knowledge. "Have you thought of who might have given them to her," she asked.

"I can't believe any of her friends would've done that."

"Maybe, if we could find who supplied her ..."

"When I find out who it was, I'll wring his bloody neck!" The bell rang and conversation ceased as a customer came in.

"Got any doughnuts, Gracie? I got the grandkids coming for tea and they eat me out of house and home. Half a dozen should do it."

Grace took up the tongs, counted out the order and took the money with a distracted air. The customer turned to go and as she reached the door, it swung open. Billy entered and blundered into her. He spun around to look, his startled blue eyes wide, his mouth open.

"Sorry Missus." One hand clamped onto his hat, slapping it back into place. He turned away, a deep flush spreading up his neck.

"Billy! Watch it!" Grace bellowed to him. "Are you all right?" she asked the startled customer in a quieter voice.

The woman waved back. "Youngsters – all rush and tear these days. I'm all right, no thanks to him, though. See you tomorrow, Gracie."

"Now Billy, calm down. I can't have you knocking my customers about, you understand?"

"Yus, Mrs B. I'm late, and Lennie's in a temper. He's always in a temper."

"Why's that, Billy?" Hannah asked him. Billy started at the sound of her voice and spun around to look. He shifted his feet awkwardly as she approached him.

"I'm not supposed to talk to strangers. Jed said."

"Oh, for heaven's sake Billy, what is the matter with you?" Grace's patience was running thin. "Hannah's not a stranger, she's a nice lady. You can talk to her anytime you want, especially if there is something troubling you."

"That's right, Billy, I'm not going to eat you."

"I know that. I'm not daft, you know."

"And, I'm not a stranger, either." Grace wagged her finger at him. "So, what's put Lennie in such a bad temper, then?"

"I dunno. Everything. This it? Can I go, now?" Billy collected his box, stuck it under one arm and left the café.

Hannah lifted a questioning eyebrow at Grace.

"Don't ask me. It's the same with everyone. The whole town's on edge since my girl was killed."

*

If Jane was unwilling to corroborate her story, it wouldn't be much good to the investigators, but Hannah had to pass the information on. She'd put it to Doug tonight.

If the wife abuse was a factor they didn't know about, then it gave a different slant to the case. Was the smooth talking Sebastian capable of killing? His wife thought so. Jane's injuries proved he could be violent, and her story illustrated his power over her.

The type of man who knocked his wife around would have no qualms about rape. He may even have used it as a device, to make the murder look like a rapist's assault, in order to conceal the true motive – self-preservation. A wife beating charge would be the death-knell to Sebastian Peach's social status and his 'great dream' of making it big time.

So, if she had found the motive for Vicky's murder, the question was, had Sebastian left his house and gone in search of Vicky? Jane had not heard the car. Who said he took the car? The distance between Sebastian's house and the churchyard where they'd found Vicky, was approximately ten minutes walking time. If she could come up with something more substantial, then her report would carry weight. All she needed was someone who had seen Sebastian leave his house that night.

Hannah left the café so preoccupied with what she'd heard, and how she could go about getting corroboration, that at first she didn't notice Jed cross the road towards her.

"How're you going?" his voice made her jump.

"Jed, sorry, I was miles away." She gave him a bright smile. He was not the sort of man she would want knowing of her vulnerability.

She waited for him to catch up. A typical outdoorsman in working gear, a singlet, jeans, and sneakers, he brought the scent of wood shavings and engine oil with him. He'd tied his long hair back in a ponytail.

She fell into step beside him. "What are you doing, playing hooky?"

He grinned. "Nah, just going up the pub for smokes. How about you, still with McKay?"

"I'm only filling in for a spell, while he looks for someone permanent."

"Yeah, life moves on, I suppose." His eyes shifted to middle distance.

They walked side-by-side the few extra paces it took them to reach The Crow's Nest. Jed stopped outside the door and looked at her. He tilted his head. "Fancy a quick drink, see how the other half live?"

The opportunity to talk to someone who lived near Sebastian's home was too good to turn up. "You're on."

Jed pushed the door open. It was cool and dark inside. Hannah looked around curiously. Her glance followed the narrow L shaped saloon, and swept up the walls, which were largely unadorned and painted a uniform nicotine tan. A row of framed photographs hung along the wall, opposite the bar. A handful of small wooden tables and chairs together with the cracked, leather-topped barstools provided seating in the dimly lit room. By contrast, harsh fluorescent tubes lit the games room, which formed the foot of the L.

The landlord leaned over the counter deep in conversation with a customer. He stopped talking and stood upright as Jed and Hannah approached. Izzy Foster looked over his shoulder to see who had come in. He turned back to the landlord and raised his hand. "Right, you'll let me know when, okay? See ya." He nodded to Jed and Hannah, and sidled out of the room.

Jed headed away from the bar to the cigarette machine against the wall. He pushed his coins into the slot and collected his pack. He nodded towards the bar. "What'll you have?"

Hannah named her beer. "Not exactly crowded is it?" Even the man behind the bar had gone back to his TV set.

"Not this time of day, comes to life in the evenings. Come on, I'll introduce you. Hey, Razor?" The man gave the screen a last lingering look and came to serve them.

"Jed." Razor walked with a slight stoop, as though used to ducking his head in small places. With the figure of a heavyweight wrestler, he looked too big for the space he occupied. He could be somewhere in his fifties Hannah guessed, though his shaven head made it difficult to judge. He looked from her to Jed without a smile. Hannah's mind double-clicked on alibis. The landlord of The Crows came up clear. His alibi had been the same as Mac's in that he'd been minding his own business all evening, and had scores of witnesses to verify the fact.

Jed performed the introduction with a touch of mirth in his voice. "And, in case you haven't heard yet, Razor, Hannah is the new barmaid up at the "Lights.""

Razor lifted his eyebrows and allowed his glance to travel her figure. His inspection complete, he nodded as though she'd passed muster. Hannah ground her teeth.

"Come to check out the opposition, have you?" he asked. He pulled their beers, and then walked away to the far end of the counter back to his wide screen TV, where horses lined up ready for the off.

Hannah sat on a barstool. She raised her glass at Jed. "Not very sociable, is he?" she whispered. "Why's he called Razor?"

Jed shrugged. "Razor? Don't ask me, maybe it's his wit!" They both laughed. "Well, what do you think? Better than McKay's fancy set up, eh?" Jed swept his beer glass around in a circle without spilling a drop.

In place of Mac's music, the sound of galloping hooves and a caller's excited voice took precedence. Hannah looked at him. "You've got to be joking. Anyway, Mac's place does a different job; it's not just a watering hole, is it?" She glanced around the bar room. The only thing missing was the sawdust on the floor and a spittoon in the corner. The caller's voice grew higher and louder as the race progressed, until it climaxed in an unrecognisable screech at the winning post, when the sound was abruptly muted.

"Jed. A word." Razor jerked his head. Jed excused himself and walked to the other end of the counter. Razor leant over and they stood head to head across the bar.

Left alone, Hannah gazed around the bleak walls. The best you could say about The Crow's Nest was that it was functional. It was a place where men drank their beer and played their games of pool or darts. No dress code and nobody minding your manners: that was the unwritten rule, so Mac had told her, and if the women didn't like it, tough, men had not been emasculated here.

She couldn't see what the photographs depicted from that distance, so taking her drink she walked over to have a look. Mostly they were ships. Old rust buckets more like, flying the Panamanian flag. As she walked along the line, she could see they were records of Razor's past. He appeared as a much younger man, in groups of men in seamen's gear, and others where he stood with his hands held high in triumph. She'd had the right idea, but the wrong sport. Razor had been a heavyweight-boxing champion.

Her path took her nearer to the two men talking urgently across the counter. She couldn't hear their words, but the tone was one of frustration on Razor's part and placation on Jed's. She heard Billy's name mentioned, and instinctively it heightened her awareness. One more photograph to go. She fixed her gaze on the last frame not really seeing its picture, and fine-tuned her ears to the voices behind her.

"There's another on the way ..." Razor's querulous voice came over clearly, but Jed's soft reply was lost.

With no further mention of Billy, the whole thing was meaningless to Hannah. Another *what* on the way? Silence followed. She remained staring at the photograph waiting for more, but it appeared their conversation was over. The tension in the air warned her. She moved back to the previous picture before twisting her head around to look at the men. They were standing together, looking directly at her.

"You have some good memories here," she said, pointing to the pictures. "I didn't know you were a champion, Razor." It was enough to break the tension.

Jed came towards her and clapped a hand on her shoulder. "No reason why you should Hannah, it was a long time ago, now." She steeled herself not to wince at his touch.

"Well, I gotta go." He checked his watch. "Catch you later"

Hannah nodded, and having no wish to stay alone in Razor's company, she finished her drink and followed Jed out, flicking his touch away from her shoulder. As she left the pub, she caught a glimpse of him with his ponytail flying, as he jogged back to the boatshed. She'd learned nothing about his neighbour, Sebastian Peach.

She crossed the road, leaned on the wall, and looked out over the water to the grey silhouette of the distant Sydney skyline. Razor was ex-merchant navy. If the drugs were imported as opposed to being manufactured here, was it likely Razor still had an interest in ships from overseas?

So far, she'd only found the two Es with nothing to tell her where they came from. Vicky had many friends in the area; Jane was only one of them. Jed's wife Cassandra was another – and she lived opposite Sebastian Peach. She was at home the night Vicky was murdered.

Would she be willing to talk about her neighbours?

* * *

12

Hannah brought the car to a gentle halt before she reached the driveway to Jed and Cassandra's home. On the way there, she had mentally rehearsed her approach to Cassandra. She would say she was looking for interviewees for a magazine article on the history of the town. Even so, she wasn't sure she'd get a hearing. If she could find a better way, she'd go for it. She'd considered phoning Cassandra first, but a refusal was too easy that way; she preferred face-to-face encounters.

She sat in the car, clicking her fingernails on the steering wheel, while she surveyed the quiet, tree-lined cul-de-sac, large houses with landscaped gardens. Kids didn't play in the streets up here. Hannah switched the engine off and studied the two homes that interested her. On the opposite side of the road, Sebastian Peach's residence had an open plan garden with lawns down to the pavement. A lawn-mowing service van parked outside while its operator set up his gear.

On her side of the road, Jed's garden was marked off with cream metal railings. Inside the fence, a row of palm trees edged a trim lawn. A carved timber, double-entry door, was partly open. Hannah's glance scoured the garden looking for the person who could have come out and left it so. A small, white fluffy creature, looking more like a fairground prize than a dog, darted out from under the bushes.

She watched the pup play. It nosed a yellow tennis ball along the top path and pounced after it. The ball reached the incline of the driveway and picked up speed as it rolled downward. The pup chased it but was not quick enough to stop it rolling between the bars of the double gates and onto the pavement outside. Dismayed, the dog peered out. After a moment's hesitation, it put its dainty paws on the bottom cross piece, pushed its head through the narrow gap and hopped out. Hannah couldn't believe her luck.

Quickly, she got out of the car, picked up the ball, and made a dive for the dog as it ran into the road. Alarmed by her sudden appearance, it turned and fled, running headlong into the gate, where it yipped in pain and surprise. Hannah bent down and gently scooped it up, Large, watery brown eyes, filled with hurt, looked back at her.

"You, little puppy-dog, are manna from Heaven," she said, cuddling it.

Hannah opened the gate and walked up the drive, the smell of the newly cut lawn strong in the air. At the front door, she called out, and then rang the bell. As if programmed to its sound the dog in her arms bristled and barked, wriggling to get away. Thongs flapped on the tiled hallway, and the door jerked fully open. A young woman with a dishevelled mass of curly auburn hair looked out at her, nonplussed. Her blue, cotton sarong strained over her generous figure. Quite clearly, she wore nothing underneath.

"Oh, I thought ..." the woman left the rest of her sentence dangling, as her eyes flickered to the van across the road. She turned her head back and an angelic smile broke over her features. "Oh, you've got Tipsy! Wondered where he'd gone. Where'd you find the littler bugger?" She held out her arms.

Hannah smiled and passed the dog over. "I saw him out on the road, so thought I'd better bring him in."

"Yeah? Must've left the door ... well, the lawn mower man's just been. In fact, I thought it was him back for something." She hugged her dog and made soothing baby noises.

"You're Cassandra, aren't you?"

"Yeah, and you, I know you." She pointed her finger at Hannah's chest, "I remember, you're the new barmaid at Mac's place, aren't you? I saw you the other night."

"That's me, Hannah Ford." She made no move to go.

"Look, why don't you come in for a minute; let me get you a cup of coffee or something?" she squeezed her little dog. "I don't know what I'd do if I lost him!"

"Love to. Thanks." Hannah struggled to hide her *gotcha* look, as she followed the plump, curvaceous figure through the house. She couldn't believe how easy it had been. Tipsy pranced around their feet. Hannah gave him back his ball, and he raced off nosing it down a passageway.

Two used mugs stood on the table in the kitchen. A joint smouldered in the ashtray; Cassandra wordlessly squeezed it out, waving the smoke away with her hand. She collected the used crockery and put it in the washer, clicked on the kettle, and placed two clean mugs on the pine workbench. She looked back at Hannah hopefully. "You wouldn't like something stronger?"

"No, coffee'll do fine, thanks. Mind if I smoke?"

Cassandra grinned. "Go ahead, doesn't worry me. I'll join you." She waved Hannah's offering aside. "Got one on the go."

Hannah sat at the kitchen table. Outside the sliding window, a brick paved patio surrounded a large swimming pool, complete with waterfall. The pool vacuum circled endlessly around. On the far side of the kitchen, tuned to a reasonable volume, Robbie Williams told everyone how wonderful he was. They sipped their coffee and Cassandra prattled on about a club she had recently been to. Hannah's ears picked up the name of the nightclub to store in her memory for her report later.

Eventually, stubbing her cigarette out, Hannah steered the subject around to Cassandra's neighbours. "Do you see much of Sebastian and Jane across the road?"

"Nah, not a lot. Stuck up bitch, she is. He's all right, but he's at work all day and God knows what she does, rarely comes out the house as far as I can see."

"I heard Vicky came to see her the day before she died."

"Oh? I didn't know that." Cassandra turned her face to look at Hannah, her hazel eyes wide, her smile brittle. "Yeah, come to think of it, they used to be friends, didn't they?"

"So I heard. What happened there, do you know?" She was angling to see if Cassandra knew why Vicky and Jane's friendship had cooled, but Cassandra branched off onto the subject on everybody's mind.

"What happened to Vicky, you mean. Yeah, gross. Even for her. Lennie shoulda taken better care of her, silly bugger. Then maybe it wouldn't have happened."

Hannah paused; Jed's wife didn't have a lot of time for Vicky. "You're not suggesting Lennie did it, are you?"

"Nah, I don't mean he killed her. I couldn't see Len doing that. I mean the way he treated her. All he wanted was a slave in the office, and a screw on demand. But him? He wouldn't commit himself, not even to shacking up together. Well, now she's gone and serves him right." She twirled a lock of red hair around her fingers. "Didn't know it was Zack, though." She giggled and took another drag from her re-lit joint.

"Mm, wonder how long that's been going on," Hannah mused.

"Yeah, she kept him quiet, didn't she? She was good at keeping secrets. I reckon it must've been when Lennie went away after Christmas. He was away a couple of weeks on a boat delivery job out to one of the islands. She changed a bit, you know?"

"Didn't Lennie notice?"

"You're joking! Since when do men notice things like that?" She stared out of the window for a few moments and then shuddered. "That night. It's creepy when you think about it; Len, drinking himself silly in the pub while someone bashes the life out of her."

"He'll probably remember that to the end of his days," Hannah said.

"Yeah, that's right, people do remember where they were when something like that happens, don't they. I was right here. There was a re-run of *Goldfinger,* you know, the James Bond movie? It was on TV that night." She raised her arms to eye level, hands clasped; fingers pointed, and sighted the imaginary gun. "Pow!" She blew on her fingers. "Fat lot of good it did me!" She laughed again and her eyes turned dreamy.

Hannah grinned back. "I heard. Jed's famous alibi, everyone knows."

"Shit, yeah? That's right, that's what I told the cops, wasn't it. My big boy – can't keep it down! Just got nicely settled – the music's up, the credits rolling – then in he comes all hyped up and ready to go." Cassandra laughed. It came out as a girlish giggle, but it was infectious and made Hannah smile. She needed to give off the right vibes to keep Cassandra talking. She needn't have worried. "He comes in, turns it off and drags me off to the den – here, wanna see it? C'mon, I'll show you."

Cassandra bopped across the kitchen to the background music. Hannah followed her down a passageway where she stopped outside a door. Hannah waited, not knowing quite what to expect. The young woman giggled again. She clasped her bottom lip with her top teeth, widened her eyes and paused for effect. "Da – daaaar!" She swung the door open.

Inside the small room, the light was dim. Cassandra flicked a switch. From the black painted ceiling, a myriad of fairy lights lit the room like stars. A mural took up the length of one wall and depicted a moonlit seascape; mirrors lined the remaining walls. A tangled unmade futon dominated the room. Hannah's mind jumped back to Vicky's different version of a love-nest. Could Vicky have picked up the idea from seeing this one?

"This is where we come," Cassandra giggled again at the innuendo. "My boy likes to play games." She shimmied and her 36 DDs wobbled erratically within the confines of their cotton covering. "Ever done it to E's?"

Hannah shook her head. "Never tried." *Keep talking woman.*

"Man – you don't know what you're missing."

"Don't suppose they're easy to get around here – it's not like the city, is it?"

"Don't kid yourself." Cassandra grinned. "Just because we're a small place doesn't mean we're behind the times. I can get you some, if you want." She winked heavily at Hannah.

"Anything you want in fact." She swooped on the little dog, lifted it up and held it above her head, playing with it. "There's nothing's too good for my baby's saviour, is there Tipsy-Wipsy?"

Maybe the joint had loosened Cassandra's tongue, or maybe she was on something else as well, but all Hannah's senses told her to play along. "Thanks for the tip. At least I'll know where to come."

Anything? Hannah wanted to ask. Had she found a lead to the hard drugs as well as the so-called recreational? Was this where Vicky had obtained her Ecstasy?

"Me and Jed, we're cool!" Cassandra returned the dog to the floor.

Hannah could believe her. Cassandra's earth-mother figure seeped sensuality like sweat in a gym. She wondered what sorts of games Jed liked to play, and was he using, or dealing, or was it only Cassandra's game?

She was beginning to feel uncomfortable with the sexy innuendo and the ease with which Jed's wife was giving out details of such private matters. Backing out of the stuffy little room, she held onto her self-control like a drowning man an oar. It wouldn't do to dissolve into a flashback now. She swallowed hard.

"Did Vicky ever see your den?" she asked.

"See it?" Again that slow brittle smile spread across Cassandra's face. "Yeah, she'd seen it." For once, she didn't enlarge. Had Jed been screwing Vicky? Had she been part of his games even? How did Cassandra and Lennie feel about that, or were they all into swinging? Cassandra turned the lights out and shut the door.

"So, you didn't know about Vicky and Zack Henderson?" Hannah asked retreating from Cassandra's personal zone. She wanted to be clear on how many people knew Vicky had a lover.

"I thought she might have someone. Asked her once: she just sort of smirked and did this, you know?" She tapped her finger to the side of her nose. "He's a married man, so she had to keep quiet about it, didn't she?" The sound of the front door slamming echoed through the house.

"Cazz – I'm home!"

Hannah's stomach took a roll as she recognised Jed's voice. Would he wonder what she was doing here so soon after he'd seen her at The Crow's Nest?

"Hi, Honey, we're down here," Cassandra called back. "Shit. He's back early."

Jed appeared around the corner, kicking out at Tipsy still chasing the ball. His smile for Cassandra changed abruptly as he locked eyes with Hannah.

"What's she doing here?"

"It's okay Jed, I'm not stopping," Hannah said, "I found your dog out on the road, and brought him in, that's all."

"Don't mind her. What happened to you?" Cassandra asked. Jed stood in front of them, shirtless, barefoot, in a pair of bright, red and white striped boxer shorts. Two patches of blue spread across his thighs like giant bruises. "I've heard of Ever Ready, but this is getting ridiculous!" Cassandra giggled again and Jed flashed another look at Hannah. He put his arm around his wife and led her back to the hallway.

"That clumsy shit Billy spilt a bloody can of paint over me. Lennie went ballistic, more worried about his soddin' floor than my jeans. Had to ditch them. Anyway, couldn't very well work on in my jocks, could I?" He released his wife and moved away. "Need to get another pair ASAP and get back there. Do you need a lift somewhere, Hannah?" His voice had a rough edge.

"No thanks, I've got my car. I'll get off and leave you to it."

"Yeah, you do that," he opened another door and disappeared inside.

Hannah walked on with Cassandra who was still laughing at Jed's predicament. Her question about Sebastian leaving his home that night was superfluous. There was no point in rousing Cassandra's curiosity by asking it. She had been so pre-occupied, she wouldn't have noticed if a herd of cattle had paraded outside her house that night, let alone a solitary pedestrian bent on murder.

Back at the entry, Cassandra, appearing oblivious to the tension between her husband and her visitor, opened the door.

"Okay, Hannah, glad you dropped by. See you later, may be down the 'Lights' one night?"

Hannah nodded. "Are you coming along to the sailing club's dinner tomorrow night?"

"Oh yeah, that. Same old stuffy faces. Me and Jed always go to anything they put on. Some of us are going on to a rave afterwards. Hey! You wanna come? We can squeeze a little one like you in, no trouble."

The thought of going to any party that the likes of Cassandra enthused over sent shivers up her arms. Hannah smiled back. "Ah, that's too bad; I can't, I'm working tomorrow night. Anyway, thanks for the offer, and the coffee."

"Okay, well, see you at the dinner, then." Cassandra waved as Hannah walked away. "And tell them to cut the speeches shorter this year, right?"

Hannah waved and hurried back to the car. Jed had changed his attitude. Was it because he caught her listening to Razor's conversation? Or had he also been running a second agenda when he asked her in for that drink? She stifled a grin. Those who play the devious game are quick to accuse others of doing the same. At least she'd learned plenty from Cassandra.

The lawn mower man had moved on. A short way up the road, she saw a black car parked at the kerbside. She debated whether to call on Jane to see if she was all right after this morning's talk, but she didn't want Jed to see her canvassing the neighbourhood, so decided to leave it.

Hannah drove to the end of the cul-de-sac and circled back, glancing curiously at the black Magna as she passed. It looked vaguely familiar, like the car that had squealed to a stop when she was at the boatyard that first day. Automatically her mind registered its number. Through the dark tinted windows, it looked empty. She drove on, her mind running through

Cassandra's story, emphasising the relevant pieces before she forgot them. This 'interviewing' without tape or notes was proving a great exercise for her memory.

Hannah approached the next corner, checked her rear view mirror, and did a double take. The black Magna was tailgating her. At The Harbour Lights, the car was still with her, though it had dropped back a few feet. She swung into the car park and checked again. It turned the other way.

Once in her room she opened the French windows to let in the fresh air. She walked out onto the balcony. The Magna was parked across the road on the wharf. She returned to her room to start work on her laptop. An hour or so later, she rubbed her eyes and stretched her back. Oh, for a smoke. It wasn't time. In her efforts to cut down, she had allocated set times when she could indulge and not feel guilty about it. She'd already had an extra at Cassandra's today. But that was business. Restless, she got up from her table and went out on the balcony for a breather.

The Magna was still there. Its brooding presence renewed her uneasiness. Determined to put her suspicions to rest, she ran down the stairs and out onto the street.

The black car was gone.

* * *

13

The following afternoon Hannah worked alone, laying the tables for the sailing club's dinner that evening. She heard the outer door open. Doug, all six foot four of hunky geniality, strode through the public bar.

"G'day Hannah! How're you going?" he asked as he reached the dining room.

"Just the man I need to see. Is this a good time?" Hannah asked.

"Where's Mac?" He draped his leather jacket across the back of a chair.

"Down in the cellar, had some work to do there."

"Okay, what's the go?" He pulled out a chair and waved her down into the next one.

"It could be another lead. Yesterday, I went to see Cassandra, Jed's wife. Do you know her?"

Doug smiled, "Yeah, I know her." His hands shaped the air into a voluptuous figure.

"That's the one." She grinned back briefly and told him about her visit.

"Good, it's a start. Interesting to hear she has access to different sorts of drugs. Her use of the word 'anything,' I wonder if she means that literally. Are we looking at something more than Ecstasy?"

"Short of asking, I can't tell you at this stage."

"It might be worth someone watching her at the rave you mentioned."

"Do you want me to go?" If it was part of the job, she'd have to do it.

"You mean, take up Cassandra's offer to go with them? I don't think so. Judging from Jed's reaction, you wouldn't be welcome, and if they were dealing, they'd make damn sure you didn't see them doing it. Leave it to me. I'll pass the info on and the boss can decide what he wants to do with it. Anything else?"

"I can't be sure yet, but I think someone is taking an interest in my movements." She told him about the Magna and the way it followed her back from Cassandra's place.

"Was it just the one incident?" Doug asked.

"No, I've seen it a couple of times. The first time was the day I looked around the town. On that occasion, I was walking up the ramp towards the boatshed. I knew that's where Vicky had worked and I was having a sticky-beak. I stopped to look back and this car screeched to a halt in front of the gates. Whoever it was stayed there long enough to have a good look and then drove off up the road."

"Is he a local? Have you seen the car anywhere else?"

"I've seen it on the forecourt of Izzy Foster's garage. But I was too far away to identify the driver. When I looked back I saw both him and Foster together."

"So the driver was male and known to Foster. Was he tall, short, thick or thin?"

"Against Foster he looked tall. Remember, I was seeing this through my rear view mirror. They just stood there watching me leave."

"Probably passing comment on the colour of your car," he teased.

"What's wrong with purple? I'm very fond of my car."

"You got his rego?" He made a note of the registration number she recited. "I'll check it first thing in the morning. Could it be someone simply playing silly buggers and trying to scare you?"

"Obviously, but why? Anyway, that's it for now." Hannah had made her report and she wanted to change the subject. "Are you just dropping in, or are you here to stay for the club's do tonight?"

"I'm here till closing, Mac's sure to need a hand tonight. Home without Mara and the kids is deadly dull."

"So, which hat are you wearing, sailor, barman, cop or plain old Doug McKay?"

"Tinker, tailor, soldier, sailor, eh? You forgot husband, father, diver," Doug grinned back at her. "Delete most of it. Officially, I'm off duty, but if you need anything, I'm your man. Have you mentioned it to Mac, about the car? He's the one that lives here. I know the locals, but not necessarily their wheels."

"Did I hear my name mentioned?" Mac popped his head around the kitchen door. "Hi Doug, what's that Hannah should be asking me?" He came in drying his hands on a towel.

"Who drives a black Magna round here?" Doug asked.

Mac pursed his lips and shook his head. "I know all the local boats, but cars leave me cold. Why?"

"Some idiot was tailgating me yesterday, that's all," Hannah said, wishing Doug hadn't brought it up.

*

One group at the end of the table sang in hearty voice to Don MacLean's *American Pie*. The beat from the overloud music reverberated from the walls. It vibrated up through the floor into Hannah's aching soles as she pirouetted around the dining room, serving jugs of beer and trays of shorts to the club's party.

Sebastian seated at the top table was in lively conversation with his immediate neighbours, his wife demurely by his side. Cassandra, amongst those boogying to the music, waved cheerily to Hannah. Izzy Foster, ignoring his skinny wife beside him, made a show of leering at Hannah. More than once she had to avoid his touchy-feely hands until, ready to crown him with her tray, she steered away from that area of the table. Apart from the Club Commodore and the more serious officials on the top table discussing club politics, most of the members were only out for a good time. Her face ached with smiling.

Later, in the comparative quiet of the lounge bar, she leaned against the rear counter for a moment's respite. She was dying for cigarette, but smoking behind the bar was a no-no. She caught herself breathing in second hand smoke as it wafted in her direction. Had she gone loony? What was she doing here stuck behind the bar in an insignificant little town, who's only claim to fame was an ancient death and a modern murder. It had been years since she'd waited on tables; she'd forgotten how tough it could be. The thought of her room and her laptop upstairs loomed as a quiet, attractive alternative. And that black car. Had someone observed her quiet canvassing? Steele had a man in custody. The magistrate had refused Henderson's plea for bail. If Steele had it wrong, the killer-rapist was still on the loose with no one out there even looking for him. She rubbed the goose bumps sprouting on her arms.

Mac was coping with the party group adequately. Doug was slack in the public bar. She walked down and tapped his shoulder.

"Taking five, can you keep an eye on the lounge for me, please?"

In the dim hallway, she turned and headed for the stairs, to her own bathroom rather than the public one. As she drew level with the pay phone, it rang. She jumped at the unexpected sound. It was unlikely anyone else would hear it over the noise of the music, so she answered it.

"The Harbour Lights, can I help you?" Silence. She tried again. "Can I help you?"

Half swamped by background music, Hannah heard a voice say, "Pack your bags and go back home. Do it now. We don't want your sort here."

"Excuse me?" The hairs on the back of her neck prickled.

"Whoever you really are, you're nosy bitch. Get out while you still can." The caller terminated.

Hannah stared at the buzzing receiver. How did he know she was within range of the telephone at that precise moment? She jerked around, peering into the shadowy alcoves of the deserted hallway.

The door to the public bar opened and a woman came out in a blast of music. She smiled and raised a hand. Hannah acknowledged her with a nod and watched her walk down to the Ladies. As soon as the woman disappeared into the restroom, Hannah realised the melody she'd heard when the woman came through the door had been the same as the one on the phone. The caller was in the bar. He'd watched her leave, just as she imagined someone had watched Vicky leave. She returned the receiver to its cradle, ran up the stairs to her room, slammed the door and locked it.

In the en-suite, she washed her hands, splashed cold water over her face and dried herself briskly with a towel. She dabbed cream on her face, rubbed it in, pulling at the ever-deepening crow's feet ... she stopped and stared at her reflection.

"You have to go back. You're a cop; you're not afraid of anything. You wanted this job, get out there and do it." The face narrowed its eyes; its lips pressed together in a thin line, and then it spoke back to her. "Go back as though nothing has happened; don't let him see he's got to you."

The pillowcase fell from the towel rail. It felt dry. She took last night's pillowcase off her pillow and replaced it with the clean one, smoothed it down, and then put the other one in the basin to soak. Time to go back.

Somewhere in the crowded room downstairs, the person who had made that call would be waiting to see what effect it had on her. If he thought she was going to pack her bags and meekly head for home, he couldn't be more wrong.

Doug smiled when she returned to the bar. "Had a rush on as soon as you'd left."

Hannah intended her laugh for whoever might be watching her this minute. Where was he? Who was he? She hadn't heard him long enough to recognise his voice.

*

101

To give her hands something to do, Hannah picked up a cloth and polished a glass. Sebastian Peach's booming laughter carried across the room. Beaten your wife lately Sebastian? What would he do if he knew she was aware of his secret? Would he use the phone to make her leave town? She still hadn't ruled him out as Vicky's attacker. Her glance shifted down the table. Lennie looked alone, as he always did, even in a throng of people. He brooded quietly over his drink, picking occasionally at the food on his plate. Even if he did resent her taking Vicky's place behind the bar, would that be enough for him to warn her off?

"A Scotch, please. Make it a double."

Hannah jumped as the voice broke into her reverie. "Colin, how are you? A double coming up. Ice?" She swung back into her role.

"Will you have one with me?" he asked. "Don't usually drink alone."

"Thanks." She gave him a cheery smile, and poured herself a mineral water laced with ice and lemon. "They haven't got you playing the piano tonight, then?"

He slumped onto the stool. "That's only Friday nights after the darts match."

"And, I take it, you're not a sailor."

"Me? No way, I have better things to do with my time than get wet."

She laughed. "So, what's new with you?"

"I'm still trying to get my head around Zack's arrest."

Her instincts told her to get him talking. His earlier drinking had already loosened his tongue; he only needed a little encouragement. "You know him well?" she asked.

He shrugged. "How well does one man ever know another? I wouldn't say we were dyed in the wool mates, but we teach in the same school, play golf, and sing together ..." he paused, and she raised an eyebrow. "Oh, it's only amateur stuff – Gilbert and Sullivan's Pirates of Penzance, you know the sort of thing.

We put on a show up at the school every Christmas. We're doing Mikado this year."

She looked around over his shoulder. Groups of patrons nearby were all intent on their own business or engrossed in conversation. "What makes you think Zack couldn't be involved?" she asked.

He sighed, an expression of resignation on his face. "I thought I knew him. But this business ... don't get me wrong, I don't believe he's guilty of murder. Okay, so he had a bit on the side, like they say, but Zack's not violent. Not the man I know, anyway."

"Did you know about him and Vicky?"

"Didn't know it was our Vicky, but thought it must be something along those lines when he started missing rehearsal nights." He shrugged and downed half his drink.

Hannah found it interesting how many men referred to Vicky as "our" Vicky. It said a lot about her, and how she'd infiltrated the hearts of her customers, and yet, one of them had found it necessary to kill her.

She looked back at Colin. "Your practise nights, Wednesdays somebody said, didn't other people notice he was missing?"

"Not as far as I know. He dropped out of rehearsals after we finished Pirates. It's not like he has a big part in this one, he's only in the chorus and he knows the score backwards. He said he wanted a break, and that he'd come back to it later."

"He just forgot to tell his wife?"

"Hmm, well that's his business. His marriage – his purgatory."

Hannah looked up as a man pulled away from a knot of drinkers behind Colin. Morgan Draper approached the counter. She put her glass down ready to serve him, wondering uneasily if he had overheard any part of their conversation. Wearing a tartan lumber jacket, an open neck shirt and black jeans, he walked up behind Colin and dropped a hand on his shoulder, making him jump.

Colin turned his head, recovering quickly. "Morgan! How're you doing? Can I get you a beer?"

Hannah watched the gravedigger and waited for his order. Morgan nodded curtly to Colin, and the dented, hand-rolled cigarette dipped from the side of his mouth. He perched on the next stool. His weathered face, limp black hair and permanent three-day stubble put Hannah in mind of a hobo. He sniffed wetly, and shifted his attention to her.

"For a barmaid and a stranger, you ask a lot of questions, Missy!"

Hannah caught her breath. Had he made that call? She stared at him straight in the eye. "Nothing wrong with that, Morgan, I'm a good listener, a necessary qualification for a barmaid, wouldn't you think? Now, what can I get you?"

* * *

14

Eleven thirty and Hannah's shift was over. She bade Mac goodnight and climbed the stairs to her room. Glad to be out of her shoes, she sank onto the bed and rubbed her aching limbs. Her head pounded from the constant noise, smoke, and the mental drain of being on her guard. All she wanted was sleep. Her fingers pulled a curl of hair around to her nose. First, she had to take a shower. In a fit of self-discipline, she turned the tap from hot to cold. It shocked her body out of its lassitude. She grabbed a towel, scrubbed herself dry and welcomed the warmth of the hairdryer.

Dressed in an over long T-shirt, she took out her laptop, opened it and brought up the DW file. Without bothering to read what had gone before, she simply added the information she had gathered since her last entry in an effort to empty her mind and let it sleep. Too tired even for her quiet time on the balcony with a cigarette, she piled into bed and blacked out.

Hannah woke abruptly. She raised her head to look at the luminous digits on the clock radio, nearly four-thirty. The French windows rattled. Alarmed, she raised her head, but it was only the wind. She turned over and tried to get back to sleep, but instead became more alert as she listened to the rhythmic slapping of halyards beating against the masts of boats on their moorings. Turning onto her back, eyes wide open she abandoned all thoughts of sleep.

Finally, she got up and went to the loo. Wrapped in a towelling robe, she slipped her feet into her trainers and picked up a packet of cigarettes. When she unlocked the French windows, the wind in her face felt warm and the night beckoned her out. She lit her cigarette before stepping outside to take up her customary position leaning over the balustrade.

The telephone message insinuated into her thoughts. *"Go back home."* She looked up. Clouds scudded across the sky in long narrow bands, racing across a full moon. *"Do it now. We don't want your sort here."*

In the clear moonlight, she could make out the boats jigging and jiving on their moorings. On the wharf, the single yellow streetlight melted into insignificance as between the cloud cover, the moonlight cut a swathe across the scene like a giant spotlight sweeping a stage. Hannah's eyes followed its passage *"Get out while you still can."* The jetty came into view, and the angular lines of the yardarm stood out pale and stark. Hannah stiffened. The voice in her head silenced.

Her eyes returned to the yardarm. Something looked different. A bulky shape swayed gently back and forth. The hairs on her arms stood erect as Mac's distant voice echoed in her head. *"And some say the ghost of Willie Draper still walks."*

Her cigarette fell from her fingers. Distracted, she leaned over and looked down in time to see its flurry of red sparks as it hit the street below. Then, lifting her eyes, she searched the moonlit scene again. The light was confusing. With the fast moving cloud now covering the moon, she waited a few seconds for the next bright patch, and again peered carefully at the crosstrees.

The shape still hung there. No way did she believe in ghosts. Hannah ran along the balcony towards Mac's room at the end. She banged on his open French windows.

"Mac! Wake up! Get out here! Quick!"

*

The ocean at this depth appeared the darkest of greens. He was back at work on the sunken oilrig. The familiar feeling of foreboding clenched him. He knew he was dreaming and tried to wake for he knew what was to come. As always, the dream dragged him down into its terrifying grip. He couldn't move. One foot caught by the wreckage on the sea floor. He pulled and the metal moved, trapping him still harder. He tried to wriggle out of it. His suit snagged on broken steel spikes and his airline fractured. He was conscious of his partner grabbing him, shaking his arm, and thumping his shoulder – a voice shouting at him. Different this time. The words finally penetrated.

"Mac, wake up, damn you! Come on, there's something on the yardarm."

The ocean rolled away and he was back in bed. He reached out to push away the tentacles of his recurring nightmare. It was Hannah's voice. He opened his eyes to see her anxious face above his as she violently shook his shoulder and called his name. She stood back once she realised she'd woken him.

"Whatsamatter?" He raised himself onto an elbow, shaking his head to clear it. "Okay, start again. Tell me slowly, what's the trouble?"

"There's something hanging on the yardarm. I want you to come and have a look." She said it slowly, enunciating each syllable. Her expression put him in mind of his old diving instructor trying to din something vital into a thick-headed recruit.

"Oh, is that all? God, I thought the place was on fire." He lay back on his pillows and grabbed the duvet.

"Come on Mac; wake up! If you don't believe me, come and look!"

"Okay, okay, wait a minute." Like most heavy sleepers, he hated being woken abruptly and then be expected to function with full mental capacity. Hannah was already on her way out to the balcony.

"Shit and bloody women!" Mac dragged himself away from the warmth of his bed and followed her, shivering, as the sweat of his nightmare cooled.

"Can you see it? Look, there."

"No." He squinted at the yardarm, but the moonlight dimmed and he couldn't see a thing. He returned to his room and hunted around his bookshelf for the binoculars.

Outside again he adjusted the lenses and waited for the moon's re-appearance. He sucked in his breath. "Yep, you're right."

"What is it, can you see?" Hannah asked.

"Something's hooked up." He tightened his lips. Bloody sailing club. There had been one particularly loud element at the party tonight. They'd left the pub as high as kites. Up to their stunts again, no doubt this was their handiwork. Great fun, stick an effigy up on the yardarm to resemble Willie Draper's ghost, and it wasn't the first time they'd done it, either.

"It's a prank. Don't worry about it."

"What do you mean 'a prank'?"

"Why don't you go back to bed, I'll sort it in the morning?"

"Aren't you going to check it?" Hannah asked, clearly annoyed at his lack of urgency.

"Oh God, woman, is there no peace? Some of the lads from the club have stuck an effigy up to frighten the old ladies. That's all. You expect me to go down there and clear up after them? God, what's the time?"

He swept his hair back over his head and studied his tormentor. Her short blond hair had that tousled, straight out of bed look. Her blue terry-towelling robe showed tantalising glimpses of bare leg beneath it. The old hormones wriggled their antennae. He stamped them down. Forget it man. If her behaviour in the shack the other day was anything to go by, there was no way she'd be travelling that road. He became conscious of his own clothing – a skimpy pair of black jocks and nothing else. He turned away from her to shield the rising evidence of his interest.

Back in his room, he grabbed a pair of jeans. "All right, all right. It's only something stuck on the yardarm, but I'll go and check it out, if I must."

"Only something, not somebody?"

"Don't you go falling for that old ghost story. That's exactly what they want you to think. It's their idea of a joke. If you're coming with me, do your shoes up." He slipped his feet into a pair of loafers, while she tied her laces.

"Okay, call me gullible if you like, but I'd like to make sure. What if you were wrong about it being a prank?"

He gave her hard look. "You'll see."

Hannah turned as though to go out via the balcony. He called her back and opened his bedroom door. "This way – we'll need some light."

*

Hannah ran down the stairs ahead of him. She knew he was only humouring her, but at least he was moving. In the hallway, Mac stopped to collect a flashlight from a cupboard under the stairs. "Knife?" she asked.

Mac rolled his eyes and sidetracked into the back room. He returned brandishing a diver's knife. He unlocked the door. Hannah pushed past him, raced across the road and down the wharf. She could hear his feet pounding the timbered jetty behind her.

Hannah reached the yardarm and pulled up short. She covered her mouth to stifle a cry. The moon lit the scene with brutal reality. The body, hanging by a rope, swayed slightly in the wind. Barely a foot above the ground, heavy boots clunked against a wooden crate at the base of the mast. She looked up into his face, the chubby features immediately recognisable.

"It's Billy!" she shouted. "Quick, cut him down!"

"Christ!" Mac stepped onto the wooden crate and reached up beyond Billy's head. "Can you take his weight just for a second?"

Hannah put her arms around Billy's hips and braced her knees to hold him. Her body convulsed as the smell of urine overwhelmed her. She averted her face from his soiled clothes, and squeezed her eyes shut. Her teeth ground together in her efforts to control her revulsion. Billy's weight increased as Mac cut through the rope. She bore his full weight for the few seconds it took Mac to step off the crate and grab him under his arms. They lowered him to the ground. Hannah swallowed the bile burning the back of her throat at the sight of Billy's contorted face. His open eyes bulged, staring at her in a look of total incomprehension.

Mac pulled at the rope deeply embedded in Billy's throat and loosened it. He felt for a pulse. He shook his head.

"Nothing. Too late. He's dead."

*

Mac stood in the shadows; he listened to the slurp and suck of water washing around the legs of the jetty. He heard the wind scything through the wire stays of the boats clanking nearby. Somewhere along the wharf, a rubbish bin had fallen over and scraps of airborne litter fluttered like bats on the rampage.

Part of his mind had become detached as he looked down on a theatrical scene. A spotlight threw a cone of light over Billy's corpse. Busy people slid in and out of the surrounding darkness, doing the things they had to do. He saw Hannah a few paces away, hugging her robe around her, bare legs shining whitely on the edge of the harsh light. She appeared agitated, scraping her nails through her hair scratching her head.

The wind increased. Somewhere, a loose tarpaulin cracked the air and Mac flinched at its gunshot sound. He dragged his attention back from its sojourn to his place on the wharf, outside the tape that now cordoned off the jetty. Redundant and relegated to the wings he and Hannah could only watch while the official performance was under way. The coroner, two constables, and Detective Sergeant Ingram, who was Doug's boss from the water police, and others Mac didn't know had taken over. He kicked a stone to relieve the tension in his legs.

"Why did he do it?" He heard Hannah's desperate question. It demanded an answer, but he had none to give. Sergeant Ingram came and stood beside him as a new set of headlights approached the jetty.

"That'll be the body wagon." Ingram said. "We're finishing up here now. You're free to go if you want, Mr McKay. There'll be someone around to see you again in the morning to go over your statements – well, should I say later today?" He nodded towards the first light of dawn seeping in over the eastern sky.

"I'll stay and see him off." Mac realised how silly it must sound, as though he was seeing Billy off on a journey, not a trip to the morgue. "Do you want to go back?" he asked Hannah. She shook her head.

The unmarked wagon moved in quietly beside them. Its driver got out, and gave them a brief nod. He leaned against the side of his vehicle waiting his cue. Mac moved out of the way, as an officer took down one section of the tape to let the officials through. The driver and his partner collected Billy's body and took him away. The State Emergency Services dismantled their temporary lighting, and the police cars moved on leaving a solitary constable to watch over the site.

Mac turned to Hannah. "Ready?" Tentatively he stretched out his hand. She took it, and he drew her near. In the greying light, he could see the sorrow in her face, her eyes too dark to fathom. He put his arms around her. She didn't flinch, but moved nearer to hug him. He could feel the rhythm of her heart against his chest. He laid his cheek against hers and she snuggled into his neck. He waited. She didn't pull away; she had accepted his touch, his closeness. He wanted to absorb her sorrow and take it from her. The break, when it came occurred naturally with no sign of her earlier fears.

"Let's go," she said, and kept one arm behind his back. At the door of The Harbour Lights, he stopped. The moment he opened it the atmosphere changed. Hannah broke away from him and made a dash for the stairs.

"How about a hot drink?" he asked. "You look like you could use one." But he was talking to her back.

Already halfway up, Hannah looked down at him, her eyes haunted. "I've got to clean up. Must wash my hair."

"I'll be in the sitting room when you've finished." He watched her run the rest of the way without stopping. "Come and join me if you want – Hannah?" She'd gone. What had he done to change her mood?

*

The story she'd told Mac about her rape had been the truth, but not the whole truth. The second man was still out there. In the bathroom, Hannah stared at the drawn face in the mirror. With both hands, she scraped through her short, uncombed hair. She pulled it away like wings each side of her head. Once, it had been long and had hung like parentheses each side of her face. It had swept down in a gentle wave that curved and broke across her shoulders. The type of hair that Hollywood starlets would kill for, someone had once told her. She gazed deeper into the mirror to the darkness beyond its reflective surface.

The big man finishes. He zips his trousers and waves his mate forward. Still she can't move; the paralysis is complete. She sees the shadow of the second man, a smaller silhouette, against the glare. His face: a black hole where his mouth is open, his laughter: fiendish in the night. They drag her out of the van. Drop her on the ground. The laughing man undoes his fly. A stream of hot, yellow liquid hits her face and drenches her long hair. She can't move out of the way. Drowning ... drowning ... drowning in piss. His laughter ricochets around her head. The smell engulfs her.

Her awareness returns to the face in the mirror. She hadn't been free of that hated smell since. Her memory was patchy, the drug, Rohypnol or 'roofies' for short, had seen to that. Scenes pulsed in and out of her mind. Some so clearly, others appeared through banks of fog, and others she had no memory of. By his laugh, she'd recognise the second man. Its sound: *demonic*. It came to her in unexpected moments. It echoed through her nightmares. She waited every day to hear it again and when she found him...

Hannah frowned at her reflection. Billy was dead and all she could think of was herself?

The smell of Billy's piss filled the tiny bathroom. How much longer was she going to let that smell rule her life? Her rapist was dead, but the lout who used her as a urinal and laughed as he did so was out there – still laughing.

It came to her in a startling moment of enlightenment. The energized eyes in the mirror stared back. Why hadn't it occurred to her before? Every time she succumbed to her phobia, she was granting him another conquest. Why did she do it – why give in to the bastard? She took a deep breath and inhaled the hated smell. Again, and again, she breathed in Billy's odour, long and deep, both from the air in the room and her soiled clothing.

The walls did not fall in on her.

Imbued with a new sense of liberation, Hannah felt light headed. She turned the shower on. She washed her hair and lathered her body with sandalwood soap. Wrapped in the bath towel she stared at the misted mirror. She felt good, clean, even a touch feminine again. A sensation she had almost forgotten. Then thoughts of Billy returned and doused her lightening mood.

There was no point in going back to bed. She wondered if Mac were still around and if it wasn't too late to take up his offer to join him. She'd left him abruptly. It wasn't his fault. She dressed in fresh clothes and went downstairs. Mac was in his private sitting room, stretched out on his sofa, holding a mug. He'd lit the fire.

"Hi, you all right?" he asked and she nodded. "Hot chocolate?" He leaned over, picked up a jug keeping warm in the grate and poured its contents into the second mug.

"Thanks." Hannah took it and sat down in a large, saggy armchair curling her legs beneath her. Mac seemed content without conversation. They sat, mostly in silence, until Mrs Bates arrived to get the breakfasts.

* * *

15

Shortly after eight, Hannah sat alone at her usual dining table next to the window and sipped her coffee. It was still too hot. She glanced across the room at Mac, his sleeves rolled up, his tie hidden behind a navy blue and white striped apron. He served breakfast to the four other guests who had stayed overnight. The smell of bacon lingered in the air.

She stared out of the window. All that was left of the nightmarish scenes on the wharf was a strip of yellow tape across the jetty. Her mind was still too raw to view the events with any objectivity. Had Billy's death been suicide? Ingram had told her that he viewed suicides as suspicious deaths until proved otherwise. With the additional factor of the barmaid's murder still unresolved, he was taking no chances.

Hannah buttered her toast, added the marmalade and began to eat. Food settled like concrete in her stomach and she pushed her plate away before she'd finished. More than food, she wanted a smoke. The cravings were getting worse. Perhaps it was time to think of patches. Mac had returned to the kitchen. He still didn't know the real purpose of her visit here. After his comforting presence in the early hours of this morning, she felt bad about that. It was a kind of deceit.

The picture of Billy's eyes haunted her. Although she'd only known him a week, she vividly recalled each time they'd met. The first in Grace's café, where he'd stood before her in his paint-spattered clothes, twisting his hat around in his hands. *Not very bright, but he looks after his mum well,* Grace had said. Was that to be Billy Draper's epitaph?

Again, the time he'd blundered into the café, and nearly knocked a customer flying. He'd been troubled then, she now realised. Didn't anyone care? Was it because he was slow that nobody bothered to take the time to listen to him? It wouldn't have taken much to find out what his problem was. No one bothered, including her, and now he was dead.

A movement on the wharf caught her attention. The police patrol car drew up and Detective Inspector Steele got out of the passenger seat. He spoke to the constable on duty. Sergeant Pike followed him inside the taped area. After a few moments of conversation, Steele nodded his head and made his way across the road towards the hotel's entrance.

"More coffee?" Mac approached with the tray of jugs. "What's going on out there?"

"Steele's just turned up." Hannah proffered her empty cup, "looks like he's on his way here." Their eyes locked as they heard the outer door open.

"Good morning, Mr McKay, Ms Ford, we meet again." Steele stepped into the dining room. "Bad business over there, wouldn't you say?" He accepted Mac's offer of coffee and sat at the table with them to drink it. "I know you've already given your statements to Sergeant Ingram, but if you wouldn't mind, I'd like to hear the account first hand."

"Sure. And I'd like to know what the hell's going on?" Mac asked him. "Two violent deaths in just over a week in a place like this. It doesn't make sense."

"Wouldn't we all," Steele sat back. He interlaced his hands, as though in prayer, then turned them to point his index fingers at Mac. "They're not necessarily connected, but that's why I'm here. According to the statement you gave to the senior sergeant, you two were first on the scene. So, will you tell me exactly what you saw, what you did and, what made you go down there in the middle of the night in the first place? McKay?"

Mac went through his story from the moment of his wakening to when the police arrived. "And that's about it," he finished.

Steele nodded and turned his attention to Hannah. "Righty-ho, you were the first to realise something was going on. What woke you up, Hannah?"

Hannah, who'd listened quietly to Mac's account, twisted her fingers in her lap. "I've no idea. I'm a very light sleeper, so it could have been the wind rattling the windows. Once awake, I couldn't get back to sleep. I needed a smoke. I know, I know, filthy habit. I've been trying to cut it down." She had seen the mild flicker of distaste cross his features; obviously, Steele didn't go for women that smoked cigarettes in the middle of the night. "So anyway, I went out on the balcony." She paused to recall the sequence.

"Right. You're outside – did you see anyone in the street, or on the wharf?"

"No one. Apart from the wind, it was a beautiful night. The moon was full; the light was alternately bright and then dark as a cloud passed over. There were a lot of moving shadows. Then, in a bright spell I saw this ... this shape on the yardarm."

"That's when you woke McKay, and you both went running down to see what it was. How long did it take you to get there?"

Hannah and Mac exchanged glances. Hannah shook her head. "Five, ten minutes I suppose? I don't know; we weren't timing it. Mac sleeps like the dead. Took me ages to wake him up. Look, we didn't know it was a person. Mac looked through the binoculars, he said it looked like an effigy – said they'd done it before," she added defensively. Although Ingram had told her the coroner believed Billy had been dead for at least a couple of hours, she felt guilty for not getting to him sooner.

"Who do you mean by 'they'?" Steele turned to look at Mac.

"The sailing club," Mac answered. "You always get some spoilers. They had a do here last night. There was a particularly noisy element amongst them. When I saw the shape looked like a man, I took it to be one of their practical jokes. As I said, they did just that a couple of years ago. Caused a bit of a stir at the time, but no harm was done. Would have left it but for Hannah. She was the one who insisted we check it out." He inclined his head towards her, giving her a supportive wink.

"Ten minutes?" Steele gave them both a speculative look, and then turned to Hannah with a half smile. "Is he usually so hard to wake up?"

Hannah's lips tightened. She was in no mood for jokes, and if Steele thought they'd been sleeping together at the time, he was wrong. Protesting would only add value to his belief. She left the quip unanswered. Mac intervened, his face stiff, his voice low.

"Inspector, Hannah is a guest in my hotel. And, it was as a guest with a problem that she came to wake me up. I would prefer it if you didn't embarrass my visitors."

"No offence intended," Steele smiled and looked back at Hannah, unrepentant. "Getting to be a habit this, isn't it? Hannah Ford being present when a new discovery is made. And this time, a body, no less."

About to reply, Mac held his hand up, silencing her.

"Hannah has already explained how she learned about the fisherman's hut, and she couldn't possibly have known anything about last night's tragedy."

"And, your other guests, where were they while all this was going on?"

"Asleep. Last night I had two retired couples travelling in tandem, but you won't get anything out of them; their rooms don't look out on the wharf. I asked them before breakfast if they had been disturbed in the night, but they said they heard nothing. They're still here if you want to speak to them."

Steele nodded. His pager beeped. He looked out of the window to see Pike and the constable staring in his direction, in front of them stood a woman holding something up. He lifted his hand in acknowledgement and tucked his notebook and pen away, and finished his coffee in haste.

"Excuse me," he said, scraping his chair back. "It seems I'm wanted. I'll be back shortly to see your guests, McKay. Would you mind asking them if they'd wait? Thanks for the coffee." With a final smile and wave for Hannah, he hurried away.

Through the window, Hannah watched him cross the road. He'd enjoyed baiting her, but at least he hadn't broken her cover. "Prick. Why does he needle me so?"

"He's not known for his patience with journalists. He thinks you're after the story."

Her conscience tweaked, she changed the subject before he went any further down that road. "It looks like there's been a development."

Mac nodded towards the group. "What's that she's holding up, a shoe?"

*

Lennie Cooper sat in front of his computer nursing a hangover. The accounts needed doing. A couple of weeks back he would have left all this to Vicky. The blank screen stared back at him. After last night's piss-up, his head was not up for this today.

Jed was handy with the computer perhaps he'd take it on. Staggering out of his chair, he used both hands to stop his head from wobbling as he lurched across the room to the coffee machine. He brewed a pot, poured a cupful and drank it black.

Jed still wasn't in. After last night, it was not surprising he was late. The club's party had gone with a swing. It's all right for those who liked parties, but Lennie hated them. He only went because it was good business to keep in with the yachties. His stockroom was as good as any boat supplier and most of the club members bought their stuff from him. The least he could do was turn up when invited to their shindigs. He swallowed down another couple of codeine.

Where the hell was Jed? Even Billy hadn't turned up for work. Did Billy think he was getting the day off or something? He hadn't even been to the party. Slow and daft he might be, but

119

he was good with a paintbrush and usually reliable as far as attendance was concerned. Anything to get away from that demanding mother of his no doubt; must be worse than being married – he didn't even get any nooky.

Lennie glanced out of the window towards Billy's cottage. The car parked in the driveway belonged to one of the health care people who came to sort out Annie Draper on a regular basis. With them in the house, there was no excuse for Billy not to be here.   The wail of a police siren sounded in the distance. It can't be for him this time. They'd got a man for Vicky's murder. One was enough, wasn't it? He peered through the window, Jed, at last. He was dragging his feet, too. Clothes looked crumpled, like he'd slept in them. He'd lost some of his bounce. A ripple of amusement surfaced through Lennie's pain. He wasn't the only one suffering a hangover.

He left the window and turned in towards the workshop to watch Jed stumble up the stairs to the office. Without a word of greeting, Jed moved passed him straight in to look out the window. "It's the cops again. Can't they leave us a-bloody-lone?" Jed touched his forehead gingerly as if his voice had triggered another wave of pain.

Lennie went outside the office, stood on the catwalk and looked down on the approaching officers. "G'day. What can I do for you guys this time?"

"Lennie Cooper? Detective Sergeant Ingram and Constable Baxter, of the Water Police," the senior officer said, as he climbed the stairs holding out his ID.

Lennie tried hard to concentrate. Water police? What were they after? He hadn't had any stolen boats lately. He led them back to the office. Jed turned from the coffee machine and nodded to them curtly.

The senior officer spoke first. "I understand you employ a man by the name of Billy Draper."

"Yeah, we do, but he's not in yet. You want him?" Lennie looked into the cop's clear blue eyes searching for clues as to what the short stocky man, with cropped grey hair could possibly want with Billy.

"You mean you haven't heard?" Ingram put a hand to his face and smoothed it down as though feeling the quality of his shave. "In that case, I am sorry to say, I have bad news for you. Draper was found hanged this morning."

"No shit!" Lennie shot a quick startled look at his partner. "Why ... how?"

Jed's face paled. "Silly bugger! What's he do that for?"

Ingram turned to look at Jed. "Had he been depressed lately, do you know?" When both men shook their heads, he went on. "We'd just like to ask you a few questions, and look around Billy's place of work, if that's all right with you. Did Draper have a work area of his own or a locker for instance, where he kept his personal things?"

Accompanying the police officers, Lennie led the way to Billy's locker. Jed tagged on behind them. Lennie produced a key from the counter drawer and opened the narrow metal door to a waft of sweaty socks and decaying food. Stuck on the inside of the door was a metre high, well thumbed poster of Elle in her skimpiest bikini, walking along a beach, her blond hair sweeping around her face and an enticing smile on her lips. "Billy loves Elle," scrawled across the side in Billy's childish handwriting, accompanied by red hearts and X shaped kisses.

Constable Baxter snapped on a pair of latex gloves. He took out Billy's old sneakers and comics, half-eaten packets of chips, bottle of juice, a large rubber torch and other sundry items. He put them all, including the poster, in plastic bags and took them out to the car.

"How long have you known Draper?" Ingram asked Lennie.

"Two, three, years I suppose. He's our next-door neighbour. As a kid, he was always hanging round the gates, watching us work on the boats. When he finished school we started off giving him part time jobs, like sanding down, or sweeping the yard and before you knew it he was part of the set up."

"Has he ever shown any signs of violence?"

121

"If he has, I've never seen it. What about you, Jed?"

"We-ell," Jed shrugged his shoulders as though reluctant to tell. "I've seen him lose his cool a couple of times, especially when people laughed at him. He couldn't take that. Chased off a whole bunch of kids once, swinging a dinghy anchor, like a lasso, around his head," Jed laughed, "nearly got one, too."

Ingram looked from Jed to Lennie and back, as though not fully appreciating Jed's sense of humour. "What was his relationship with Victoria Brown?"

"He didn't have one," Lennie answered shortly. "Other than neighbourly – they got on. Sometimes, up in the office, she let him comb her hair. He used to say it was like Elle's. Every long haired blond looked like bloody Elle!"

"To your knowledge, did he ever try to take it further?"

"What with Vicky? You gotta be joking! She'd have laughed in his face."

* * *

16

Steele stood in the incident room looking up at the wall chart, at the photographs taken of the dead woman, the crime scene at the graveyard and lists of names cross-referenced with alibis not yet considered solid enough to warrant the eraser. He examined the list of the victim's effects that were still missing. In a whole week they'd found only one shoe. Was it a coincidence the shoe only surfaced after the death of Billy Draper?

Ingram had already instigated a second search of the area around the wharf. He'd let Steele know if he came up with anything relevant to the barmaid's case. Steele turned back to glower at his sergeant, who was sitting on the corner of a desk, swinging his heel against its leg with an irritating thump.

"We going to release Henderson now?" Pike asked.

"Not yet. One shoe doesn't convince me that young Draper should change places with our prime suspect. It certainly doesn't seem likely he would've acted alone." He tapped his teeth with his marker pen then pointed it at Pike. "I want to talk to Zack Henderson again. On the face of it, there seems to be no connection between young Draper and Zack Henderson, but we've got to dig deeper. Get him up."

*

Paperwork – Doug hated it. Being a diver didn't get him out of it. He couldn't concentrate. Far from being with the job, his

123

mind worked over the latest news from Draper's Wharf. How was Hannah coping? From a straightforward surveillance operation, she'd unwittingly become involved in a murder and a possible suicide. Doug picked up the desk-phone and tapped in a number.

"Mac? Just heard the news."

"Oh, it's you. God, it's unbelievable, in a place like this! We've been up half the night with your Sergeant Ingram."

"Yeah, this one's ours, so close to the water. You okay? What about Hannah? I heard you two found him. What were you doing out that time of night?" He doodled stick-men hanging from scaffolds on the pad as he listened to his brother's voice.

"We've just had Steele in asking questions," Mac said. "He's not on Billy's case, but he's trying to find out if it overlaps with Vicky's. Han's okay, she's upset of course; seems she'd taken a shine to young Billy. Can't understand it, why would he do a thing like that?"

"Don't ask me, didn't know the lad all that well. I'm waiting for a call out. Might see you later; if not, see you tonight."

The call came through ten minutes later. "Doug, job for you," it was Ingram's voice. "We need another search of the Draper's Wharf area, around the jetty where they found Draper. It seems a training shoe similar to the one missing from the murdered barmaid's effects has turned up on the beach nearby."

Doug shook his head. "Odd. We did all that area the day after Vicky's murder, didn't find anything then."

"Could you have missed it, one solitary shoe? Anyway, give it another go will you? I'll send someone down with the details."

Doug put the phone down and punched the air. "We're on!" he shouted to his colleague, Robbie Naylor. Robbie – or Rusty Nails, as most of the guys knew him, for his red hair that stood up in spikes, raised his thumbs and grinned. Nobody was keen on office work.

On board the police launch, Doug stood with his legs braced against its movement, chest drum tight, full of optimism. Perhaps, today, they'd find something vital. Anticipation set the old heartbeat quickening. It was always the same at the beginning of a search. He heard Rusty laugh at the punch line of some joke one of the crew was rehashing. It was their way of coping. Sometimes the things they brought up from the sea-bottom were the stuff of nightmares, and if you didn't snatch a laugh when you could, your sanity might not make it through the day.

Wind ruffled through his hair. Salt water sprayed his face as the launch turned about and accelerated across the river. The powerful diesels trembled beneath his feet as the boat's sleek bow scythed through the wakes of other craft. He wouldn't swap his job for any other in the world. A days' work could mean anything from a lost wedding ring, a sunken boat, jettisoned evidence, to the more macabre, the recovery of the dead. The job, the sea and the weather, no two days were the same.

He flexed his arms, as their destination loomed nearer. The launch slowed in a welter of white water as they slewed around in a semi-circle in the approach to the shallow horseshoe bay. One of the crew dropped the anchor a short way off shore; another lowered the inflatable craft from its davits.

Doug gave Rusty a brief nod. They were ready. He fixed his mask and slipped over the side into the Zodiac. Rusty climbed in beside him. The helmsman started the outboard motor, and steered the inflatable towards a buoy belonging to the sailing club. They had already designated the search area and were using the striped buoy as a marker for the beginning of their run. With a last look at the clear blue sky and the sparkling bay, Doug signalled his partner and rolled over backwards into his element.

He surged ahead through the haze of air bubbles into the green sunlit water. This was his real work, the place where he could make a difference.

Using hand signals to communicate with Rusty, Doug took the shore side and adjusted the space between them to double their range of vision. He slowly cruised above the seabed, skimming over jagged bottles embedded in the muddy bottom, cans and rusty bits of bikes.

The water grew murkier nearer the shore. He searched out every piece of detritus, looking for the second shoe, or any other item that might be relevant to the two deaths ashore. Plastic bags, like giant jellyfish, swayed softly into his slipstream.

He moved on into the shallows. The legs of the jetty loomed into sight. Here the depth at low water was just over two metres, the light reasonable. What was that? He jerked his head with a stab of recognition.

On the murky riverbed, tangled amongst the remnants of an old shopping trolley, lay scattered clothing and a solitary grey training shoe. No way had these been here the last time he'd looked. He raised a thumb to signal Rusty and surfaced to wave the Zodiac in.

*

Zack Henderson, nursing a hollow feeling inside his gut, pulled the chair out on one side of the table in the interview room. He'd been unable to face breakfast this morning, and the watery tea they'd dished up slopped around his stomach like bilge water.

His solicitor grunted and sat beside him. Oscar Benson, a small man with the figure of a potbelly-pig, wore a grey suit, pale shirt and striped tie. His black, square-rimmed glasses didn't suit his round face. Zack had not met him before this case. He'd never had much to do with solicitors in the past. But it was good to have someone batting on his side, even if he did wear a pink shirt.

Meg had abandoned him. At first, convinced of his innocence she'd broken down in tears when she learned of his arrest. Later, when she heard irrefutable evidence that the barmaid was pregnant by him, it had destroyed the fabric of trust that had existed between them. She'd shouted at him. He was no longer the man she thought she knew, so how could she *know* that he wasn't a murderer? She hadn't been in to see him since.

Steele, with Pike beside him, went through the formalities for the tape.

"Okay, Mister Henderson, let's have it one more time." Steele began the questioning. "I want you to go through your movements step by step on that Friday night." He laid Zack's earlier statement on the table in front of him, as if to double check every word.

Zack sighed. Wasn't it enough that Vicky was dead, without them blaming him. He'd loved her; he would never have harmed her. He raised his eyes and met the inspector's steady gaze. "I don't know what more I can say to you. Haven't you any different questions to ask? I've told you everything I know, again and again."

"And, as we all know, you took your time about that! I want to hear it once more."

Zack looked across the short space between them. He put his elbows on the table and lowered his head into his open hands. Aware the sergeant was watching him with a hint of amusement in his sharp little eyes, he took his hands away, put them back in his lap, and sat upright. He glanced sideways at Oscar, but the man had no objection to make about this repetitive questioning, so once more he launched into his story, his voice a flat monotone. "Vicky Brown telephoned me at school on Friday morning. She asked if we could meet at the cabin later that night as she had something to tell me."

"You said earlier that it was against your rules to phone you at school, if that is so, why didn't she wait until your next planned date?" Sergeant Pike asked, squaring his shoulders.

"Like I told you; we were not going to see each other that day. I had a PC meeting, and I wouldn't be able to make it. It happened like that sometimes."

127

"Righty-ho," Steele elongated the word smoothly as though to get him back on track. "So, you agreed to meet her that Friday night. The usual time?"

"No, we normally met at 7.30, but Vicky was working that night and said to make it around 9.30. Even then, she would have to make an excuse to leave work. I left the pub about 9.20, I suppose, and went straight there. I saw no one on the way, I saw no one on the way back. Zilch, nothing, nobody until I got back to the pub's car park to pick up my car and it was chucking out time."

"As your date was so late in the evening, why didn't you wait for her outside somewhere and go on together?" Steele asked.

"We couldn't risk being seen together." Zack hesitated; they knew all this. "We had always been very careful not to show any signs of our feelings for each other. I have a wife to consider and a position in the community. Vicky had a relationship going that she didn't want to break off."

"Didn't that bother you? You know, that she was screwing around?"

Trust the sergeant to turn it into something dirty. Vicky was a tease; Zack knew that. Many a bloke might think her easy, but he knew better. When it came to make or break time, she was very picky. As for her relationship with Lennie, Zack would not admit it to the sergeant, but he did mind. He cringed every time he thought of Lennie's hands on Vicky's body. He lied.

"No, it didn't bother me. And she was not screwing around. We're adults – as I said already, I had a partner. Why shouldn't I extend the same courtesy to her? Lennie was her sauce for the goose, if you like. I think we both understood ours was not a permanent relationship." At least, Vicky had understood that. For him, it was an exciting interlude and one he never wanted to end. Vicky had threatened to break it off if it became public knowledge.

"Sauce ...?"

"Not a permanent relationship," Steele repeated, homing in on a different slant to his sergeant. "So, the news of her pregnancy would have come as an unwelcome shock?"

"I suppose it would have. But like I said, I never heard it from her."

"Okay, so now you've gone on ahead – why not wait for her somewhere along the track, somewhere you would not have been seen? It's a rough track for anyone to follow in the dark – especially a young woman." Steele sat back, formed a steeple with his fingers and tapped them on his teeth.

"Vicky was familiar with the track. She would have had her torch, and anyway ..."

"Torch? You made no mention of this in your earlier statement." Steele cast his eyes down the typewritten sheet then looked back at him.

"Perhaps nobody asked. We both carried torches; as you said, it was dark. I think Vicky's was one of those large black rubber ones."

Steele made a note on the pad in front of him. "Right ... and anyway, what?"

"Umm, oh yes, and anyway that's the way we always did it. I go straight there, unlock, get the place ready – get the lights going, the music playing, and Vicky turns up when she's ready. I make it nice for her," he added, then wished he hadn't as he caught the smirk on the sergeant's face.

"These training shoes: on the night in question, when did she change into them?"

Oscar Benson shifted in his seat. "I don't think my client would know that, Inspector, as he wouldn't have been there at the time, would he?" he murmured softly.

"That's okay," Zack said. "I don't mind answering: it's true, I don't know about that night, but normally she used to come straight from home and was already wearing them. She's a runner. People are – were – used to seeing her jogging. The track along the water was a normal route for her. The fact that it was deserted was the one thing she liked about it. But I don't know about Friday. She must have changed before she left work."

"Where was Billy Draper when you left?"

"Billy? What's he got to do with it?" This was a new question. He looked at Steele.

"He topped himself this morning," Pike said.

Zack turned and stared at the sergeant. "Billy! He'd never do that. I know that boy, I taught him at school. What do you mean – he topped himself, how?"

Steele gave his sergeant a warning look, as though he were in danger of saying too much. "Billy Draper was found this morning hanging from the yardarm on the jetty. It appears to be suicide, but," he looked sideways again at Pike, "that is speculation until the autopsy results are in. So, back to the question: when you left, what was Billy Draper doing?"

Billy – why, in God's name, hang himself? He cast his mind back, trying to see Billy in the context of Friday evening, but he didn't figure as being out of place. He stared at his hands; they were shaking. He tried to recall the early part of that night, and could vividly remember his own worries. Why had Vicky called? What had happened? Had Lennie found out? Was Vicky going to call it off? All evening he'd been jumpy, checking his wristwatch constantly, and watching her behind the bar. He knew her smiles and flirtations were part of her job, but it killed him to watch her all the same. What was so important that it couldn't have been said quietly over the counter? Billy – yes, he was there, along with Jed and his mates as usual on a darts night, nothing out of the ordinary.

"He was playing darts with The Crow's team," he said.

"Think. Was he still there when you left?"

"As far as I remember, yes."

"How soon after the end of the game did you leave?" Steele's eyes stared hard at him, and Zack realised that the emphasis of the questioning had changed. They were gunning for Billy. No wonder his solicitor had been willing to sit there and say nothing. They were going to put the blame on Billy. Hot saliva hit the back of his mouth.

"Answer the question," Steele insisted.

Zack swept the hair back off his face with a hand. It masked the action of wiping away the sweat prickling his forehead. The moment of nausea passed. He licked his lips.

"Five minutes, or so? I made my move while the crowd was still round the bar. Colin was just getting to the piano. Vicky hoped to leave as soon as the singing started. The bar work usually quietens during the first couple of songs. I wanted to be out of her way when the time came. Like I told you, I went straight to the cabin – I waited. But she never came." He looked at his hands again, and bunching them into fists, he squeezed them between his thighs. "She never came."

"What time did you eventually pack it in?" Pike asked.

"I stayed on till nearly eleven. And no," he anticipated the next question. "I didn't hear anything, or see anything on the way back." He sensed Oscar's nodding approval beside him. For a brief, he hadn't had much to say, but it was comforting to know he hadn't fallen asleep. "I gave her every chance. Even after I had given up any real hope she'd make it, I stayed on." His voice had taken on a defensive note that embarrassed him. He cleared his throat and continued in a gruffer tone. "Eventually, I closed up and walked back to the pub to collect my car. I had to be home at the normal Friday-night time so as not to arouse any suspicion from my wife. Vicky would have known that. People were coming out of the pub. I mingled with them looking all the time to see if I could see her. But she wasn't there. I assumed she couldn't get away in time, and had gone on home once she realised it was too late."

"Wouldn't she have called you, if she was going to cancel?"

"That part of Draper's Wharf is a dead spot as far as mobile phones go."

There was a knock on the door. Steele got up and opened it. Outside an officer handed him a large manila envelope. "You said to let you know when this came."

Zack heard the words and looked from Steele to Pike and back to Oscar, wondering if the latest development had anything to do with him.

Steele returned to the table, a smile on his face. He looked across to the solicitor. "Righty-ho, Mr Benson, I think we'll take a break.

* * *

17

The cheerless day passed slowly for Hannah, punctuated by wretched memories of the hanged body, the dead man's eyes and the smell of his dying moments. She tried working on her computer, but couldn't concentrate. Instead, she mooched around the dining room, clearing up, refilling the condiment containers and other minor jobs.

Earlier, she'd spotted the police launch's arrival in the bay, and had seen the divers go over. She and Mac stood on the quay to watch their progress and saw them load the inflatable with a net full of sodden material.

Sergeant Ingram came around lunchtime to go over the statements they had made the night before. In particular, he wanted to know how the scene had changed from when they first saw it, to when the police arrived. Hannah knew he meant the fact that they had cut Billy down. In doing so, they had contaminated the scene. What were they supposed to do, leave him there? What if there had been a breath of life still left in him?

Doug arrived just as Mac was locking up. "Sorry I'm late, couldn't get away."

Mac collected a bottle of Glenfiddich from the bar and waved it at Hannah. "Coming in for a night-cap?" He gave the bottle to Doug, "Here, get it started. Be with you in a minute, got the till to empty."

Hannah followed Doug through to the sitting room. He looked questioningly at her, but she shook her head. She'd done nothing towards uncovering the drug scene that day. She flopped down into the same worn but comfortable armchair she'd occupied in the early hours of that morning, and curled her legs beneath her. So long ago, it hardly seemed like the same day. Doug opened the bottle, took three glasses from a corner cabinet, and poured the whiskey into two of them. He held the bottle up.

"Same for you, Hannah, or would you rather something else?"

"That'll do nicely, thanks, with lots of ice and water."

"Philistine." Mac returned with an armful of logs. He added a couple to the dying fire and kicked it back into life.

"Some of us have more respect for our livers; we don't all take it neat."

"But not for our lungs, eh?" he teased. "Thanks." He took his glass from Doug's hand and reclined full length on the sofa, crossing his ankles over the edge.

Doug twisted the lid back on the bottle and placed it beside the water jug.

"For God's sake, sit down Doug. You take up too much room." Mac said.

Doug shifted a couple of books from the remaining armchair and sat down heavily.

"We saw you bring up that load of stuff," Mac said. "So, how come you didn't you find them first time around?"

"Because they weren't there. They've only just been dumped."

"We heard they'd found a training shoe on the beach," Hannah broke in.

"Yeah, we now have the pair. It was like one of the rubber shoes floated while the other sank where it dropped. The theory is that Billy, in a fit of remorse, chucked the evidence into the sea just before he hanged himself."

Hannah shook her head, still in disbelief. The whisper, that Billy Draper had topped himself because he had killed Vicky Brown, had been flying around town all day. No one knew where the rumour had started, but the story was on everyone's lips. Grace had been shocked when Hannah had called on her for a brief visit after lunch. She said she couldn't believe the stories she was hearing. She'd known Billy since he was a boy, and there was no way Billy would have done that to Vicky.

"What if Billy didn't do it?" Mac echoed her thought. He circled the top of his glass with a damp finger, making it sing. The noise resonated in the tiny room, setting Hannah's teeth on edge.

"The message buttoned in his shirt pocket could read as a suicide note."

"We didn't see that. What did it say?" Mac asked.

"You didn't go through his pockets? It didn't say much. It was written on a small scrap of notepaper, in big childish writing, *'I did it.'* That's all he said."

"And you're interpreting that to mean he killed Vicky. Bit of a jump isn't it?" Hannah stared at Doug. "It could mean anything."

"Exactly." Mac downed the remainder of his drink and held it up for a refill. Doug obliged, topped his own up, and checked Hannah's glass. She shook her head.

"Okay, I agree, it's a bit of a jump, but that's only one theory. What do you reckon *'I did it,'* means in these circumstances? Come on, let's have your ideas."

"Grace says she's known Billy all his life and she's never seen him anything but placid. Why should he act so out of character now?" Hannah said.

"It could've been an accident. Look at the size of Billy; he probably doesn't know his own strength." Doug extended a hand palm up.

"You don't think he and Vicky – no way!" The ringing glass stopped suddenly as Mac fixed his eyes on those of his brother.

"Being slow of mind doesn't mean he doesn't have the same physical needs as any other man. I'm just arguing the point. You say she's always been friendly with him, maybe he tried it on, and things got out of hand. Think about it, Mac. This is only one scenario. *'I did it.'* I did what? *I did hide the clothes. I did throw them in the river.* They're not hanging offences. You,

Hannah, you said yourself the other day how upset he'd been after Zack's arrest. If he did do it – accidentally kill Vicky – his guilt from that, added to what he'd done to Zack, could've led to him seeing no other way out."

"If he did do it, then his alibi is wrong." Hannah cradled her glass in both hands and gazed into the pale amber liquid. Her head felt light with the lack of sleep, yet her mind was sharp and strangely clear. "You said he was in the bar with the darts team until 9.30, and spent the rest of the evening in the loo with the runs before Morgan took him home, sometime after 10.15. That doesn't sound to me like a man about to try his luck. Can anyone verify he was in the toilets all that time?"

"Nobody actually saw him in there," Doug said.

"That's quite possible. He would've been in a stall, and most of the guys wouldn't notice anyone was in there at all." Mac said, trying to hide a yawn.

"Those toilets have access to the outside too, haven't they, Doug?" Hannah asked.

"Yeah, the hallway next to the men's toilets goes out to the car park."

"What are you getting at, Hannah?" Mac asked.

"Just playing devil's advocate, I really don't believe he did it, either. But, for the sake of argument, I was trying to follow Doug's line of thought. What if Billy left here at 9.30, would he have had time to commit the deed and get back by 10.15, say? Didn't somebody say they'd seen a man running into the pub's car park just after ten? He could have come in that back entrance by the toilets and feigned his tummy troubles to cover his absence."

"No way! Billy didn't feign anything. He'd messed his pants; the shits were genuine enough. He stank," Mac protested. "And, one thing you're both forgetting, he didn't have the grey matter to think up something like that. If Billy had accidentally killed someone, he'd have left the body where it happened and fled back to his mother!"

136

"Hold on a minute," Doug waved his brother's protests down. "We're just discussing whether it would fit in with his time scale. Three quarters of an hour is a long time. Time enough to rape and kill, but not time enough to clean up and bury her in a grave. As you say, mentally, the cover up was too well planned for Billy."

Mac smiled as though he had won the debate. "Exactly, so we're agreed. Now, can we talk of something less stressful; I've had a gutful of Billy Draper today! How's Mara?"

"No sign of her coming home yet. Her sister's overdue. I wish she'd get on with it; I'd like my wife back – not the same coming home to an empty bed every night."

'Tell me about it!"

"Unless ..." Hannah, deep in thought, murmured the word as an idea began to take form. It went unheeded as Mac teased Doug about the advantages of a bachelor's life

* * *

18

U nless, there were two of them, the words echoed through Hannah's head the next morning. She sat at the table in her room, her laptop open, her thoughts sharply focused on Billy's pathetic little note. 'I did it.' What did he do? He was a big man; he could easily have overpowered Vicky, maybe Grace had only seen the gentle side of him. The real question remained, was Billy capable of raping the girl next door?

And Vicky – was she a flirtatious barmaid or a young woman working hard to better herself? And yes, it did matter. Vicky's behaviour could provide a clue to motivation. Would she give Billy the come-on then back out as soon as he tried? Or, more likely, would she have run rings around him if he'd tried to make a pass at her, or worse, laughed at him?

Hannah reviewed all the information she had previously entered. Apart from growing up as childhood neighbours, and working in the same place part of the time, Billy and Vicky had little in common. To go back to last night's discussion, the plan to cover the crime had been too complex for Billy. But, what if there were two of them? The discovery that the time gap between finishing the darts match, Billy's exit, and his re-appearance in the bar was long enough to commit the deed was significant.

Steele's team had Zack Henderson. From what she had learned of Zack, he also seemed an unlikely suspect, but again, what if Zack and Billy worked together? Zack was a small man. If he had wanted to get rid of the evidence of his affair, and had succeeded in overwhelming Vicky, moving her body to the grave would not have been easy. Maybe he'd needed a large, strong man to help him. Would Billy have come to the aid of his one-time schoolteacher?

She looked again at their alibis in this new light. Zack had been playing darts. He was there for the last throw. Billy had left the room after the end of the game, say 9.30, ostensibly for the toilets. No one in the pub had seen Zack again until closing time, around 11.00 when several punters spotted him in the car park. Meg, his wife, had given him a firm time of arrival at home shortly after. Who was the man seen running into the car park just after ten? Nobody had yet put their hand up for that one.

Both Billy and Zack fitted the frame on the time scale for Vicky's attack. If Zack's motive was to hide Vicky's pregnancy, that would not have affected Billy. Secondly, it didn't cover her burial. Billy was away from the bar for a maximum of forty-five minutes, Zack an hour and a half. Together they might have had time enough to carry the body to the gravesite, but not enough time to complete the burial, unless one of them had returned during the night. '*I did ...*' bury her?

The forensic evidence indicated someone had washed Vicky's body prior burying it. What likelihood of Billy coming up with that idea? Zack would not have had the time to do that and get back still clean and tidy to the pub's car park by eleven. Although it was a logical line to follow, every avenue she took came to a dead end. Zack's own version, spread to all who would listen by his distraught wife, of setting out to meet Vicky at the love nest had a more authentic ring.

The concept of two people being involved opened up a new field. It made a difference to other alibis. It meant that two people in cahoots could have halved the time they were each without an alibi. Anyone, not just Billy leaving the pub early and clocking back in before closing time, could be in the frame, because the second partner in the crime could complete the task of removing the body whilst the killer was in the company of others.

She worked through the alibis again to see if she could come up with a likely pair who might work together, and have suitable motives. As she read, her thoughts flitted from one name to another. There was something in both Jane's and Cassandra's accounts that she'd missed first time around, an anomaly she needed to sort out.

The phone burbled from beneath her pile of notes. Irritated at the break in her concentration, she snatched it up. "Yes? Oh, Mum. Hi, how are you?"

Her mother's voice sounded plaintive, she'd phoned the office first and Peggy had told her Hannah was away for a few days. Hannah rolled her eyes and absorbed her guilt.

"So, when are you coming over to see me?" Her mum asked. "It's been ages. I haven't seen you since your Simon's funeral; and that coming so soon after your dad's."

"I know Mum. Look, don't worry, I'll be over shortly, really, I will, but I have an assignment to finish up here first. Okay?" She closed her eyes, listened to her mother's chatter. The warm familiarity of her voice stirred distant memories until she ached for one of her mum's comforting hugs. Mum didn't know about the rape. And there was no way she would ever tell her about the aftermath.

"So, you're busy working then, are you, dear? Your dad was so proud of you. Everything is all right, isn't it?"

Hannah eyed the packet of cigarettes on the table and reached out for one. She extracted it from its box, tapped the end on the table and held it, unlit, between her fingers. "Everything is fine, Mum. I've had a break, since Simon ..."

"I thought it might be something like that. Well, I'll let you get on. Just wanted to make sure you were all right."

Hannah closed her phone. The colourful swirling shapes of her screensaver drew her eyes into its dark vortex, leaving her mind free to wander. Her thoughts became disorganised.

In choosing to terminate the rapist's leavings, Hannah thought she was doing the right thing. At no time had she seen it as a baby, even in the pre-abortion counselling. But only as something alien, something the rapist had left behind, something that had to be cleaned up before she could become whole, again. With fierce determination, she had shut her mind to any alternatives. But for her understanding boss Peggy, who helped her through it all, she would never have climbed out of the black despair that followed the procedure.

Afterwards, they had tested the foetus for DNA in the hope they could later match it to any suspect they caught for the rape. They told her the scrap of humanity was older than they'd first thought. Some nights she still woke screaming and lathered in sweat, as the cries of a lost baby echoed through her dreams, Simon wept, and the devil laughed. *She had aborted Simon's baby.*

In the weeks following Simon's death, Hannah in mourning hadn't even noticed her missing monthly. Afterwards, although she grieved for Simon in the normal way, she was unable to cope with the pain and guilt of killing his child. She pushed the thought out of her mind by burying the memory deep inside her heart. Only then could she get on with the process of living.

She jerked her head away from the screen to stare out of the window. A bright sunny day out there, in a world full of real people, gotta get out; take a break. Opening the French windows wide to allow the breeze in, she turned the air conditioner on for a few minutes to get rid of the smoky smell. Mac'd kill her for smoking in the bedroom.

A walk to Grace's café for lunch would be good. She'd sit by the window and watch the comings and goings in Lennie's place. How was he coping with Billy's death? It wouldn't tell her much, unless she could get in there, but at least it would give her a rest from the keyboard, time for another smoke and, if Grace were in a talkative mood today, someone to give her a different perspective.

*

141

Hannah opened the café door to a buzz of voices. Grace, standing behind the counter, was in animated conversation with the two old ladies, Betty and Violet. They looked across at Hannah as she entered. Grace acknowledged her with a small wave of the fingers. Violet stopped talking, glanced dismissively at her, and then turned back to Grace to resume her discussion. Hannah didn't want to appear too intrusive, so she approached a different part of the counter to study the array of cakes inside the glass cabinet.

"Be with you in a minute," Grace said. "Sorry, Vi, what was that?"

"I was just asking you if Morgan had been in to pick her lunch up today."

"He does know Billy got her lunches from here, I take it?" Betty added.

Grace shrugged her shoulders. "All I know is he's in there now; I saw him go in. Maybe he's cooking something up for her."

"Huh! He wouldn't give anyone the time of day," Violet scoffed. "He's never had a good word to say to his sister-in-law, why should he start now?"

Grace turned towards Hannah to include her in the conversation. "We were just discussing what to do about Annie Draper's lunch."

"Maybe one of us should take it over? I'll go, if you like." Hannah volunteered. She'd never met Billy's mother. It was unlikely the old lady would have any answers, but people who sat and stared out of their windows all day sometimes saw things other people didn't. She could probe the angles, but then she remembered that Annie was just as much a victim as Billy and Vicky.

Violet straightened her shoulders and towering above her small, plump sister, pursed her lips, deepening the lines on her long face.

"I'll take it over," she said. "Annie won't want to see strangers, not at a time like this." She turned to Hannah. "Nice of you to offer, but we look after our own here."

Hannah smiled thinly at the implied rebuke. They were closing ranks and she was the outsider.

"I understand, Vi, that's okay. By the way, that was a good observation on your part – the lights on the beach, I mean. You did well."

"Humph," Violet huffed, but she looked pleased at the compliment. "Well, like I said, some of us around here keep our eyes open." She turned to her sister. "I see your shed light's been on in the middle of the night again, too."

"Oh, spying on my tenants again, are you? Told you, it's none of your business, nor mine either." Betty's soft cheeks flushed with indignation.

Hannah's interest piqued. "Which night was this?" She had sussed out Violet's weakness the last time they met. Vi might pretend to be reserved with those she didn't know, but underneath that formal façade, she liked nothing better than being the harbinger of news.

"Must've been the night the wind woke me up. I went out to the kitchen to make a cuppa and, like I said, I can see down to Betty's shed from there. I don't need to spy, as you very well know." She poked Betty's arm. "Now, do you have Annie's dinner ready, Grace? I'll pop it off on my way home. You coming?" she asked her sister.

Grace spooned a serving of chicken paella from the hot cabinet into a tinfoil dish, fixed the lid and put it in a plastic bag for Violet. "On the house, tell her. If you see Morgan, you might try to find out what future arrangements he wants to make about her lunches. Though, it's my guess he'll pack her off to a home somewhere."

The door closed behind the two ladies; Grace let out a sigh of relief. "Chalk and cheese those two, never did get on, yet you rarely see one without the other. Anyway, I'm glad you came in, Hannah. I was just about to call you when those two arrived. I meant to mention it yesterday, but completely forgot, what with the shock and everything. I wanted to have a word with you about young Billy."

"Oh?"

"I know what they're saying about him and Vicky, but like I said, I can't get my head around that. What I wanted to say was did he get in touch with you on Sunday?"

Hannah shook her head. "Was he supposed to?"

"Well, not really supposed to, it's just that he was here, he'd been talking about you. He called you the nice lady. I told him that you listened to people who wanted to talk about Vicky, and about the town and that sort of thing. He got a bit agitated, and I had the impression he wanted to say something. He wouldn't tell me what it was, so I suggested he talk to you. I wish now I'd insisted; he might have told me if I had taken more time."

"Don't go blaming yourself, Grace. You've enough on your plate without adding that to it," Hannah said, trying to control an uneasy feeling. What had Billy wanted to talk about? She'd been working Sunday afternoon and evening for the sailing club dinner and hadn't visited the café all day. Had she been available for Billy ... what then?

"Has anyone from the boatshed been in for the lunch order yet?" she asked.

"They phoned it in earlier, but no one's picked it up yet. Don't worry about it; they've got a couple of blokes working on the beach. Jed will probably send one of them."

"I'd like to go over there. It would give me an excuse. What about it, Grace?"

Grace raised her eyebrows. "What are you up to? I never know with you. All right, don't tell me. I won't be a tick." She loaded a cardboard box with the depleted lunch order.

"I don't think you'll have much luck talking to them, if that's what you're after. They must be in shock after poor Billy's death. All this trouble ... and they say it comes in threes. A word of warning, Hannah – the way Billy was talking, some people think you've been a little too interested in what's going on around here. So, watch yourself, okay? I don't want you getting into trouble. There, that should do them."

Hannah hefted the box under her arm. No way was she looking for trouble. She'd watch her back every step of the way. "Be back for mine shortly."

* * *

19

The white concrete forecourt glared into her eyes as she walked up the slope. Hannah had never been this far inside the gates before. She turned to look back at the roadway behind her, and then at the cottages to the side. Her range of vision now took in the latticework of a carport belonging to the first cottage. The dark coloured car parked inside looked very much at home. A black Magna.

Her heart logged an extra beat. Morgan Draper? Morgan had been hostile towards her from the beginning, but why would he keep track of her movements? The voice on the telephone had sounded nothing like Morgan's gruff pitch. He'd made a point of breaking up her discussion with Colin across the bar. Her stomach tightened. Was there anyway he'd seen through her cover? Was he watching her, even now?

She walked on, left the hard brilliance of the sunshine and entered the shade of the massive barn-like boatshed. On one of the sliding doors, a notice with an arrow directed visitors towards the Boat Shed Supplies around the back. A second notice read, No Unauthorised Entry. She hesitated on the threshold and called out. "Hey, Lennie, Jed, anyone here?" No answer. No matter. As a lunch delivery person, she was authorised should anyone challenge her.

Sunlight filtered through the Perspex skylights in the roof, giving the huge workshop a light and airy feel. Hannah recognized the cadence of a radio playing nearby, and the lingering smell of turpentine and sawn timber. She moved around several boats in various stages of disrepair looking for someone.

To her right, the only sign of life appeared to be her own reflection gleaming from a fibreglass yacht beside her. The luxury boat rested on its keel, held upright by tall wooden legs bolted into its hull. A ladder, heavily padded at the top, leaned against the side. Here the acrid smell of fresh fibreglass resin tainted the air. Someone was tinkering around but could see no one. She stopped to listen.

On the left hand side of the building, a set of metal steps led up to the office, a glass-fronted area on a long platform halfway up the walls above the workshop. Beneath the office area, stood a low counter with a telephone and a grubby looking computer on top, together with a roll of plans, or blueprints spread out with a weight at each end. Behind the counter, a row of metal lockers stood against the wall. Between them and the door marked Males, a peg-board held an array of keys.

Through the upstairs window, she saw Lennie, back to her; hunched over a desk and on the telephone. This was Vicky's place of work during the daytime, when she wasn't bar keeping for Mac. She headed in the direction of the steps.

"Hannah!"

She nearly dropped the cardboard box. A face peered down at her from the gunwales of the white yacht above her head.

"Jed! Hi, I've brought your lunch," she tapped the side of the box, "where would you like me to put it?"

Jed, in a singlet and stained shorts, stood up in the cockpit. He held a strip of fibreglass tape in one hand and a brush in the other. "Be with you in a minute." He spoke through the protective mask that covered his nose and mouth, then ducked down and disappeared into the cabin.

Hannah walked on towards the office steps to wait for him. He resurfaced, without his mask, climbed down the ladder and came towards her, rubbing his hands on a cloth. She couldn't read his expression. His eyes looked wary, but didn't appear hostile like the time he'd caught her at his house talking to Cassandra. Perhaps he didn't like people seeing his wife stoned.

"I'm sorry to hear about Billy," she said.

147

"Yeah, well, don't waste your breath. He's not too popular round here right now." He raised his eyebrows indicating the office.

Hannah looked up. "Lennie, you mean?" She considered Jed's words. Billy had worshipped this man, followed him around like a dog, somebody had said. "What about you? You probably knew him better than anyone. Do you really think he killed Vicky?"

"Why not? He's admitted it; cut and dried, I'd say."

She had expected more loyalty from Jed, at least the benefit of the doubt, but here in his work place, Billy's pathetic guilty plea already had him tried and convicted.

"What do you think?" Jed's eyes narrowed as he spoke. "Bloke goes and hangs himself, says he's done it. What's your interest anyway, you didn't even know him?"

Jed's blond hair, tied back at the nape of his neck, looked dusty. His eyes, more confident now, held her gaze as though challenging her to argue with him. She caught a hard edge to his voice. He took a couple of paces towards her. She could smell his sweat and his eyes took on a predatory flicker. She took a step back as a cold draught skipped across her skin.

Jed grinned, as though he'd won a bet with himself. He backed off.

"Look, no need for you to bother Lennie, I'll take that." He held his arms out for the cardboard box. Hannah surrendered it reluctantly, as though giving up her badge of office. He swung away from her and made for the metal steps. "See ya."

Hannah scolded her oversensitive imagination. Her mind was too quick to see danger where none lurked. The office door swung open and Lennie came out in a hurry. He put his hands on the railing, and to the sound of cars driving into the forecourt, he shouted down to Jed.

"It's the bloody cops back again! What for, this soddin' time?"

"Shit!" Jed bounded up the stairs to join his partner. Ignoring Hannah, they hurried back into their office. Through the glass wall she could see them arguing and gesticulating.

"Hannah Ford, I believe." The voice behind her made her jump. She turned as D I Steele approached. A small delegation of police officers fanned out across the workshop.

"On the spot again, I see." Steele's mouth looked stern, but his eyes held a glint of amusement.

Hannah ignored the sarcasm and returned his smile with an equal portion of warmth. He had a knack of making her feel guilty, as though he thought she was crossing the line from her brief into his case. She had to admit that in her mind that line was fading fast.

"I brought their lunches over, that's all. I was just leaving."

"Good. I was about to ask you to do just that."

Lennie came out of the office and stood on the catwalk, waiting. Steele nodded to Hannah, walked away and mounted the steps.

"G'day Mr Cooper," Steele said, handing him a document, which, in the circumstances Hannah took to be a search warrant. Lennie looked bemused.

"We're shutting shop for a while." A young police officer approached her and smiled "So, if you wouldn't mind ..." She indicated the door. Then Hannah was outside in the glaring sun, on the other side of a tape drawn across the doors to prevent interruptions.

Hannah threaded her way through the police cars parked on the forecourt, and out of the double gates. So preoccupied in trying to interpret the meaning of the police presence, she stepped into the path of an oncoming car. The driver beeped his horn, his tyres squealed on the tarmac. She leapt back and waved apologetically to Morgan Draper's glowering face. Taking more care, she crossed the road behind the black Magna. Well, at least he didn't try to run her over. That must count for something.

Hannah returned to the café, shaken. She shrugged her shoulders at Grace's enquiring gaze from the open door. "Don't ask me. I don't know. Whatever it is, they appear to be turning the place over. They're obviously searching for something."

"But what?" Grace asked, wide-eyed. "It couldn't be drugs, or they'd have found them yesterday, when they brought out that bag of stuff."

Since Grace learned that Vicky's pills were Ecstasy, she'd been seeing drug caches everywhere, or so it seemed to Hannah. Unfortunately, her sightings had no substance.

"Yesterday; they examined Billy's workplace and his home." Hannah said. "They'll be looking for reasons why Billy died. I don't know what's got them going today." She'd give a lot to be a fly on the wall over there this minute.

Twenty minutes later, she sat at a window table hands wrapped around a hot coffee cup, the remains of a cold meal littering the table.

Grace paced between the door and the counter. "Looks like that was a waste of time," she said, when the officers returned to their cars, apparently empty-handed. Lennie and Jed's faces appeared in the office window looking down on the departing police cars.

Grace collected Hannah's empty dishes. "I know they've got a job to do, but I can't see why they keep bothering Lennie. What's he got to do with Billy's death?"

Hannah left the table and followed Grace to the counter to pay her bill. From the beginning, Hannah had insisted on paying for her meals even though Grace had tried waving her money away. She remembered the elusive thought that had occurred to her just before her mother's call. Grace would probably know the answer, but if it wasn't necessary, Hannah didn't want to remind her of the night her daughter died, when she could ask others. "See you later, Grace."

Leaving the café, she angled across the road, where she stopped and leant on the seawall, staring into the sunlit world. Yachts, motorboats, colourful dinghies, and the bright sails of the wind-surfers bounced across the wavelets in the breeze. A gaily-painted ferry furrowed a deep white vee in the dark waters, as it chugged down river taking passengers from Parramatta to the distant city. The peaceful scene appeared at odds with her persistent thoughts of rape and death. She ground out the last of her cigarette, along with her morbid thoughts. Time for work. Cassandra, or even Jane, should have the answer. Jane: she'd try her first.

* * *

20

Hannah peered through the window of the real estate office. Between the rows of advertised properties, she saw Sebastian in his red working blazer. He looked busy, sitting behind a desk talking to a young couple. She walked away opening her mobile.

"Jane Peach speaking."

"Hi, it's Hannah. Can I pop in and see you for a minute?"

"Why?" Jane sounded jittery.

"I need to check something we discussed. Don't worry; it's not personal, more about timing on the night Vicky died. I won't stay long. Promise." She'd chosen Jane to ask, because with Jane wrapped up in her own problems, she was less likely to wonder why Hannah would ask such a question. Cassandra might have been more curious.

"I don't know what time Sebastian's coming back. If you were here ..."

"Well, he's in his office right now, talking to customers." She didn't want to put Jane at any risk from her bullying husband. "How about I meet you away from the house? Would that be better? Can you suggest somewhere nearby?"

Jane hesitated. Obviously, the idea did not appeal to her at all. "I sometimes go for walks around the park, by the children's playground, you know, feed the ducks. I could see you there, that wouldn't be out of the ordinary. But really, I don't see how I can help you any more." She sounded tired and Hannah felt bad that she was coercing Jane into something she didn't want to do, but it was too late to back out now.

Hannah collected her car and made it to the park in five minutes. She kept a check on the rear view mirror, but there was no sign of the black Magna. In the empty car park, with no other vehicles around it, her purple Honda stood out like a fluorescent billboard. She walked quickly along the path. There were few people about. She slowed as she reached the empty swings; the kids were in school. She sat on one, and idly moved it back and forth. It would have been easier to ask her question on the phone, but people lie more readily when you can't see their eyes. And Jane was practised at lying.

"Hi!"

Hannah swung around at the sound of her voice. Jane, in a slim white skirt and a long-sleeved, rose-coloured silk blouse, stood behind her.

"Hi, yourself!" She left the swing, and caught up with Jane as she walked on towards the shrubbery edging the duck pond. "How are you?" she asked.

"I'm okay. Look, what I said before, I wish you'd forget it. If he ever found out, I'd told you ... I know what you said, but I can't report him. Right? Just forget it." She tossed her blond hair behind her shoulders and turned her head away. "Sorry about you having to come here, but if he saw you at the house he'd want to know why you'd come. It's not like you're an old friend or anything, and if he got suspicious, well, you know."

Hannah shook her head; she'd never understand women like Jane. They sat down on a bench beside the pond and watched the mallards searching through the waterweeds.

"What did you want to know?" Jane asked.

"It's about the night Vicky was murdered. When we were talking before, you said Sebastian came home at 9.30, and that he was ratty because they delayed the film he wanted to watch for the football going overtime. You also said that he could have gone out later, after you went to bed, as you didn't see him again until the morning. Right?"

153

"But he didn't go out. I would have heard his car, I told you that, too."

"Okay. Can you tell me what time you left him to go to bed?" Jane was bravely sticking to her story; how far would she go to protect her husband?

"About ten, I suppose, the footy was still on. He phoned the TV station to complain, that's when I went up."

"Which channel was it, do you remember, or the name of the film he wanted?"

Jane shrugged. "Ah – wait a minute. Don't know what channel, but," she clasped the bridge of her nose with her thumb and forefinger as she searched her memory. "It was one of the old Bond films, gold something. He has a thing about James Bond, probably all those sexy women." She smiled wryly.

"Goldfinger?"

"That's the one." Jane clicked her fingers; a smile lit her elfin face as though she had done something right at last.

"What time did it eventually come on, any idea?"

"Don't know. I'd left him to it by then."

"Well, thanks Jane, you really have been a great help."

"Is that all you wanted to know? You could have said that on the phone." Jane's brief look of annoyance made Hannah feel guilty at the stress she'd put her though.

Hannah delved into her shoulder bag and took out a small white card. She pressed it into Jane's hand. On it was printed a simple number and nothing more. "But I couldn't give you this on the phone. It's a helpline, Jane, if you change your mind, you can call them day or night. They're very discreet. You can tell them anything. Keep it safe."

*

"Where do you keep your old newspapers?" Hannah asked Mac when she got back.

"Out in the storeroom, Mrs Bates keeps them for the recycling, why?"

"I'm looking for the TV magazine for the week before last."

"Try there. If not, we could've burnt it. By the way, I have some good news for you." He gave her his best granddad look, with a closed lipped smile to go with it.

"Great. You're giving me a pay rise!" Hannah grinned back.

"Nope, better than that, I'm relieving you, getting a regular in."

"What do you mean?" Hannah held her breath. Had he found out what she really did for a living, was he angry at her for not telling him?

"You, working behind the bar – it's not for much longer. I'm interviewing the day after tomorrow. Izzy had a word with me on Sunday. He knows a lass looking for bar work. Hey, Han, what's the matter?"

A customer approached the bar. Always the bloody same in this place, no sooner had you got involved in conversation, someone had to interrupt. She backed away, had to get on, things to do, that paper to find, questions to answer. Time had concertinaed.

"Han! I'll talk to you later, right?" His voice followed her.

Hannah rummaged through the piles of stacked newspapers and TV magazines. Eventually, she found the one she wanted. Her fingers flicked through the pages until she came to the night Vicky died. Back in her room, she phoned Channel Nine.

On the computer, she checked Jed's alibi again: left pub at 9.30, went straight home. Cassandra had confirmed Jed's arrival at around 9.40. But, she'd told Hannah that Jed came in just as *Goldfinger* was starting. The credits were still rolling, was the way she'd put it. Had the film started on time, 9.40 would have been about right. But *Goldfinger* had not gone to air until 10.15 that night.

Had Cassandra simply forgotten to mention the film's delay, or was she a football fan, in which case, she could have watched the game and not noticed it running over time. And being Cassandra, she probably would enjoy watching those hunky males jumping all over each other. Or, was she stoned? On the other hand, she could be deliberately lying about the 9.40 time slot. And if so, why?

*

 Hannah greeted Mac with feigned disapproval in her narrowed eyes when she joined him in the bar at the start of her evening-shift.

"So, you want to get rid of me?" She teased, as she placed a bag of lemons on the Formica top beside the cutting board. Selecting a sharp knife from the drawer, she made a start on slicing them, ready for the night's orders.

Mac walked the length of the bar and came up beside her. She tilted her head and let her smile show him her words were light hearted. Of course, she understood his need for a permanent worker. But, the thought of leaving her major source of information, not to mention Mac's company which she was beginning enjoy, disturbed her.

"As soon as you want out. But Han, it doesn't mean you have to go. You can stay as long as you like, be a proper guest, not a working one." He extended his fingers and traced the knuckles on the back of her knife hand. "I know you're not here for long."

Lowering the knife, she dropped it on the counter and turned towards him. His hands moved to each side of her arms, above the elbows. She took another step towards him, their aprons touching.

Mac's eyes were near enough for her to see their dark brown colouring, as they looked into hers. She'd never noticed their warmth before. He bent his head. The fleeting contact between their lips felt firm, but gentle. The old familiar flick, a yearning she hadn't known in a long while, took her by surprise.

The door creaked open and they broke their clinch. Inevitably, the customer claimed his attention. She turned back to her lemons, short of breath with her awakening emotions, and strangely comforted by the thought that Mac wanted her to stay.

Izzy Foster had approached Mac on behalf of a girl who was interested in the bar job. Hannah's mind went back to the notes on her computer. Knife poised, she looked up. That phone call, it could have been Foster. His voice held a slightly nasal sound that would make it right. Mac returned to her area of the bar.

"When did Izzy Foster first ask you about the barmaid's job?" she asked.

"Sunday night, at the sailing club party, I wasn't sure if he was serious at first or whether it was the drink talking, but he kept on. When he wrote her name down on a card, I said I'd see her, but I made no promises."

"Is this when you were serving around their table? Did you happen to notice if he made a phone call when I left the bar to go upstairs?"

Mac shook his head. "He came to the bar with that suggestion; maybe he didn't want his wife to hear. I didn't notice him on the phone, but it probably wouldn't have registered if I had. Come to think of it, I did see someone on the phone, but that was much later just before the party broke up." He screwed up his face trying to remember. "No, that wasn't Foster. Jed's phone, I heard it ring. Why, is it important?"

She told him about the anonymous telephone call. "It could have been Foster."

"Why didn't you tell me before?"

"What with Billy's death, there's been so much going on, perhaps the same reason you didn't tell me of Foster's plans to get rid of me," she retaliated.

"You think he warned you off, so he could put this girl in your place? A bit snaky."

"He is snaky. How much do you know about him?"

"Not a lot. Bit of a tearaway in his teenage years, successful with the girls, though, I can't think why with his weasel looks."

"Who's the Old Goat?"

Mac smiled. "His father-in-law. But they don't get on. The old man put up the capital for the service station franchise as a wedding present. Word has it that the old man thought Izzy

157

would settle down if he had a business of his own to run. A sweetener some people called it. The bride was heavily pregnant at time. Izzie's a good mechanic, but he'd never have done it on his own."

"And, did he settle down?"

"I don't think it stopped his philandering. Reading between the lines, I get the impression the lass he's talking about now is more than a casual friend."

"He's slimy enough to make threats to get me out of town. The more I think about it the more convinced I am that it was his voice. *"Get out while you still can,"* sounds like a threat to me. What does he plan to do, if I don't?"

Mac looked at her sideways. "You're not thinking he eliminated Vicky for the same reason, are you?"

"No, I'm not suggesting that; she was well entrenched. I don't like Foster, but even for him it's hardly a big enough motive for murder. Is Doug coming in tonight?"

Silence. He had turned away to serve a customer and she was talking to herself.

The banter and the arguments around the nightcap routine that she, Mac and Doug were falling into made her evenings. So far, she and Doug had managed a few minutes alone to liaise on work matters most nights, while Mac dealt with the closing-time routine.

One day, she'd tell Mac the truth about her role here. What would his reaction be? In his own dealings, he appeared to be so straightforward. Would he turn against her?

* * *

21

As Mac called for 'last orders,' Doug tapped Hannah on the shoulder and indicated the back room. She nodded and followed him through.

"What's new?" she asked.

"Briefly: to keep you in the picture, Billy didn't top himself, he had help."

Hannah closed her eyes and leaned against the doorframe. "How did he die?"

"Asphyxia due to overdose of narcotics, the pathologist said she found a single needle mark buried amongst the mozzie bites on the back of his knee."

Her body sprang to attention; a groan escaped her lips. The very thing she was here to look into. Apart from the so-called recreational drugs, she'd made no inroads into finding the source of the hard stuff. She bit her bottom lip as a groan escaped. If she'd been quicker, she may have been able to save Billy.

"It's not your fault," Doug said. "You've been told to take it slowly. You couldn't have done any more in the time. But, now we *know* for sure someone here has access to heroin."

Hannah pulled herself together and started thinking. "Did they turn up anything on the search of the boatshed?" she asked.

"Clean as far as drugs go. That search brought nothing new, but as you know they emptied Billy's locker earlier on, and that search turned up Vicky's black torch, and inside his biscuit tin, they found her watch, smashed."

"Shit, who did that?"

"Find that person and we'll have Billy's killer."

159

"What time did the watch say? It could give us the exact time she died."

"True. It said 9.40 – But it's no good as evidence. Anyone could have wound it to that time," Doug answered. "Obviously, the items were planted to put Billy in the frame."

Hannah cast her mind around for ideas. "We know Cassandra has access to Es. How about conducting a search of her place?"

"Smoking a joint in her own home comes under 'personal use,' it's not enough to get us a warrant We need more. Keep at it; see what else you can unearth. I'll let Mac know the score about Billy; it'll be all over the papers by morning."

She looked at him. "Do you tell Mac everything?"

He caught her look of concern and smiled. "No, I haven't mentioned you. We do discuss things obviously, but I don't tell him anything marked for police eyes only. Give me some credit."

Mac brought in the bottle of Glenfiddich. He looked from one to the other curiously, then handed the bottle to Doug to pour. "You two taking time off? You left me to load the washer." He threw another log on the fire, dropped onto his settee and stretched his legs out along its length. "Okay, Doug, what's the go? You're up to something, I know. Didn't expect you so late."

"Got held up." Doug handed around the nightcaps. He raised his glass and swallowed half his tot. "God, I needed that."

"Rough day?" Mac asked.

Hannah listened as Doug and Mac talked. Her eyes locked on Doug's for a disquieting moment as he went into more detail of the pathologist's findings on Billy.

"She had to look hard to find it," he said. "Says it was cleverly done. Billy wasn't a user who had accidentally overdosed. This was cold-blooded murder. The only mercy is it would've been better than hanging."

Hannah shivered in spite of the heat coming from the fire.

"But why would the killer go to the trouble of hanging him afterwards?" Mac asked. "He must know a post-mortem would discover the drugs. It doesn't make any sense."

"Perhaps he's a weirdo and sees the hanging as fitting," Doug said.

"Fitting! What do you mean by that?" Mac spluttered over his drink.

"If Billy *had* killed Vicky, someone might see hanging as symbolic. Like a death sentence – a more fitting punishment than the current law would give."

"Or, if he is a weirdo," Hannah said, "could the killer have planned it as a re-enactment of Willy Draper's hanging? Like something bigger and better than the effigy they used last time."

"Old Willie Draper's death wasn't an execution," Mac said.

Hannah caught her breath. At the word execution, her mind turned to the newspaper pictures of her rapist, sitting in his car on the hard shoulder of the highway, with a bullet hole in the centre of his forehead. The papers had called that a gang related execution, but that punishment had nothing to do with her rape.

"Any theories on who might have done it?" Mac broke the lengthening pause.

Doug shook his head. "Seems young Billy spent his last night drinking, playing pool down the Crows. From all accounts it sounds like he had a few too many and was shouting his mouth off. In the end, Razor took him in the back room and gave him a coffee. He said Billy left at closing time and, as far as he knows, went straight home."

"*Went straight home*," reiterated Mac, "where have I heard that before?"

Hannah's internal antennae twitched. "What was he shouting his mouth off about?"

"Don't know exactly. According to witnesses, Billy was drunk and being a pest, getting Vicky mixed up with Elle, and fantasising what he'd done to her."

"What's up, Han? Look like you've seen a ghost," Mac said.

161

"It's something Grace said. She had a notion Billy knew something about Vicky's murder, but he wouldn't tell her what it was. Then, on Sunday, he said he wanted to talk to me, only I didn't go to the café that day, so I never got the message."

"Why would he ask to talk to you?" Mac asked. "You didn't know him that well."

"Apparently, he thought I was a 'nice lady.' Grace knew how upset he was about Vicky, and told him I was good at listening. I think she was hoping I would pick up some clue from him and pass it one to her. Except, it never happened."

"Maybe he saw something he shouldn't have seen, and said something the killer recognised. In which case, the killer would want to shut Billy up before other people cottoned on. It's a possible theory," Doug said.

Hannah sat quietly, thinking it out. "What about the mechanics of the thing? Billy was a big man. It wouldn't have been easy to force an injection on him."

"If he was drunk like Doug said, or comatose, it would have been easy enough."

"He wasn't comatose, Razor said he left on his own two feet," Doug said.

"Didn't someone take the trouble to see him home?" Hannah held her glass out for Mac to recharge.

"Seems not," Doug said, grimly. He filled his empty glass with iced water, took a long drink and passed the jug to Hannah. "If you remember, Morgan, who might have walked him home, was here that night."

Hannah remembered Morgan's scowl when he broke into her conversation with Colin. "Okay," she said. "Let's take it a step further. Billy's dead. The killer has to dispose of his body. He thinks up this scheme to make it look like suicide. He then has to transport the body to the wharf, carry him out to the jetty, where incidentally, cars can't go, and then has to hang him up, all without anyone seeing. Even if he could accomplish all that, the risk of discovery at any point along the way would be enormous. How did he do it?"

"What if the killer walked with Billy to the wharf, and then did the deed there." Mac suggested. "That would have been the least obvious way of doing it."

"Doesn't work," Doug shook his head. "The doc said he died somewhere between midnight and one in the morning. She reckons he was dead at least an hour before he was hanged. So, that rules out walking to the wharf theory. The killer isn't going to leave his dead body out in the open all that time before coming back to hang him."

"Could his body have been taken by boat?" Hannah asked.

Mac considered this. "Theoretically, I suppose it could, but the weather would have been against it. The chop would have made it difficult to tie up, and you've got to think of how one man could lift the body out of the boat. It's not like there's a winch to do the work. And with an unstable base like a rocking boat – I can't see it."

Doug looked thoughtful. "If he came in on the lee side, there's a minimum depth of two metres of water there. It's not as if he was restricted to a dinghy. You could get a sizable craft in there." He took out his mobile and tapped the keys.

"True. What are you doing?" asked Mac.

"I'll have a word with my man at the weather bureau." Doug turned his attention back to his mobile. Hannah and Mac listened to Doug's side of the conversation. After a few affirmative grunts, and some rapid scribbles, he finished up.

"Where's that got you?" asked Mac.

"According to his records, at midnight the wind was westerly 12 knots," Doug looked up from his notes at Hannah to explain, "that's a moderate breeze. It increased gradually. At 2 a.m. it was 20 knots, here you're looking at a fresh breeze and white caps on the water. An hour later, it was up to 25 knots. It peaked around 5 a.m. at 30 knots overall – that's near gale force."

Hannah stared into the fire mulling it over. "So, Billy died between twelve and one, you said, and was hanged an hour later. At the earliest estimation, we're looking at one o'clock for

163

the hanging part of it. Which means the wind would've been somewhere between 12 and 20 knots, say 16 – right? What would it have been like around the jetty then?"

"On the windward side it would have been choppy; on the lee, hard against the jetty, it would have been reasonably calm." Mac answered.

"Any good going out to have a look, compare that to what it's like now?"

"Wha-at?" chorused the two men, comfortably ensconced in their armchairs.

"Well, it makes sense. Here we are arguing the toss as to whether anyone could land Billy's body there. Let's go and look at the place and we might get a better idea."

"But it's dark!" Mac objected. "What are you going to see?"

"So much the better, we'll see it from the same perspective as his killer did."

Doug grinned. "She's got you there. Get the torches."

Hannah kneaded the queasiness from her stomach, as they walked across the road to the wharf. Above them, the moon, minus a portion of its roundness, shone in a clear sky. She slowed, and looked up at the tall, white painted mast and spars of the yardarm. In her mind, it stood out as a ghostly memorial to Billy and his long dead ancestor. Mac and Doug had reached the end of the jetty, and were playing their torches over the water when Hannah caught up with them.

"I think that answers one question," Doug said. "Even with a few knots more on the wind scale I reckon our killer could have tied a boat up alongside the jetty here. You're the boat owners' expert, Mac, any ideas on who would have a boat of suitable size."

"Off-hand, I can think of several boats capable of getting into this spot."

"Mm," Doug stared down into the dark, rippling water. "If he tied it fore and aft, that would have given him good control, and make it easier to move the body. What do you reckon, Mac? Think we're onto something?"

Mac turned his mouth down. "No one could lift that man's weight out of a boat."

"What if there were two?" Hannah said. She was convinced two men were involved in Vicky's killing and cover-up, why not two for Billy – the same two?

Doug rubbed the side of his face. "Two men could lever him onto the quay. He's dead, so he wouldn't be fighting. Put the noose around his neck, thrown the end of the rope over the spar ..." Doug flashed his torch onto the relevant crosspiece.

Mac took over from his brother. "Then the second man could jack him up with a fireman's lift, whilst the first hauls on the rope until he's so far up. They stick the crate in under his feet, haul a bit more together, to straighten him up possibly; knot the rope around the cleat like we saw; kick away the crate for good measure, and the job's done. Put like that, I reckon it's possible. Hannah?"

Hannah shuddered as it all became too real for her.

* * *

22

Ned and Maggot, the two old codgers, as she'd dubbed them, were normally inseparable.

It was unlike one of them to order lunch before his mate had and turned up.

"Where's your friend today?" Hannah asked the grizzled old man leaning on the bar.

"He's gone in to have his prostate seen to." Ned looked like he'd lost a marriage partner.

"Poor old Maggot, that's not so good." She poured Ned a large beer, placed it on the counter and fetched a meat pie from the hot cabinet.

"Nah, you're up pissing half the night, he says. Don't give you no rest. Not supposed to drink much, so someone told him, but he reckons lunchtime drinking don't count."

"Want some more sauce?" Hannah handed over the bottle of tomato sauce, and watched Ned squeeze a dollop into the hole in the middle of his meat pie. He stirred it around with a finger.

"Where's the boss?" he asked, licking his blood red finger.

"Gone out for a while, I'm filling in until Mrs Bates gets here at two." She didn't go into detail, but it had been her idea that Mac take advantage of her presence and take a few hours off to continue the work on his boat. He'd invited her along to see it later in the day, but she hadn't made any promises. She had work of her own planned.

Instead of taking his pie and beer to a table as he usually did, Ned pulled out a stool and stayed at the bar to eat. Food and conversation for him went hand in hand, and with his partner away, Hannah, apparently, was the next best thing. Stuck with him, she prepared to turn the disadvantage into her favour. She turned the music down and, with a few discreet comments, eventually steered his conversation towards Vicky's last night in the bar.

"Yeah, I remember that night, it was Maggot's shout ... no, it was my round, that's right, I remember now. Colin, the teacha fellow, he was at the piana ..."

Hannah had already heard the basic story several times from different people, but listened hard for any angle she might have missed. The old man looked pleased to have an attentive sounding board and needed little encouragement. Words tumbled from his mouth along with a frequent spray of pastry crumbs.

"Maggot, he's been telling me all about this operation he's gotta have. Then I go an' get the next round. It's the big fella, Doug serving by that time, 'cos our Vicky's gone on home. Anyways, I take the beers back to the corner table, over there." He pointed it out for her. "That young Billy had the next table, I was sittin' facing him and his pal Jed, you know, the one with the long sissy hair, looks like a bloody girl, wouldn'ta done in my day, I tell ya. Anyways, I was saying, he gets up an' goes off to the bog..."

"Who, Maggot?"

"Nah, Jed. I'm telling you, aren't I? He goes off to the bog first. I take it that's where he's gone; he went out that way and left young Billy to watch his beer. He hadn't hardly started it." He chuckled, licked his lips and took another bite of pie. "But he's been gone some time and Billy gets up and goes after him, leaving his beer only half drunk, an' all. Well, when they don't come back – you know, me an old Maggot, we look at each other, like. I mean, we can't abide waste, either of us..."

Ned's weathered face crinkled and his pale blue eyes, misted with the years, managed a twinkle. His shoulders shook and his breath wheezed through his lungs. He laughed so much he

167

choked on his crumbs. Beneath his white bristles, his face turned puce.

Hannah soothed him down and offered him a glass of water.

"Nah, none of that shit," he gasped, then grabbed his beer, quaffed it down and belched, tears streaming from his eyes. "Tha's bedder."

"Didn't Billy want to know where their drinks were when he came back?"

Ned's laughter returned. "He wasn't in any state to be drinking by then. No wonder he'd been gone so long – phew – you shoulda smelled him. No wonder that Jed didn't come back."

*

Hannah wiped the counter down, turning the old man's story over in her mind. She knew the time Jed had left the pub, but what made him leave his beer? That was not the action of a man simply leaving to go home. Either he intended to come back, or he was leaving for an unexpected reason. To catch up with someone else who had just left, maybe?

Mrs Bates arrived promptly at two o'clock. Hannah ran upstairs to her room, eager to get going. She added Ned's story to her journal before changing into jeans and a loose top. She paused over her choice of footwear, flat casuals or go for the running shoes. Uncertain of the terrain she might meet, she decided on the lace up runners.

Outside The Harbour Lights, she checked the time on her watch and turned left. Vicky's watch had been smashed at the time of 9.40. No good as evidence, as Doug rightly pointed out, but she could use it as an exercise. She set off at a brisk pace, gauging her speed to that a young, athletic woman might take when going out to meet her lover. She walked along the main road and branched off to the right. A short way up the track she passed the clearing around back entrance to the graveyard that Mac had pointed out. Checking the time, she continued up the track towards the fisherman's hut Vicky had been heading for. Ten minutes later she stopped.

Here, the mangroves grew thick and dense to her right, a bank of tea-trees to her left. The track was at its narrowest point. Good for an ambush maybe, but it left no room for the attacker to manoeuvre. Even supposing the watch had been broken during the attack, she had no means of knowing at what point – in the beginning, or the end.

No need to go further, she retraced her steps to the clearing. Vicky had started out in high heels. Mac had confirmed she was still in high heels when she left the pub.That would have reduced her speed, and therefore her distance.

She would've stopped somewhere along the way to change her shoes, another delay. In Vicky's place, where would she have done that? Out on the main road, in a shop doorway, say, would have been too obvious. The first place hidden from curious eyes, but with room to move, was here. The track widened into a small open space. A gate led through to a narrow stony trail back to the graveyard.

She sat on a grassy bank to one side of the path and faced the river where the mangroves were thin enough to watch the water moving around their roots. The sun warmed her back; birdsong filled the air. Vicky could have sat here in the dark, her torch on the ground. She would have breathed in the same faint smell of river mud. Maybe she heard the scuffle of nocturnal creatures, or perhaps the footsteps of someone following her as she laced on her running shoes for the rougher track ahead.

In between the grassy tufts, the ground was hard, small rocks and stones abounded. Vicky died from injuries to her head, believed caused by someone bashing it on the ground. But, Zack had passed this place later in the evening on his way back to the pub, had her body originally been left here, he would have seen it. The crime investigators had covered the area but, due to the rainstorms, had found no evidence of the killing ground. Ironically, those same storms had washed away the earth in Old

Marty's grave to reveal Vicky's naked corpse to the burial party.

Mac said the graveyard wasn't far away. She shivered in the warm air and rose to her feet. The wrought iron gate, painted black looked to be in good repair. It opened silently. It would have been good to have Mac here with her, but as she still hadn't told him, he would think it odd she was taking such an interest.

Hesitating only for a moment, she walked on through the gate and followed the narrow trail between trees and shrubs. Had Vicky's body made this journey, or had her murderer forced her to walk in here before he did the deed. He had plenty of cover.

The rough trail ended abruptly as she came out onto a tarmac path, the back-end of the graveyard. Hannah stopped to take in the scene. The headstones on the nearest bank of graves appeared to be relatively new, not yet softened by lichen and weather. The church stood at the furthermost corner of the deserted cemetery. She turned to her right and followed the tarmac path that skirted the outside of the graves. She didn't know which grave the killer had used. They'd refilled it and allocated Old Marty another plot.

A large garden shed appeared, almost hidden by the overhanging branches of trees that lined the edge of the grounds. She studied the landscape to the left and right before she approached the shed. This was Morgan Draper's patch. He was responsible for the upkeep of the grounds and was the last person she wanted to run into. She had her mobile, but there was no back up she could call on apart from Mac. She could break it off right now, and return to the safety of The Harbour Lights. This had nothing to do with the job she was here to do; it was simply to satisfy her own curiosity.

After another quick look behind her, Hannah leaned forward and peered through the shed's dusty window. Just a normal garden shed – a home for tools; shovels, spades, forks, and a variety of implements she had no name for that hung on the walls inside.

It was too small for the mini-backhoe used for digging graves. Presumably, Morgan kept that elsewhere, and anyway the murderer wouldn't need it. He only had to deepen the hole that was already there. Shading her eyes, she peered further into the shed. A large wheelbarrow took up an expanse of floor space. She pursed her lips and pulled away from the window to check the door. Padlocked.

On the outside wall of the shed hung a roll of green hosepipe, wound tightly around its drum; for cleaning tools, she supposed. One end of the hosepipe locked onto a tap; the other end capped with a small, brass nozzle for adjusting the power. Goose pimples shivered up her arms.

The sound of a bird's alarm call caught her attention. She listened, but could hear nothing out of the ordinary; could see nobody. Which way to go home? She could take one of the public paths between the headstones; walk to the church and go out the conventional way. It would be a long way round, but easier walking, or she could find the turnoff and go back the way she'd come. That way she would be nearer to the place where Mac was working on his boat.

Hannah found a turnoff, hesitated, not certain that it was the right one, but it led in the right direction, so she took it. If it didn't work out, she could always turn back. She strolled along the path, not in any great hurry. It was necessary to get her thoughts in order. If Mac was in a talkative mood, she could bounce her theories off him. So preoccupied with thoughts of Vicky, her mind was slow to register the sounds her ears recorded.

The sound came again. This time she stopped and listened. A crunch of leaves? Silence. She held her breath to listen. Nothing. Okay, it's scary; she was alone and slap bang in the centre of an area where murder had been committed. She needed to curb her imagination, that's all. She was a cop; she had to get over her fears if she wanted to continue her career in the job. The noises were probably perfectly natural. Probably.

She moved on. A few seconds later the sound came again, like an echo to her footsteps. Was anybody there, she wanted to yell, but fought the urge. She was unarmed so if someone was following her without identifying himself, she wasn't going to stay around to have a conversation with him. A stick cracked behind her. No doubts now, her breathing quickened. She hastened her pace.

The path narrowed then petered out. It wasn't the one she'd come in on. She stopped to take her bearings. Her choices were few: she could either retrace her steps towards whoever was following her, or blunder on through the undergrowth until she came out, hopefully, somewhere along the main track. If she went sideways, she could be in this maze forever.   Mustn't panic. Straight on. She pushed her way through the undergrowth, ducking under branches, skirting fallen trees, and all the time making herself aware of the direction she was heading. The canopy was light, and she kept the glimpses of the sun behind her. She could hear the sound of blood pulsing somewhere in her head. The footsteps grew louder as she fought her way through the bush.

Her pace became more frenzied as she searched out the easiest routes. She no longer cared how much noise she made. Speed is what counted. No one was going to do *that* to her again. She found another trail and raced on. Her loose top snagged on the bushes each side.

"Run, baby, run!"

A voice on the wind sang out to her. It was a real voice, not one in her head. Her pursuer had given up any pretence of subtlety, his footsteps crashed along behind her. His words echoed in her ears.

Driven by adrenaline, her legs powered her forward. Feet, fists, knees, elbows, teeth, nails, if he caught her, she would fight with all the weapons at her disposal. He wouldn't get away with it this time.

Suddenly she was out in the bright sunlight and back on the familiar track. She skittered around, arms wheeling to keep her balance, feet slithering on the gravel stones, as she made the ninety-degree turn.

Her stride lengthened as she raced along the clear track heading for town, and the safety of people around her. She didn't look behind. No longer hearing anything above the pounding of her heart and the rasp of her breath, she sprinted for home and didn't slow down until the track entered the main road and civilisation.

It was only then did she chance a look behind her. The track was empty. There was no one there. She slowed to a stop. Feet apart, she bent double, hands holding her ankles she fought to bring her breathing under control. Drops of sweat fell from her face to darken her running shoes.

"Hell of a way to keep fit!"

She jerked her head up and stared straight into Mac's eyes.

"Where the hell did you spring from?" she asked accusingly as he approached her.

"Down there," he adjusted the strap of a tool bag hanging from his shoulder, and indicated the laneway that ran down to a shore beside the sailing club. "If you've come to help on the boat, you're a bit late. I've put the tools away. Hey, are you all right, you look a bit stressed out?" He stopped a couple of metres from her.

Hannah swivelled her head to look again at the empty track. She returned her glance to Mac; his breathing was relaxed and normal. She scraped her face with her forearm. "I thought I was being followed." She gave him an apologetic smile for her ungracious thought. "What with this and the black Magna, you must think I'm paranoid. I guess it's an overactive imagination."

"Where have you been?" Mac looked over her shoulder as though following her glance. When she told him, he was angry.

"Shit! Hannah! Why didn't you tell me, I would've come with you? Did you see who it was?"

"I didn't see anybody. I think I heard him. All right, I *know* I heard him. I was in Morgan's territory; it could've been him, I don't know. I know Morgan's not a young man, so if it was, he's fit. He kept up with me, at least through the bush."

"When I saw you it looked like you were running a two-minute mile. It didn't look like imagination to me. Whatever got into you, to go there alone? You laid yourself wide-open, Han." Mac shook his head at her foolishness.

"Yeah, yeah, right, I know! Won't do it again. Promise," she added flippantly.

"It wasn't Morgan Draper, I can tell you that. Listen," he held up a hand. "Hear the machinery working? That's Draper, he's mowing the council verges. I've seen him."

Hannah put a hand to her mouth to suppress a nervous giggle.

Mac dropped his bag and came towards her. He looked startled, as though he thought she was on the verge of hysteria.

"Han?"

The laughter welled inside her, bubbling like gas under water. He didn't understand. She'd won. She'd lost the bastard. Her laughter exploded. Tears mingled with her sweat. Mac stared at her as though she had taken leave of her senses. He put his arms around her and held her tightly to quell the spasms.

She got herself under control, back to earth and sanity. "Ah..." she jerked away from him, slapped his arms down, and then held onto her sides to stop the cramping pain of stitch. "I'm okay. God, that hurt."

"Let's get you home."

"Mac, I'm all right! Honest, I'm fine. I couldn't be better. You have no idea!" She stared around, as though looking at the place for the first time. People crossed the road, cars passed by and pedestrians looked in shop windows. Everything appeared in sharp focus and newly washed colours. It was a wonderful day. The sun's warmth penetrated her cooling skin, and the blue sky had not a single cloud. She laughed again, gently this time. Boy, did she feel good!

"With your history, I would have thought you would avoid risky situations. Whatever possessed you to go there, Han?"

"At the time, I didn't see it as a risky situation. But, I have learned something. I may not know the 'who,' or the 'why,' but I think I have a good idea on the 'how,' and possibly even the 'where.'"

* * *

23

At The Harbour Lights, Hannah left Mac talking to Mrs Bates and ran upstairs to the cool safety of her room. Her euphoria rapidly evaporating, she locked the door behind her, stumbled over to the bed and sat down. She hugged herself, rubbing the clammy skin of her arms. Twigs didn't snap on their own. "Run, Baby, run!" The whispery words had not been a voice in her imagination. Someone had chased her out of the graveyard. Was he the killer, or just some fruitcake that got his jollies from chasing women and frightening the hell out of them? Was the chase all the excitement he needed? But not for Vicky, some freak had caught her.

She moved into the en suite intending to start the shower. Her face in the mirror looked exhausted – her hand went to the side of her head.

The dog snuffles at her face. Voices, lights, movements; she wakes in a hospital bed to the pungent smell of urine. Her hair is sticky and matted with it. She cries out. She knows something bad has happened, but can't remember what. She begs for a shower, a bath, anything. At the nurse's gentle persuasion, she agrees to the examinations first. She closes her eyes and grits her teeth against their probes. At last, blessed clean water and soap and her hair cleansed of its filth

But it doesn't stay that way. Back home she can't escape the smell. She washes her hair two, three, sometimes four times a day. The smell lingers. She can't sleep, she changes her pillows but the smell keeps coming back. She stares into the mirror at home. Her once silky, blond hair is dry and brittle, the colour of dirty straw. One day, she takes the scissors to trim the split ends. She cuts another inch off, and another. She watches the hands in the mirror working of their own volition as they chop and chop and chop. Her fouled hair falls to her feet on the bathroom floor. And she rejoices.

The images fade. The new face in the mirror is the one she has learned to live with. Thanks to remedial work of a hairdresser, it sports a short and stylish bob. She turned away and into the shower.

*

Wednesday was her night off, same as Vicky's, Hannah reflected. The evening hours stretched enticingly ahead as she sat down to her laptop and opened her journal. After updating the DW file, she stopped to make a cup of coffee and reached for a cigarette. The pack was empty. Shit. That meant going downstairs. Since Billy's death, her smoking timetable had gone to hell.

Instead of a smoke, she immersed herself in work. Her under-cover progress was too slow. So far, Cassandra was still her closest lead. From her sojourns behind the bar, she watched, looking for those with money to chuck around, for surreptitious deals taking place. She hadn't spotted anything out of the ordinary. Perhaps she was looking in the wrong place – would she have more luck in the Crows? It was something to consider. In the meantime, she worked on her own theory that the two murders and the drug running were connected. The manner of Billy's death had confirmed it.

Going back to Vicky's case and the list, prioritising suspects who had motives and alibis, she studied it once more. If she worked on the premise that the person who chased her *was* Vicky's killer, then she could begin an elimination process. Morgan Draper for starters: It was a mystery why he was interested enough in her movements to follow her around in his Magna, or stand nearby and listen to her conversations in the bar, but she could exclude him from this afternoon's events. He had been busy mowing the verges.

Izzy Foster: he wanted Hannah out of town. He'd made that plain. Was it because she stood in the way of the girlfriend's job, or did it connect to Vicky? His backroom light was on the night Vicky died. Why? Foster dismissed it as 'left on by mistake.' When someone pointed out that it was off when he went to work at dawn the next day, Foster's explanation was that the globe had blown. His story, although unverifiable, could well be true. Or, could he be using his back room for dealing purposes? Was he Vicky's supplier? Did the fact that soon he would have money enough to pay off 'the Old Goat,' have any bearing on the subject?

Hannah continued working until her concentration lapsed. She rubbed her eyes with the heels of her hands. God, she wanted a smoke. Leaving everything as it was, she picked up her bag, left the room and descended the stairs.

The machine stood in the dimly lit hallway, near the public telephone. She inserted her coins and collected her prize, her feet tapping in time to the heady thumping of music coming from the bar room. She changed her mind about going straight back up and went in to buy a bottle of mineral water. Hannah glanced around, it seemed to be the regulars there and Mac was coping well, he didn't need her help. He waved away her money and she nodded her thanks.

"Just going out for a breather," she told him.

"Is that what you call it?" he said, looking at her packet of cigarettes.

"Need some company, Hannah?" A punter called over the heads of his mates.

"Get back in line Squiffy, she needs someone with a bit more muscle, don't you, Han?" another answered with a friendly laugh.

"Goodnight boys." Hannah grinned at the ribaldry and gave

them a mock salute.

"G'night!" they chorused.

"And, sweet dreams, baby."

Hannah slipped out of the front door and crossed the road to the wharf. With daylight fading fast, the tall yellow lights were winning their evening battle for supremacy. She didn't go as far as the jetty; too many memories of Billy's corpse lay that way. Instead, she leaned over the rail and watched the gentle movement of the black water. She lit her cigarette and took a deep, satisfying drag, savouring the moment, waiting for the guilty pangs her weakness always brought her when she thought of her promise to her dying dad. On the second pull, she looked up and watched, as the lights of the town grew brighter. Her thoughts turned to Foster's service station; his backroom, why the light was on the night Vicky was murdered. Did it have any relevance?

After the fourth puff, she pinched it out. Only one thing for it, go and have a look. A quick glance in through the window may give her the answer, or even eliminate Foster altogether. Given the circumstances, she'd take the car; its shell would provide a place to sit, unobserved, while waiting for him to close. She'd not forgotten the cemetery chase.

It wasn't for another hour that Foster showed signs of shutting up shop. Finally, he turned off the workshop lights and closed down the big roller door. He looked around as though sensing a watcher. Hannah sat very still. She'd parked her car along with others to one side of the garage, behind a row of ragged bushes. In the dark, she hoped he wouldn't pick out its hue. Purple was not the colour of car to go sleuthing in.

Foster doused the bright forecourt lights and disappeared into the shadow. The security lights came on, but no Foster. Maybe he'd already left. He could have parked his car around the back, and gone out the side-road without her seeing him.

Hannah waited another ten minutes, then picked up her torch, and slipped out of the car, through a gap in the hedge, crossed the boundary fence. The yard was empty. The light in the backroom cast a yellow splash that spilled out through a small window high off the ground. Her luck was in. With a quick look around to check no one was watching from the side road, Hannah stepped up onto a small retaining wall. It brought her face level with the window.

Standing on tiptoe she peered inside, then drew her head away. There was movement in the room. Unsure of what she'd seen, she peeked again, and quickly absorbed the situation. Inside the storeroom, a sofa bed, opened out and covered with a tartan rug, stood directly below the window. Stretched across the bed, entwined figures bounced in rhythmic harmony. Izzy Foster's naked back concealed all but a spread of plum coloured hair over pale blue cushions. The girlfriend.

Hannah watched for a few more seconds before she became aware her curiosity had become voyeuristic, when she drew away from the window. Her feet slipped on the broken wall. Stones rattled onto the tarmac below. She fled back to her car. In the quiet of the night, the car sounded overloud. Its muffler was going. She changed gear with care.

So, Foster was using his storeroom to have it away with his girlfriend. So, why, if he was bonking her the night of the murder, hadn't he produced her as his alibi? Maybe, if the 'Old Goat' was holding the franchise over his head to keep him on the straight and narrow, Foster didn't want it made public. But, in keeping quiet, he'd only brought suspicion on himself. She pulled into the pub's car park satisfied with her evening's work.

* * *

24

Hannah hurried up the stairs. Not intending to leave her room for longer than it took to pick up her packet of cigarettes, she'd left it unlocked. As soon as she opened the door, her relieved glance fell on her laptop still in its place on the table.

The computer had shut down, the screen black. She touched the key to bring it up but the sleep mode had turned off and it needed rebooting. Instead of her desktop appearing, a purple message sprang onto a deep black background. "Primary Master Hard Disk Fail," the text read. Ah, shit! It'd crashed big time.

She stared at it as though her eyes alone could bring it back to life. A quick check showed the power leads and jacks were still in place. She slammed a fist on the table.

"Why?" she yelled at it. The notice remained. What did this mean in terms of her work? If the hard drive had gone, she'd lost everything not already backed up. And, that meant all the stuff she'd entered in the last twenty-four hours.

She rubbed her face and pulled at her eyes; she'd have to go right back through her notes and doing the whole thing again. She couldn't even make a start until someone had repaired it, and however long was that going to take? She looked at the manila folder on the table. It was flat. Her hands shook as she opened it. Empty. All her scraps of paper, scribbled-on envelopes, napkins, notepads, and sheets of rough workings had gone.

Trepidation touched the back of her throat as she looked around the room. The bottom drawer of her bedside cabinet was slightly open. She never left them open, too frightened of the funnel-web spider getting into her underwear. The bed appeared more rumpled. Her shoes, peeking out from underneath it, had parted company, and one had fallen over on its side. She got up and went to the drawer, pulled it open and drew in a sharp breath. It didn't look very different, but she knew. Someone had rummaged through its silky contents. She checked the other drawers. Nothing missing, but someone had been there.

"No-o!" she ran to the wardrobe. She stretched her hand up and ran it along the top. Her fingers touched the cardboard box. She grabbed it and opened the lid. Relief swamped her as saw her back up still intact. She looked around for somewhere safe to put the memory sticks. If he could get in here, nothing was safe. She tucked them into her bum-bag and strapped it around her waist.

A quick check around the rest of the room indicated nothing else was out of place. In the en-suite, the laundry basket was on its side. Of the four items she knew to be in there, only three remained. Yesterday's panties had gone. Rage outstripped disquiet in the base of her belly.

She ran down the stairs and into the bar. Doug sat on a bar stool, a glass of beer in hand talking to his brother. Mac raised a hand and indicated her as she approached.

"Here she is you can ask her yourself. Hannah, just telling Doug about your adventures this afternoon," Mac said.

Doug swung around to greet her. He had a big grin on his face. "It's a boy!"

"What's a boy?"

"My sister-in-law's new baby."

"Oh, right. Bully for her."

Doug's grin slipped from his face.

"Are you all right, Hannah?" Mac asked. "Can I get you anything?"

Hannah touched her lips with her fingers. "I'm so sorry Doug; I didn't mean it to come out like that. Truly, I didn't mean it that way. Well done, I'm glad it's all over for her. I suppose that means you'll be getting your wife back soon."

"She'll wait until the littley is home with his family. Then she'll leave them to it. What's up with you, still spooked from your chase? Want to talk about it?"

"Someone's been in my room."

"What do you mean, been in your room? Didn't you lock it?" Mac the landlord demanded.

"You mean they've broken in?" Doug asked, putting his glass down on the counter.

"I was only going out for a minute. I came down for cigarettes. But then I went outside for a smoke and ... yeah, I know, my fault, forgot to lock it."

"Come on, let's take a look." Doug swung his legs around the stool and stood up.

She led the way back to her room, Doug following and asking questions as to how long she'd been out and what times. He examined the door. "As you say, the lock's okay. They must have just walked in; talk about making it easy for them."

"All right, don't keep on. I don't always lock it, not if I'm downstairs or around nearby, only when *I'm* inside. It isn't as though I have anything in here worth pinching, other than my laptop, of course."

"But that's still here." Doug jerked a thumb at the computer on the table. He gazed around the room. "It looks tidy enough. What makes you think anyone's been in here?"

"My computer's crashed," Hannah said, slowly, barely able to control her fury. She stood beside the table, and jabbed a finger at her useless laptop. "Somebody's been messing with it." Doug raised his eyebrows.

"And my notes have gone! I had them all collected together in that folder. I was only going to be a couple of minutes; I didn't even shut it down. I was updating my report, it was probably right there on screen when they came in."

"Not very clever. You got it backed up?" He looked at her sideways.

"First thing I thought. Most of it's in here," she patted her bag. Doug seemed more concerned with the loss of her report than the fact a villain had been trespassing around her room.

"Wake up, Doug! Can't you see? Whoever has been in my room has seen my work and destroyed it. Not only is my cover blown, but *that someone* could be the man we're after."

"Okay, apart from your notes, have you checked to see if anything else is missing, your purse and money, for instance?"

"No, I had all that with me. He's a sicko. He's taken my underwear!"

"What?"

"Not even a clean pair, the jerk."

"Oh God, one of those. Okay, I'll get the boys in. You'd better ask Mac for another room tonight while we deal with this one." He looked around as Hannah pointed out the small differences she had spotted.

"I've been targeted twice today. He's got to be an opportunist. It's possible he followed me to the cemetery, but he couldn't have planned for me to be out this evening. Even I didn't know I was going out."

"Mac'll know who's been in tonight. Not much to go on. No break-in, an unlocked door, a wad of papers and a pair of used knickers missing, but, put that with what we've got, and it's gotta be more than coincidental."

"You might have a man in custody, allegedly for Vicky's murder," Hannah said, arms hugging her body, "but, there is still another killer on the loose. Zack Henderson didn't murder Billy Draper."

"True." Doug took his mobile from his back pocket. "Don't worry, we'll look into it. Hopefully we'll find prints other than yours on the laptop."

"I wouldn't bet on it," she muttered, between clenched teeth.

*

Hannah couldn't sleep. The day had been too long, too full. The knowledge that someone had penetrated her cover, meant that she'd have to pull out, and just when she was getting into the job. Her new room wasn't any different from the old one except its colour scheme, but it felt different, not so lived in. All her things were still back in the old room. She got up and went out onto the balcony, wrapping the hotel's bathrobe around her. The night air was cool; it lacked the wind of the night Billy died. The moon lurked behind an overcast sky; the yardarm barely visible.

Mac's light was still on. With her role here coming to an ignominious end, she needed to tell Mac about it before anyone else did. She walked silently towards his window. The sight of him sitting up in bed, wearing glasses, brought a smile to her lips. Granny glasses with the half-moon shaped lenses. Although he had the mannerism of peering over the top of glasses, she had never seen him wearing them. It made him look vulnerable. Her tap on the window roused him from his reading.

"Can't sleep?" he asked, putting his book and glasses aside.

"Can I come in?" She stepped through the French windows. Her heart banged against her ribs. Although she'd been in here before, she'd had a very different reason. Instead of bringing him a deathly message, she was looking for something else, though she wasn't sure what, comfort, or security maybe – or, to tell him she'd been living a lie under his roof. He smoothed out and patted the side of his bed. "You can sit here if you want. I hope you haven't come to drag me out of my bed again." His genial smile drew her on.

"You should be so lucky, it's freezing out here."

"You're welcome to share my duvet." He said it without guile, and she was grateful for that.

He lifted the corner of the dark blue cover, and she slipped into the cosiness of his bed. She sat beside him, her legs outstretched. Her shivering body had a life of its own, and it wasn't all down to the cold. Without saying a word, he stretched his arm out and dimmed the bedside light. Turning back to her, he put his arm around her and held her still. "Are you all right with this?" he asked.

Their bodies warmed together beneath his quilt. She nodded.

Tears watered her eyes. He understood. At this moment, she had absolute trust in him. When he made no further movement towards her, she realised he was waiting his cue from her.

The choice was hers. She snuggled lower into the bed. Mac held back as though expecting her to withdraw any moment. She smoothed her hand across his chest; he responded by caressing her shoulders. Their movements became a game of 'follow my touch.' For every movement she made, he followed in kind.

The hard little knot in the base of her belly unravelled. Hannah led him all the way, instigating every move until they lay together, naked in the gentle light. Barely moving they held each other close, letting the sensation of skin on skin work its magic. She leaned forward and whispered in his ear. "Do you want to use a condom?"

On the pill and cleared of any infection the rapist might have left, she had no worries for herself, but Mac wasn't to know that and she wanted him to feel safe.

"Might have one here somewhere." His fumbling hand found one in the bedside drawer. He stuffed the packet beneath his pillow and taking her head in his hands, he nuzzled her throat, and then her lips. Their first real kiss was long, slow and sensual. Eventually they broke for air. And laughing at their clumsy efforts to un-wrap the condom they put it on together and started all over again.

* * *

25

Doug who had been propping up the bar for most of the evening was in a celebratory mood. When Mac closed for the night, Doug fetched a bottle of Champagne from the fridge and popped the cork. He grabbed the ice bucket, and with the foam effervescing down the cold bottle, he darted away into the sitting room.

He poured the sparkling wine into three flutes. "Come on you two; help me wet the baby's head."

"Hah!" Mac laughed. "Thought you'd been doing that all night. Better make the most of it, Hannah, when he gets Mara back, he'll have better things to do than spend the evening drinking with us then."

Doug winked at Hannah and raised his flute. "The bairn!"

"The bairn," Mac and Hannah responded.

Hannah sat in the armchair and pulled her feet up under her. So far, today, neither she nor Mac had made any mention of their lovemaking the night before. But, whenever he looked at her, she could sense the warmth in his eyes, and it made her smile.

"Any news on Hannah's computer?" Mac asked Doug.

"Yeah, I called in before I came over." He turned to Hannah. "Mainly your prints are on it, and not many at that. It looks like he wiped it clean, all bar one spot. He left a group of three fingertips on the base of it, as though he'd moved it and forgotten to wipe that bit. So far, no one's found a match for them, but once we get the perp, we can at least tie him to your room."

Hannah treated Mac to a 'told-you-so' look. So much for his

scepticism, that anyone would bother to crash her computer deliberately.

"I believed you!" he said, wounded. "I'd give a lot to know who came into my place and walked into a guest's bedroom, even if it was unlocked!"

Hannah wrinkled her nose at him. He hadn't forgiven her for that indiscretion.

"Anyway, Han, forget that, you were going to tell us your ideas on the 'how and the where.' Still game?" Mac asked.

Doug cocked his head. "This should be good," he said it with a smile that took the sting out it. "Only remember, before you get too carried away, as far as Vicky's murder is concerned, Steele's team is building a sturdy case against Zack Henderson. I doubt you can find anything that will sway them otherwise, but okay, let's hear your theories."

"I'm not ruling Zack out necessarily, just looking into alternatives. There are others whose alibis that are also weak."

"Like whose?" Mac asked.

"Do you want me to cut to the chase, or go through an elimination process?" Hannah asked Doug.

"Let's hear your reasoning, all of it. Whose alibis are not holding up?"

"Sebastian Peach's for one," Hannah continued. "Your worthy real estate agent had no alibi after 10 pm, in spite of what you've been told. We know he was angry with Vicky. They had words across the bar. We also know that Vicky had learned only the day before that Sebastian knocked his wife about. Vicky had seen Jane's bruises."

"He'd hardly kill her for that, though," Mac protested.

"Sebastian is a toady, a social climber. He's a man who needs to get to the top no matter who he tramples along the way. There's no way he would want that side of his life to become public knowledge. Look at you, you've lived here all your life, did you know he was a wife basher?"

Mac shook his head.

"There you go! Now, suddenly, someone does know about

it. The barmaid no less, how's he going to keep her mouth shut? So, what I am saying is that Sebastian, like Zack, has both motive and opportunity."

"So, why didn't Jane tell Steele about it?" Mac asked.

"It's an old problem," Doug said. "We hear about it almost on a daily basis. When wives are bashed, they rarely dob their husbands in. Sometimes, even after they've been hospitalised and have agreed to press charges, at the last moment they withdraw."

"Basically, it's because she's more frightened of him than she is of you," Hannah said, pointing a finger at Doug. "Look at Jane; she's in denial. She truly believes that unloading her problems onto Vicky led to Vicky's death. Then, having got that off her chest, she begged us not to say anything. She was terrified of what Sebastian would do to her if she reneged on his alibi. She said she would deny everything if I told Steele."

"So, you're suggesting Sebastian committed murder to prevent his reputation becoming sullied, although you know we have no sightings of him outside his home after 9.30?" Doug said.

"Jane says he was there until at least 10 pm, after that she went to bed, and didn't see him for the rest of the night. For what it's worth, I don't think Sebastian did leave his house that night. But if Jane *is* covering-up for him, then I think someone should be aware of her situation, for her own sake. Also, in case it dovetails into something the investigation already has on him." She looked Doug in the eye to make her point.

"Can't see Sebastian getting his hands dirty to dig out the grave," Mac said. "Not like him at all. He hasn't got that sort of bottle." He drained his flute and changed it for a whiskey tumbler. "Here, you two finish the fizzy stuff. Can't stand it."

"Okay," Doug said to Hannah. "So, you've dismissed Sebastian. Who's next on your hit list?"

"What do you know about Razor?"

"Razor: landlord of The Crow's Nest?" Mac answered, surprise in his voice. "Tough looking guy, ex-boxing champ; he used to be a cook in the merchant navy in his earlier life. Came here about two years back, not short of money, known gambler on the gee-gees. Don't think his life crossed Vicky's anywhere. Anything else you know, Doug?"

"We haven't anything on him as far as I know. He floats on the edge of respectability, bankrolls various business enterprises. Although no one really knows where his money comes from, we've never caught him on the wrong foot. Why? He doesn't fit the frame. No motive, alibi as sound as Mac's here. What interest do you have there?"

"I went to his pub the other day. I met Jed outside and he asked me in for a drink. He introduced me to Razor. Not exactly a woman's man, is he? Got distinctly unfriendly vibes. He took Jed away to talk to him. I only heard a few words and they didn't make sense. He said something about 'another one was on the way' and something else about Billy." She made a face and forestalled Doug's burgeoning quip, "and no, I don't think he was talking about babies. I caught them looking at me when I got too close. I tell you, it gave me the shudders."

Doug laughed. "Whispers in the wind; they're meaningless, Han. If that's all you heard, you have nothing on him. Just because you don't like him, or he gives you a bad look, doesn't mean he's a bad boy."

"Okay, try this one: Jed's alibi of getting home at 9.40 doesn't hold up. Jed left the pub at 9.30, but didn't get home that night until sometime after 10.15 – that's thirty-five minutes, or more, later than the time he told you. His wife, Cassandra, says he came in as the credits were rolling on *Goldfinger*. And that particular film was delayed for the footy going into extra time. It gives him sufficient time to catch up, rape and murder Vicky."

"Why would he do that, what's his motive?" Mac asked.

"Not sure about motive, yet. I'm looking at available times. Okay, I agree he couldn't have done the burying in that time, but maybe he went back. Or, more likely, there were two of them, like in Billy's murder."

"You're not suggesting Billy did the burying?" Mac asked.

"No, but how about Billy's uncle?"

"Morgan?" Both Mac and Doug chorused.

"Old Ned told me an interesting tale yesterday." She recounted Ned's story of the how he'd seen Jed leave through the back door leading to the toilets, and Billy following him shortly after. "They both left their beer half-drunk on the table. Ned thought it was a great joke, him and Maggot swilling their drinks. Later, Billy came back alone, having messed his pants, and the rest you know."

"Not like Jed to leave his beer," Mac murmured, shaking his head.

"Again, why didn't Ned tell us? We took statements from everyone who had been in the bar on that night. He didn't mention it then, and as far as I am aware, neither did anyone else. Sure he's not having you on?" Doug smiled, and raised his eyebrows.

"He didn't want to admit to nicking their beer, in case you took them in, more like!" Mac laughed. "Anyway Han, what's all this got to do with Morgan? He was at the bar all the time, I can vouch for that."

"Hear me out: Billy appeared to be well throughout the evening, no one mentioned him running to the loo like he would have if he'd had tummy troubles building. Didn't it occur to anyone to question his abrupt diarrhoea? Why, does he lose control of his bowels so suddenly? What other reason makes you do that? Fear. Fright. Shock maybe? What if Billy had seen something so bad it made him shit his pants?"

The silence grew; she had their attention, now. "Look at this scenario and pick holes in it. Instead of going to the loo, as Ned thought, Jed follows Vicky out. He comes onto her and she refuses, he rapes her and ends up killing her. Billy, who tends to follow Jed everywhere, catches up with them and sees what's going on. Terrified at the violence he needs a shit badly, turns back, runs into the car park around ten, goes in the back door and into the toilets, but too late – he's already messed himself.

"He emerges from there confused, and not knowing what else to do, he comes back into the bar, acts like he's been in the toilet all the time. He says nothing to the cops, because Jed is his mate, and he knows you never dob a mate in. Next thing, Morgan gets the job of taking him home. Supposing Billy, unable to keep it quiet any longer, tells his uncle what has happened."

"That's an awful lot of supposing, Hannah. And, why should Morgan care enough to mop up after Jed?" Doug asked.

"Okay. What if Billy had been made to help Jed, say in hiding the body or something, so becomes an accessory?" Hannah insisted.

"You mean Morgan thinks he's cleaning up after Billy?" asked Mac.

"Yes, would he do that?"

"Wouldn't surprise me, Morgan did look out for him."

"Okay, taking it on from there," Hannah went on, "Morgan took Billy home. Billy's mother verified the time they came in, but what happened to Morgan after that? Living alone, he had no alibi for the rest of the night. He had hours at his disposal. If Billy had told him where the body was, Morgan could have been the one to move it."

"Somebody would have seen him, surely." Mac said.

"Not if it happened along the track to the cemetery. And, we know somebody did transport her body to the grave." Hannah persisted. "What if she stopped in the clearing by the back gate to the cemetery to change her shoes? It's after that spot the track gets rough. That delay would have given Jed the opportunity to catch up with her. We know Jed would not have had time to complete the burial, even with Billy's help. I suggest that whoever did bury her, had access to the cemetery shed's keys. He could have used the wheelbarrow to transport her body, the tools to dig the extra niche out of the grave, and the hosepipe fitted onto the shed to wash out any evidence remaining inside her. He had everything he needed right there. And, what better candidate than Morgan, the gravedigger? It's home ground to him. It couldn't have been easier."

"And that would account for Morgan's interest in you. If he heard you were asking questions, he'd have to protect Billy." Mac suggested.

"Until the time of Billy's death, since then he's paid me no interest whatever. But before that, for some reason he was interested in me from day one. Remember," she looked at Doug, "I told you about the first day I walked into the boatyard, Morgan's car went past the gate, braked suddenly, and rolled back. I thought then that he was watching me. Though, why I couldn't fathom."

"Maybe you reminded him of Vicky. There's a certain resemblance between you, same size, same build, colouring. From a distance, it wouldn't be difficult for someone to mistake one for the other," Doug said.

Mac sat upright, his face animated. "Are you saying that happened when you were walking into the boatyard, where Vicky worked?" He turned to his brother. "What about it, Doug, what if, Hannah's scenario is right? If Morgan buried Vicky, then three days later, thought he saw her walking into her place of work? Christ! It must have given him the fright of his life! Do you think she's got something there?"

Doug had been quietly listening to this last idea with a neutral expression on his face. He emptied his glass and put it back on the table. "On the whole, you have a neat hypothesis, Han, but have you any evidence to back it up, at all?"

She looked up at him her bottom lip clamped between her teeth and shook her head in frustration. "Not the sort of evidence you need, Doug. Nice idea, Mac, I like it."

But at Doug's dismissal of the theory, Mac subsided back into his sofa like a deflating airbed. "So, nobody does anything."

"Did anyone do forensic tests in the cemetery shed and its contents?" Hannah asked.

"The crime scene guys examined it thoroughly. The business ends of all the implements were clean and oiled. The handles bore Morgan Draper's prints, of course. The wheelbarrow was clean. Morgan might look like last week's laundry bag, but he keeps his tools and machinery in pristine condition, and then the hose..." Doug stopped, his expression darkened. "As crime scenes go, it was a disaster. What with the destructive weather, and the funeral party trampling the ground there was nothing left for the investigators to find."

Hannah, silenced for the moment, turned the scene over in her mind. "What about her clothes? Have you found all the missing items now?"

Doug's face relaxed now that they were on his territory. "Everything's accounted for, bar one earring, one of those gold dangly things, but the chance of finding that is pretty slim, most likely buried in the mud under the jetty."

"You said the clothes had only been in the water twenty-four hours. Where had they been kept for a whole week?"

He shrugged. "Don't know yet. The lab says some of the clothes contained fibreglass fibres, flakes of paint."

"The boatshed?"

"No, the paint on the fibreglass is an old, out-dated variety and so far they haven't found a match for it in the boatshed." Doug, nursing his newly refreshed glass, looked decidedly mellow.

"What do you know of Lennie?" Hannah tossed the question in like a coin.

Mac took it up. "He's okay. Sailed around the world a few years back. Landed here and bought up the old boat shed. Keeps himself to himself mostly, he's no socialite. Can't see what Vicky saw in him, never could. Good at his job, not short of a buck or two. Great voice, wasted here."

"How would he have taken the news if he heard Vicky had a lover? Would he have been angry, jealous, tolerant, or wouldn't he have cared?"

"As far as I could see, he didn't make much of their relationship. I can't see that he would've cared that much. Boats were the biggest love of his life." Mac answered staring dreamily into the fire. Then, he turned his head sharply and looked at Hannah, as though a new idea had struck him. "Unless it impinged on his business, threatened it in some way, then he could get real shitty. But I think it would have to be something pretty substantial and we haven't seen anything like that looming."

"So, if it was a planned killing, rather than a rape gone wrong, could he have been in at the planning stage?"

"He's a cold enough bugger. But, like Morgan, he was in the bar all night so he didn't do it himself."

"Why does he rent a shed from Betty?"

Mac turned on his granddad look and peered at her. "Didn't know he did, you sure? Why should he when he has plenty of shed space of his own?"

"Betty said it was some arrangement he'd made with her husband a couple of years ago. And he pays over the odds, apparently."

"Trust Old Marty to find a scam." Mac's face creased into laughter lines at the idea. "That man could've sold fleas to a dog breeder."

"Strikes me, there's a lot you don't know about your townsfolk. I thought you couldn't keep secrets in a place as small as this?"

"Yeah, well, you're drifting off the subject now, you two. Think it's time I headed for the sack." Doug pulled himself wearily out of his armchair. He picked up the empty bottle and held it to the light. "Just as well I didn't get a magnum. I don't think you helped much, did you, Hannah. Remind me never to share a bottle of Scotch with you!" He scraped a hand through his hair and scratched the back of his head. "Think I'd better doss down here for the night, Mac. Got an empty room?"

"Yep, your old room, take that."

Doug swayed a little on his way to the door. "Good to hear your theories Han, just wish you had something more concrete to go on."

"I'll find it – somewhere."

"G'night."

When Doug had gone, the silence in the room gained depth. Hannah was comfortable with it. That was one of the nice things about Mac, you didn't feel you had to make conversation or force the pace in any way. She took a sidelong look at his face; he was watching her. For a heartbeat, she'd caught him unawares and she watched, as with an effort, he banished the longing from his eyes. "I'm going to miss this," he said quietly.

"What, the nightcaps?"

"No, the company. Doug popping in every evening, he's only done that since Mara's been away. And you," his dark eyes turned wistful. "You'll not be here much longer."

Hannah smiled gently and held out a hand between their chairs. She would miss him, too. That certainty came as a surprise. He took her hand and entwined his fingers around hers. She recalled their lovemaking of the night before. A sensation like forgotten hunger stirred in the pit of her belly.

"You're feeling better, aren't you?" Mac murmured. "Feel ready to go home and take up your old life?"

Her old life. She had to tell him.

"Mac, something you need to know. I'm not supposed to tell you, or anyone. But, I feel I'm living a lie with you if I don't, especially after last night."

His expression became wary. "What?" He let go of her hand

"My old life: you were right when you first thought I was here for a purpose. Only, it wasn't as a reporter like you thought. I'm a cop. I'm here looking into something else, not Vicky's case. I needed to stay incognito."

He swung his legs off the sofa and sat upright. "You – a cop? Does Doug know?"

"He's my liaison officer."

"And neither of you could tell me!" He stared into her eyes. "You didn't trust me. After all the talking we've done together?" He sat back. "Or, should I feel privileged at being allowed to sit in on that?"

"I'm sorry, Mac, it wasn't like that. Going under-cover

196

means secrecy."

"And now that someone else has found out, I suppose it's all right for me to know. Well, thank you very much. Now, I know where I stand." His expression wasn't one of anger, which she could have understood, but one of overwhelming sadness that cut her to the quick. He stood up and collected the empty glasses off the table.

"You're saying that not even Doug trusted me with this information? I can't believe he had so little confidence in me." He stood tall and looked down at her. "The fire is still going, if you want to stay on for a while, you're welcome, but I'm going to bed. I need to get my head around this. Goodnight, Hannah."

The door closed quietly behind him. His departure drew all the air from the room, leaving her in a vacuum. What had she done?

* * *

26

Hannah walked along the beach on the far side of the boatshed, the sun high overhead. Somebody out there knew her identity. As soon as she hears that, Peggy Dumas will take her out of the area. She kicked a piece of driftwood. Mac was still distant with her this morning. She'd hurt him. If she could only find one concrete piece of evidence that would nail Vicky's murderer, then maybe it would justify her perceived betrayal.

If she could clear up the mystery of Betty's shed, it would be another loose end out of the way. Betty had told her about the back entrance into her garden, saying that Lennie used it so as not to disturb her and Marty when he needed to use their shed. Like Foster's back room, it niggled in her mind. Maybe all she'd find was another sofa bed laid out ready for action. There seemed to be no shortage of them in this place. On the other hand, drug dealers needed premises for cutting and packing their wares.

The small wooden gate was half-concealed in a hedgerow of tea-trees along the top of the shoreline. She stopped, ran her hands along the painted surface, noting its good order. No squeaky hinges to alert the neighbours.

Caution made her look back over her shoulder at the vast expanse of Lennie's boatshed. Its corrugated metal walls had no windows on this side. In the distance, a man fished from the beach. A couple of kids romped with a dog and a stick, and out on the water the daily parade of marine craft sailed the river. No one took notice of her. She turned back to the gate. The temptation to walk in still gnawed, but if he'd locked the shed, she'd be no better off. She might still have to approach Betty for a key. Hannah decided that rather than be caught nosing around Betty's garden, she'd be upfront about it, make up a reason and simply ask the old lady's permission to look at the shed.

She retraced her steps out to the road and approached Betty's front door. The old lady greeted her like a bosom pal and invited her in. "Sit down, dear, don't mind the cat." She indicated a two-seater, where a white cat curled up asleep on one half. "Don't get many visitors these days, not since Old Marty passed on. They all came round to see him, you know, lovely man."

Hannah sensed a spirited lady lurked beneath her soft, crumpled tissue-paper face. "So, what can I do for you, dear? I haven't seen any of Vi's ghosts, if that's what you've come about."

"No, Betty, it's not that. I wanted to ask you something. After Vicky's murder, did the police show any interest in the shed you lease out to Lennie? Did they come and search it or anything?"

"You kidding me? Why would they do that? They came to the door and asked questions about that night, and whether I saw anything different, same as they did to everyone, but they didn't come inside, or search my garden. Why?"

"Well, no doubt you've heard that not all Vicky's things have been found yet," Hannah said, stretching the truth a little. "The police have checked everywhere else, but if nobody has looked in the shed, it might be an idea if we just checked it out in case. Wouldn't hurt to have a quick look, would it?"

Betty raised her hands, her eyes wide with concern. "I can't do that, it's private. Lennie rents it. It's where he keeps his personal things. He told Marty his big workshop wasn't private enough, what with all the workers and people coming and going in there, and he didn't have room in his place. Marty said it was all right. And if that's what Marty said, I wouldn't want to meddle."

"What if someone used your shed as a hiding place for Vicky's things, Betty, wouldn't Marty want you to sort it out?"

199

"You mean someone other than Lennie, like someone taking advantage?"

"Yeah, something like that; Marty wouldn't have stood for that, would he?"

"No way, he'd have dealt with them all right. Oh dear, I do miss him so. He saw to all that sort of thing. Just a minute, I'll go and find the key." Betty rummaged in a dresser drawer. She held up a small key on a large wooden tag.

Hannah followed Betty down a long path into the far corner of her back garden. An uneasy touch of *déjà vu* brushed Hannah's soul as she approached the shed. It looked so similar to the one in the graveyard. At least this one didn't have a hose attached to its water tap. Betty took a long, guilty look in the direction of Lennie's gate. Hannah smiled at how quickly the old lady had turned conspirator.

"That's funny." Betty held the padlock in her hand, frowning.

"What is?"

"He's changed the lock. This padlock's much bigger than the one we left him. Look, the key won't fit. The cheeky bugger, didn't trust us, eh?" Two spots of high colour decorated her face with indignation.

Bollocks. All that for nothing. Hannah swallowed her disappointment.

"Let's go and talk to Lennie, see if he'll give us his key," Betty suggested.

"No, don't do that!" she cautioned Betty in alarm. That was the last thing she wanted Betty doing. Her mind was already grappling with the problem of how to get hold of the key, but asking Lennie for it outright was not on her agenda. "Leave it to me. I'll make a few enquiries. Don't say anything to Lennie yet. Promise?"

"Okay, if you really think so." She frowned, looking at Hannah doubtfully. "But if there's some jiggery-pokery going on in my shed, I want to know about it. Right?"

*

"G'day, Hannah, want a coffee, or are you looking for lunch?" Grace greeted her with a smile as weak as winter's sun. Since the funeral, Hannah had noticed Grace's gradual acceptance that Vicky would not be coming home. She'd seen the anger that had kept Grace going dissolve into a sadness that pulled her down.

"Hi, Grace, both will do me right now. I have some thinking to do. How about a piece of your quiche? Will you join me?"

"I'm just in the middle of doing the take-out lunches, I'll have some later."

Empty dishes still cluttered two of the tables. While she was waiting, Hannah gathered them up and took them to the counter.

"Thanks, Han. You don't have to do that. I'll get myself in gear in a minute. I don't know what the hell's the matter with me, I feel like a lump of lead this week. Go and sit down, I'll bring it over."

"So, what's this thinking you have to do?" Grace asked when she brought the tray.

A young couple sat at the table in the corner and Hannah spoke quietly so as not to be overheard. "I've been trying to find out who's dealing out those Ecstasy tablets. But I'm not getting very far."

"Me neither," Grace said. "I keep looking at people, but I haven't seen anyone who looks like a drug dealer, yet."

Hannah smiled, "What do drug dealers look like?"

"You know what I mean." Grace's lips quivered into a ghost of a smile.

"Have you a minute to sit down and talk?"

Grace sat. "Okay, what's on your mind?"

"Might sound a funny question, but do you know what Lennie keeps in Betty's shed?"

Grace looked at her sharply. "Why do you want to know that?"

"Drug dealers need somewhere to cut and pack their goods.

201

I'm not saying it is in there. But, if anyone reliable knows what's in there, we could eliminate that. I tried Betty, but she didn't have the right key."

"I know where the key is." Grace whispered.

"You do?"

"But, I think you're barking up the wrong tree. I got the impression Vicky and Len used to meet in that shed sometimes. I've seen her come back from that direction."

"Did she have her own key?" Hannah held a breath. Could it be that easy?

"I don't think so. I only saw the key once. It had a tag on it. White tag and red letters saying OM – I remember because I asked her what it stood for, she didn't know."

"Old Marty, or Oliver Martin, perhaps? So, where is it now?"

"Back in the boatshed."

The moment of elation sank. "The boatshed is a big place to hunt for a key, Grace."

"It's in one of two places. There's a pegboard up on the wall with a load of keys hanging up. It could be there. If not, try the drawer in the middle of the counter. I've seen her put things in there."

"Who takes the lunches over there now?"

"The boy next door," Grace jerked her thumb towards the newsagent on the left, and checked her watch. "He comes in for his dad's packet of sandwiches, and then he takes Lennie's order over and leaves it on the counter. I'd better get on; he'll be here soon."

"Tip me the wink when it's ready, will you?"

Grace returned to the counter to finish loading the box. Hannah kept watch on the boatshed. She could see the back of a head occasionally bobbing up in the office window, Lennie, most likely. A few moments later, Jed strode down the ramp and out of the gate. She craned her head and watched him disappear in the direction of The Crow's Nest. She looked at Grace, who nodded to say the box was ready.

Hannah grabbed it off the counter. "Back in a minute." She raced for the door.

With Jed out of the way, and Lennie's back to her, she slipped into the deep shade of the boatshed. She kept to the side of the wall, where she knew she was invisible from the office, and marched into the huge workshop. The luxury yacht Jed had been working on was still there. Another boat had joined it. A launch, its paintwork heavily sanded. Its bulk gave her cover as she made her way forward to put the box on the counter.

In front of the pegboard, she rubbed her palms down the sides of her jeans and stared at the array of keys. Eyes searched for white tag, red letters. The blood surged through her head and pulsed in her ears. All the keys had tags. Her glance skimmed over the hieroglyphics, trying to make sense of them. She dismissed many as being the wrong size or shape for the padlock on Betty's shed door. The rapid process of elimination finally left her with nothing that looked hopeful.

She cast a quick guilty glance around. Nothing had changed, nothing moved, she took a step behind the counter. It contained three drawers down each side and one in the middle. She pulled out the middle one and struck gold, or, at least a mess of keys, pens and pencils. The red lettering OM caught her eye and she swept it up, checking the key size looked suitable before pocketing it. She walked outside, and down the slope meeting no one. Back in the café, she bubbled over with sense of clandestine victory like a novice burglar on his initiation night.

Grace was busy with customers. Not wishing to disturb her again, Hannah waved a cheery thumbs-up sign and left premises.

*

This time Hannah decided to go in the back way and not involve Betty. On the off chance that she found something useful, she didn't want Betty tramping along and possibly contaminating the evidence. She didn't know what was she going into, Vicky and Lennie's private place, as Grace suspected, or a storeroom for Lennie's bits and pieces. It was unlikely to be a drug kitchen; they gave off odours that someone would have noticed. But it could be a weigh-station for drugs, and if that were so, it would implicate Vicky. That was the last thing she wanted to do.

Hannah left the beach trail and turned towards Lennie's back-gate. No one followed her. Morgan Draper was mowing verges in another part of the town. If Billy's uncle had been involved in the disposal of the body, he must feel safe now, because with Billy dead, there was no one left to tell the tale. Mac's theory that Morgan had mistaken her for the dead Vicky that first morning went a long way to explaining his behaviour.

With another glance over her shoulder, she pushed the gate open and stepped into Betty's garden. The overgrown shrubbery hid her from both Betty's house on one side and the shore on the other. Betty and Violet were in the café. She had seen them entering on her way out. Betty had given her a big wink, as though confirming they were still co-conspirators. The butterflies in her stomach took flight. She rubbed the stolen key between her fingers and carefully slid it into the padlock. It fitted and the lock turned.

Hannah pulled the door open, replaced the padlock in the eyebolt to make it look, at first glance, to be still intact. It was dark inside. She held the door ajar to locate the light switch. Fluorescent strips along the roof beam lit the shed with an intense flickering light. A sheet of cardboard covered a window set high on the wall.

She glanced around. It was not your typical garden shed. Nor was it was a lover's meeting place. She studied the layout. Fitted with a long counter topped with red Formica it had a small sink and single tap in the corner. Her nostrils caught a faint smell of bleach. Her heart thumped that little bit louder. A kitchen of sorts, but not for the manufacture of drugs.

Beneath the counter, the unit had three side drawers built in on the right, a central drawer that was a long shallow one with a space to the floor underneath it. The space housed a plastic crate heaped with boating paraphernalia. Next to that was a large fibreglass container, like an old fashioned fishing box, and in the far corner a stack of bulging sail-bags; Lennie's personal things, maybe?

She pulled open the shallow drawer. It contained folded charts, parallel rules, dividers, pencils, and a clutch of papers. Nothing out of the ordinary; presumably part of Lennie's navigational equipment. She took out the first chart, and opened it on the counter. It covered the area of sea around The Heads and south to Botany Bay. Course and bearing lines had been drawn in, with tiny circles marking set positions around a pencilled cross. It meant nothing to her. She folded the chart in half, the way she'd found it, and checked the rest of the papers.

Amongst them, she found a set of tide tables and a computer copy of a shipping schedule. She dried her damp palms on her jeans and looked down the list of arrivals and departures for Port Botany. It showed the names of the vessels due, their types and origins and the berths allocated.

Highlighted in yellow, one line indicated Moniker V a container vessel from Singapore was due in on Saturday. Tomorrow. Was Lennie expecting a delivery for the boatshed, or had she found what she was looking for? *Another one due –* another drug run? She needed more.

She returned the chart and papers to their drawer, trying to remember the order in which she had taken them. Next, she opened one of the side drawers. It was deep and filled with new plastic bags with self-seal closures and nothing else. She raised an eyebrow. The drawer below held a set of fine-weight kitchen scales, plastic containers, small scoops and other utensils. *Gotcha.* So, this was the source of Lennie's riches. She still needed proof. Any lawyer could argue his client's way out of this one, so far. She needed hard evidence. Quickly, she checked the third drawer. Kitchen-cleaning equipment only; Lennie meticulously cleaned up after himself.

Unable to leave until she'd found something positive to take back to Peggy; she crouched to check out the bulging sail-bags.

205

They appeared genuine enough, but as she moved them, she saw something hidden behind their bulk. Fixed to the floor with hefty bolts stood a sturdy looking safe. No chance of getting into that one but her imagination flew ahead on a tangent of its own. With care, she re-arranged the sail-bags in front of it.

The large plastic container on the floor was stacked with buoys, ropes, dinghy-anchors, plastic bottles, and flags like crayfish pot markers, but nothing of a personal nature, nothing Lennie couldn't have stored in his workshop. She crab-walked a few steps sideways to take a better look at the old style fibreglass fishing box, with its chipped edges and lid askew.

Vicky's clothes contained painted fibreglass fibres. Doug said they were searching the boats for a matching pattern. She tipped the lid aside with a fingernail. Apart from an oily rag, the box was empty. She did a double take. The oily rag was a pair of crumpled silk panties. Her breath caught in the back of her throat as she recognised the frayed bow at the hipline. Lennie?

She heard a noise; a clunk, like someone had touched the padlock. Still hunched beneath the counter shelf, she worked her way backwards to get out. Her foot stood on her shirttail and pulled her up short. She heard the sigh of the opening door. Suddenly too big for its chest cavity, her heart punched against her ribs. The lights went out.

A muted shout and scuffling noises rushed at her. Something grabbed at her shirt and pulled. Hands slid up her neck, wrapped around her face. They jerked her backwards onto the floor.

And the world exploded into psychedelic colours.

* * *

27

Voices: their murmurs far away. They had an argumentative rise and fall, but the words were unintelligible through the ringing in her ears. Hannah opened her eyes against the blindfold. Hot sticky tape pulled her hair. A dry lump wedged in her mouth. She lay on her side, doubled-over; her body ached from head to toe. When she tried to stretch out, she learned her hands were bound to her ankles on a short leash.

The acrid smell of turpentine brought her mind sharply into focus. Its hateful smell reminded her of a case she'd been involved in, where a husband deliberately set fire to his wife. Fear hammered at her throat. She cut the memory short.

No longer in Betty's shed, not with that smell. The boatshed? The paint-shop, she guessed. He must have carried her. Didn't anyone see? What time was it, how long had she been out? She lay on a sheet of some kind, a tarp or a sail maybe. Had he wrapped her in this while he carried her across the beach? The sheet did little to cushion her body against the concrete floor. She moved again, trying for a more comfortable position. Cramp gripped a foot. Pain arched her body. She stretched to the limit of her bonds and pushed at the muscles to fight it off.

The voices died away. Silence. Soft footfalls, growing louder, moved towards her. They stopped. Air moved around her face. The warmth of his breath burned her neck.

"Run, Baby. Run!"

Hannah jerked away from the whisper in her ear. He cupped her head in his hands and held it rigid, putting pressure on her bruised temple. She snuffled a cry through the gag. His whispering continued. Fear made her deaf to his words. His breath played over her skin, triggering fine hairs to stand erect.

He pulled back. She panted heavily through her nose, waiting for his next move. He separated her hands from her ankles and pulled her arms above her head, tying them to something above her. She drew her knees up tighter, but he pushed them down. The weight of his body descended astride her thighs. He ran his hands over her body, probing, feeling, squeezing. Her bound fists, pulled up short by the tie, wouldn't reach him. She jerked her knees beneath his weight, impotent gestures, as useless as those in her nightmares. He laughed at her. The sound solidified the air in her lungs.

Simon wept, and the devil laughed.

That same maniacal laugh had haunted her for months. The last time she heard it for real she lay on the ground, drugged and helpless after his mate, the rapist, had finished his work. This brute had pissed in her hair. As though sensing her recognition, his laughter tailed off into chortles.

"Unfinished business, eh baby? Knew you from day one." The breathy voice whispered into her ear. "Wondered if you'd point the finger, but you didn't even know me. Funny, don't you think? Got you to myself now. Never could stomach a wet deck. Come on, give, give." He unsnapped the belt of her jeans, and moving his weight further down her legs. He lifted her hips and pulled.

Unable to see, or defend herself, and fully aware of what he intended to do, a scream gathered in the back of her throat. With her mouth gagged, it had no voice, no outlet. It ricocheted around her head like an echo in a cave before Hannah shrivelled inside herself at the inevitability of it all.

*

Mac checked his watch. Only three minutes since he last looked. Hannah had not come in for dinner. Not that she did every night, sometimes she had it with Grace, but she usually warned him beforehand if she'd planned to do that. She'd been hurt by his coolness this morning. He'd seen it in her eyes. Stupid of him, he wished he could take it back. She was due to work tonight, her shift started at 8.30. Maybe she was having dinner out and wouldn't turn up until then.

By eight o'clock, his restlessness got the better of him, and he called Grace's number.

"Haven't seen Hannah since lunch," Grace replied to his anxious questioning.

"Okay, if you do see her. Just tell her I called."

"Have you tried her mobile?"

"She's turned it off. Don't worry, she's due at work in half-hour, I'll catch her then."

*

Grace put the phone down. A sense of unease uncoiled in her mind. The last she'd seen of Hannah was when she'd left the café after lunch. Grace had read the thumbs up to mean Hannah had been successful in finding the key. But what had happened after that? Had Hannah gone to the shed – alone? Grace had not expected her to call in again afterwards, but thinking about it, if Hannah had found anything, she would have come and shared it, wouldn't she? Betty also knew Hannah wanted to see inside the shed. Maybe the two of them got together once they had the key. Could Hannah still be over there, after all this time?

She called to Lizzie to say she was going out for a few minutes. The girl was in the back room doing her homework, ears plugged into her iPod. She shrugged in reply, and Grace couldn't be sure she'd heard, but left it at that.

As soon as she stepped outside the café, she saw Betty opening the front gate to her cottage and heading for her front door. As the old lady inserted the key into its lock, Grace called out to her. "Hey, Betty, you got a minute?"

"'Course I have, what can I do for you?" Betty waited until Grace reached her before pushing the door open. "Want to come in for a mo?"

"No, I won't stop. It's Hannah, have you seen her lately?" Grace asked.

"Not since lunchtime. Why? Did you think she'd be here?" she asked mystified.

"I heard you wanted to check out your back shed, but didn't have the right key.
I just wondered if Hannah had been back to you since then."

"That was her idea, not mine. She told you about it, too?" Betty looked a little peeved. "She said we were to keep it quiet. Anyway, I saw her round your place since then. Have you tried Mac McKay's?"

"He's the one phoning round looking for her."

"Oh, well she's not here, nor at Vi's neither, I've just come from there. You're not suggesting she's gone missing, are you?"

Grace touched her lips with a hand. "God, I hope not. No one's using that word, but Mac's worried. After Vicky, well, it's hardly surprising. Right. If you do see her, tell her he's looking for her."

*

Betty closed the door behind her neighbour and went inside. She put another log on her fire, settled in her armchair and picked up her book.

Later, when she found her concentration wandering, Betty thought about Hannah and about her strange request to look in Lennie's shed in case someone had used it to hide Vicky's things. "Well, there was no way I was going to tell Grace *that* was there?" she asked her white cat stretched out on the other chair. "It would only remind her, bring all the pain back." The cat looked up and blinked lazily, yawned and went back to sleep. And, anyway, Hannah didn't get that far, what with the key not fitting.

Could she have tried to gain access some other way? There was a window. Betty frowned at the thought. A bit high up, but that young woman was not discouraged easily. Maybe she'd better go and check it out. What if the poor girl had got herself locked in down there.

Betty collected a torch off the shelf, let herself out of the back door and hurried down to the shed. Everything was quiet and dark, the padlocked still intact.

She knocked on the door. "Hannah, are you in there?" She called, feeling slightly foolish. Nothing stirred. She swept the beam along the ground. It picked up a scuffmark on the beaten earth outside the shed door. A paper tissue glared whitely from beneath a ragged bush. It had not been there this morning; she would have noticed.

Betty returned to her house worried at what she'd seen. She phoned Grace to check if there was any news. Hannah had not turned up for the start of her work shift.

Once Betty made up her mind, she didn't mess around. She went straight to the top. She picked up the card left by the telephone and called Detective Inspector Steele.

*

Steele cleared his desk for the day. He'd been working late on the Vicky Brown case. After days of intensive investigation, his team had been unable to come up with sufficient solid evidence to clinch their prime suspect to the crime.

Although Zack Henderson admitted to having an affair with the victim, he still maintained his innocence of her murder. Steele knew a confession would not be forthcoming. They'd found plenty in the way of circumstantial evidence. Henderson had motive and opportunity, but still not enough to get a conviction. They hadn't any witnesses even to tie Henderson to the victim. The affair, apparently, had been a well-kept secret. The wife, when pressed, thought something was going on but didn't know with whom. The schoolteacher, who ran the amateur operatic society that Henderson was wagging from, had a feeling something was afoot, but hadn't guessed it was Vicky.

He'd have to get the team to review the whole case starting

211

from square one. They needed something more to tip the proverbial scales. He rubbed his bleary eyes.

The office phone rang. Steele smiled as he put the receiver down. Something was about to break. This had been the second call about the under-cover cop Hannah Ford he'd had this evening. McKay had been the first. He'd already despatched two officers in that direction to take the details. In normal circumstances, he would have held off for twenty-four hours or so, but in this case, with at least one of the two murderers in the vicinity not accounted for, there was every occasion for concern. Now, old Betty Martin had something up her sleeve to tell him. Something she wouldn't say over the phone.

"Pike!" He yelled across the room to his sergeant. "Get your roller-blades on. We've a date with a little old lady."

*

He laughed no longer. Instead, he grunted and swore. Hannah's tight fitting jeans moulded to her body. Her passion killers, as she called them, were a work of art getting into, and impossible to remove without cooperation. She heard his lust, and smelled his sweat, mingled with a scent trace of something familiar. Her mind struggled to remember where she had smelled it before. She held her body rigid, fighting back with the only weapon she had left, her will.

He hit her once, twice, on either side of her face. Red and yellow flares ignited behind her eyes. She fell limp. He tried again and this time brought the waistband down as far as her hips. A new sound intruded into the lonely hollow of Hannah's mind; the rumble of a workshop door opening. Footsteps on a concrete floor; they came her way.

"Je-ed!" A voice bellowed.

"Shit!" The man above her moved away.

Jed? Hannah remembered his scent from their earlier meeting in the boatshed. But, Jed the *pisser?* He'd been in her sights all this time and she hadn't recognised him? She recalled

212

that nowhere in all her flashbacks had she seen the face of the second man. And the tell-tale laugh? Did he only laugh like that in the throes of sexual excitement?

"What the fuck do you think you're doing?" The new voice, much nearer now, demanded. Not Lennie, not a voice she knew. Hope flickered in the dark.

"Okay, okay. Gimme a break."

She identified Jed's voice now it was no longer a whisper, his tone plaintive.

"For Christ's sake, man, I don't pay you to get your rocks off. That boat ready?"

"Yeah, put her out a couple of hours ago. Caught this one snooping in the shed. Key was missing, went to have a look, and there she was, inside."

"Ker-ist almighty! Who is it?"

"McKay's squeeze; remember, works for him in the bar."

"Yeah, I got her. The lady with the radar ears, the nosy bitch always asking questions, and I heard, peers in windows."

Hannah sensed the man stepping closer.

"She's a bloody cop." Jed's voice.

"Shit! And you let her get that close? How d'you know?"

"Saw the stuff on her computer, like she was doing a report, got all our names in it, the works."

"What've you done about it?"

"Wiped it. Permanently."

"Good man. Whadda' we do with her now?" The question sounded almost rhetorical. The new voice belonged to no white knight coming to her aid. The flicker of hope sputtered and died.

"Take her with us?" Jed's query deferred to the other man.

"And drop her off, an' all. You got it."

Both voices faded as the men walked away from her. What did it mean? Fear jerked another notch up the scale. She thrashed her around, pulling at her bonds trying to free herself, without success. She tired. Pain throbbed through her head every time she moved. What did the man mean by peering in windows? How had he known that? It didn't sound like Foster's voice, and anyway he hadn't seen her face. Her mind floated and she lost track of time. Was it evening, night, had Mac missed her yet? Her teeth chattered; her body ached in the dark.

The high-pitched peeping noise of her watch alarm woke her with a start, and she realised she had drifted off to sleep. Eight o'clock in the evening. Too often when working on her computer she lost sense of time. She'd set her watch so she wouldn't be late for her evening shifts. If he hadn't twigged it yet, in another half hour Mac would know something was wrong. Would he find her in time; would he even try, given his disappointment in her? Or, worse, would he think she'd walked out on him.

Later, she had no idea how much, a couple of hours judging by the emptiness of her belly, the two men returned. She heard rapid footsteps approach and voices arguing.

"You sure?"

"I'm telling you, it was a cop's car, it stopped down the end. They're looking for her."

"Let's bag her up and get her out of here."

Through her gag, she begged them to talk, to listen to her. Afraid of their actions, she was even more terrified of their cold disregard of her. They treated her as a package, something to be dealt with as swiftly and efficiently as possible. One freed her hands from overhead, the wrists still cuffed together. He held them down with a grip of iron while the other man pulled something on over her feet.

"Once we've bagged her she won't be able to move a little finger."

They grasped hold of her body, lifted her to standing position, and pulled a bag up around her. She heard the rustle of stiff material and felt the touch of Terylene as it passed her face. They ignored her protests and violent wriggling. Her cries barely broke through her gag. Someone pushed her head down and pulled the drawstring tight over the top as though he'd bagged a sail.

"There. Tighter than her own bloody jeans, serve the bitch

right."

"Shoulda' done this to Billy, not strung him up like that," the other voice said.

"Yeah, but not as much fun," Jed answered, with a short laugh.

"Your sense of fun will get you into trouble one day. Ready?"

Hannah felt herself hefted into the air and flung head first over a shoulder. The man handled her weight with ease, his arms clamped around her legs securely in a fireman's lift. He moved off with a stride to match his size.

Upside down, banging against the man's back, her fists digging into the base of her belly, Hannah's terror-filled mind registered the sounds of a closing door, footsteps behind her, and somewhere the clink of a dragging chain.

* * *

28

Hannah snorted for air. Encased inside the sail-bag, she fought for every breath. The turmoil in her head crystallised at the sound a powerful motor starting up. The noise died to a low thrum that vibrated through her body. After the initial judder, she sensed a gentle forward movement, a vessel creeping away in the dark.

She had tried to picture her journey to this point, had even tried to count the steps her abductor was taking in order to gauge the distance, but the pain of her trapped fists digging into her stomach drove everything out of her mind.

They had lowered her into a dinghy and motored out to another boat. That had been clear enough. The two of them had manhandled her onto the launch, and holding her shoulders and feet, had manoeuvred her through the boat into the fore-cabin. They spoke no words, only grunted as they lifted her onto a bunk. She heard their retreating footsteps, and the sound of a bolt shooting home. After that, they'd left her alone.

Sweat soaked into her clothes and poured down her face. Fear whickered in the back of her throat. They were taking her to sea to drown her like a rat. Her breathing rasped through her nostrils, as her lungs grabbed what air they could.

She struggled to dislodge the gag with a shoulder, but it wouldn't move, nor could she pull the tape from her eyes. The sail-bag effectively curtailed her movements. On the edge of getting her life back together, she didn't want to die, not just yet, not now.

Dread grew like building blocks one upon the other inside her head, until, tall and unstable it tumbled down and smothered her in a strange calm. Quiet seeped into her mind like an opiate, preparing her to accept the inevitable.

Deep inside her bag, Hannah drew up her knees and bowed her head.

*

Steele had listened to the old lady's tale. He hadn't been entirely agreeable to having an undercover operative working alongside his case, but Peggy Dumas won him over. Sergeant Hannah Ford had proved useful on the ground. However, with her cover blown, it was up to him to extricate her from whatever trouble she'd fallen into.

A methodical man, he did not intend to rush in until he knew which way to rush. He had his officers out looking, but if this had been the last place the missing officer was sighted, then for him, this was the place to start. First thing was to get into Betty Martin's shed, and find out what had aroused Hannah's interest.

While he organised officers to pick up Lennie, he sent Pike off to arrange a warrant for the search. No point in bluffing it out at this stage, if there was evidence there he wanted it, all nice and legal. Lennie Cooper produced his key under protest. Once inside, Pike opened the drawers and lined up their contents on the Formica top. Steele pulled out the sail bags to examine their contents, and discovered the safe. Another delay while they returned Lennie to his home to fetch the key for that.

The sail bags produced nothing relevant, but Steele watched intrigued as Lennie reluctantly crouched beside the safe to unlock it. The younger man's face suffused a dark red, his eyes round and wary. Steele had seen that expression before. The man was running scared. The safe locks clicked free.

"Righty-ho. Over there," Steel instructed Lennie to move away. You never knew with safes, they could contain firearms.

Obediently, Lennie stood up and shuffled away. Pike pulled the safe door open. Steele smiled. It had been worth all the delays.

217

"One sealed bag, brownish powder, one bag round pills, three small packets, syringe, needles, rubber hose," Pike called aloud the items they could see. "Documents; sundry items, and cash in bundles of hundreds." He grinned, hips wiggling like a dog waiting for its Frisbee.

"Okay, Pike, that's enough. Bag it up." Steele turned to Lennie, and touched his arm. "Leonard Cooper, I'm arresting you on a charge of possession ..."

Lennie stepped back, hands half raised. He leant against the wall, tears watering his eyes. Steele continued to read him his rights, and when the protocol was over, Steele added, "It'll do for starters anyway. After that, we're looking at the murder of Billy Draper. Forensics will have a field day with the equipment in there."

"That wasn't me." Lennie rounded on him protesting, but Steele carried on as though he hadn't heard. "And then there's the murder of young Vicky Brown."

"No – I didn't touch Vicky!"

"Too busy maintaining your alibi weren't you. What was it? She found out about your little sideline, threatened to tell her new boyfriend, perhaps? Look at what we've got here: Lennie Cooper, lover of the first victim, employer of the second. What had young Billy done to you?" He paused, "And now, another woman has gone missing, and guess whose name is the first I hear in connection with it? Lennie Cooper. What was Hannah Ford to you? An irritant, a busybody; had she, like Vicky, learned something you didn't want told, eh? Yeah, looking at life, wouldn't you say, Pike?" He turned to his sergeant who was gleefully packing the last of the evidence into bags.

"Oh, at least! Thirty years in the slammer, I reckon," Pike said, with a grin.

"No, no, you got it all wrong. It wasn't me. Okay, so Vicky knew about this, but she'd known all along. It was a warning, that's all. To keep her trap shut. It shouldn't have gone that far. But I didn't touch her. Look, I can't do jail. I know who's behind this. What if I give you names? You know, the whole works, where it comes from, dealers, distributors, they're all over." The man was babbling. "I can give you whatever you want. You name it. But I want protection and no jail." His hand came up, and claw-like it scratched at his chest.

"And we don't do deals, sunshine. Now, back to the station. You can do all your talking there." Steele took the cuffs from his belt, but Lennie stepped back, hands at shoulder level.

"Wait. That's not the way I heard it. Indemnity, amnesty, witness protection, Crown witness – there's gotta be something?"

Steele stared at him. He heard the fear and desperation in the man's voice. Realisation had been slow to hit, but when it did, he smiled. "Roll up your sleeve."

"What?"

"You heard. I said roll up your sleeve."

Lennie crumpled. He slid down the shed wall to his haunches and closed his eyes.

"Want me to do it?"

Lennie shook his head. He pushed up the sleeve of his sweatshirt and turned his arm over. Needle tracks speckled the soft flesh under his forearm.

"Shit. It's only for relaxation. Lots of people do it, I'm not a junkie, ask anyone."

"I suppose, you'll be telling me next, that stuff is only for personal use." He pointed to the bulging evidence bags. "You're a fool, Cooper. On your feet."

"Told you, I can't do jail. What about it, do I get protection if I talk?"

Crown witness, eh? If Lennie Cooper was as good as his word, they could bag the whole lot. It'd be a big case. A lot of publicity, and that wouldn't harm his chances of promotion one little bit.

"That sort of decision's not mine to make," Steele said at last. "I could have a word for you, but I need something to show you mean it, something on account. For starters, you tell me where Hannah Ford is, and I'll see what I can do."

*

It was nearly midnight. Mac had polished the bar until it shone, restocked the shelves and was looking around for something more to make use of his nervous pacing. There had been no word from Doug. The police had told him to stay put in case Hannah tried to phone. They were out doing a search of the area, while he, grounded, was off his head with worry.

He grabbed the telephone on the first ring. "Yes?"

"You reckon you know all the boats around the wharf. Would you be able to identify Jed's for us?" Doug's voice.

"Yes, but what's that got to do with anything? What news on Hannah?"

"I'll send the boat in. Pick you up from the end of the wharf. Ten minutes."

The line clicked and disconnected.

"Doug ..." Mac raised his hand and slapped the wall beside his head.

* * *

29

The engine noise changed its tune; became louder and more urgent as it shifted into a faster mode. Hannah's mind registered this action and began to function once more. She lifted her head to listen to the new note. They must be out in the main river by now.

The boat rocked and bounced across the waves. It shook her out of her torpor. Wake up woman. Fight them. Use your brains; get out of here. Stumbling through cerebral treacle, she pushed the paralysis of her mind away.

Another noise alerted her. It was nearer, small and clunky. The bolt scraped back, a tiny squeak of the door's hinge. Terrified that she had left it too late, she remained absolutely still. She felt his touch on the bag, like a finger poke. She held her breath. The touch withdrew. The door closed and the bolt slid across once more. They weren't ready to ditch her yet.

Now that her panic had subsided, Hannah's mind sharpened. Foetus-like, she stirred in the womb and stretched against the confining bag. In manoeuvring herself into an upright position in the corner of the bunk, the drawstring gave a little. A small draught of air bathed her face. Inch by inch she worked her bound hands up until they were above her head. Her fingers found the opening and pulled at it. It gave a little, then stopped. The bastards had clamped the cords together on the outside. The gap she'd made was no more than a hand-span.

There had to be a way. She pushed one hand out of the small opening, and with a hooked finger, she beckoned one of the cords down through the gap until she felt the toggle that held the ties together. Sweat poured from her face like tears while she

221

concentrated her whole mind on the task.

Her fingers locked in cramp. She stretched and wriggled them; crying with frustration, until the pain stopped and she got them to work again. By jiggling the sliding clasp, she finally got it to slide away. The cords parted. The gap she had created was now large enough to push her head through.

Wrenching the tape away from her eyes, she winced as it took hairs with it. Her prison, a tiny, two-berth cabin was awash with a red and green glow from the navigation lights that reflected in through the long, narrow windows on each side.

Once free of the gag she gulped cool, clean air into her parched mouth. An unpleasant oily taste lingered. What wouldn't she give for a bottle of water? With her hands still tied, she couldn't get the bag beyond her shoulders. She worked on her wrists, ignoring the pain from the chafing cord as her mind screamed at her to hurry.

A scream of another kind filled the cabin and assaulted her ears. Startled, she looked up, recognising the sound of metal in distress. The boat baulked as if leaping the waves and skidded around in an arc that almost threw her off the bunk. She held her breath, listening. The engine stopped, replaced by the sound of the sea and men's voices shouting at each other. Had her time come?

With blood lubricating her wrists, she pulled and pushed at the knots to untwine them. Any minute one of the men could burst through the door.

The engine started again, howled horribly and died. Her head cocked, a new noise, a splash, as though someone had gone overboard. Then nothing, only the sound of small waves slapping against the side of the hull as the boat bobbed around without direction. Had they left? What was going on out there?

The faint smell of fuel filled her head with scenes of fire, explosions, and headlines screaming "Accident at Sea." Was that the way they were going to get rid of her?

Finally, the cord pulled free. She stripped the bag off her body, and started work on the ankle ties. More shouting. One of them was still aboard. Perversely, she felt a sense of relief. She pulled her imagination in and tried to think of practical matters.

How long had they been going? Where were they? Still too dark to read her watch, it felt as though hours had passed.

Movement from the stern, the boat dipped. Once more, she could hear two voices. The engine started again. This time the motor ran sweetly, and they surged forward to pick up the pace the same as before.

Free of her bonds, Hannah peered out of the right hand window. Outside, beyond the green glow of the navigation lamp, the sky was brightening. She could see lights, pinpricks from the shore, red, green and white from other boats, and the loom of a lighthouse. As she watched, the boat changed course and made straight for the paling sky. The motion of the water changed. Between The Heads, they were heading east, out into the Pacific Ocean.

Hannah unclasped the bolts of the hatch-cover above her head and lifted it an inch or two to peer outside. Facing aft, she saw little but the boat's cabin structure. She twisted her face around to look up, still nothing but the bridgework. Good, that meant they couldn't see her, either.

The cant of the boat heeled over marginally; they'd changed course again. They swung in a gentle arc around to the right. The dawn sky now appeared on her left, and the shore lights blinked on her right. Moving south, they must've rounded South Head. Undecided what to do next, Hannah stared at the dark, distant shoreline. It looked too far to swim, and as far as she could see, no other boats lay in between.

The boat slowed; her heart quickened. Was she too late? She pushed the rising lumps of panic back down her throat, and held out. If they came her way, she'd be out over the top and take her chances with the distance.

Nothing happened. What were they doing this time? The tension became too much. She opened the hatch again, and standing on the bunk, she peered out through the opening. By angling her body around, she was able to look past the structure and see a small portion of the cockpit. The boat's lights went off. In the grey, dawn light she could see Jed's back to her, his blond ponytail unmistakeable. He was fixing up a fishing rod.

Fishing! She withdrew her head, climbed onto the second bunk and peered out the other side. This time she saw the other man. He had his back to her, but the size of his body, the shining baldness of his head identified him. Razor: landlord of The Crow's Nest. By his own admission, he and Jed had killed Billy. They had strung him up, when they should have bagged him as they had her. He, also, appeared to be slotting a heavy-duty fishing rod into the side of the boat. Camouflage?

To the east, the sky had brightened into long yellow streaks, against which the sea looked black. The occasional wave broke into a lacy, white crest. Now a fishing boat, the launch crept forward, barely making way. Ahead, against the lighter sky, she had seen a headland projecting into the sea. Maybe, if they kept this course, that piece of land would be near enough to swim to when the time came.

On the seaward side, in the distance, Hannah could make out the navigation lights of a ship heading towards the coast. She hoped those two in the cockpit were aware that big ships also sailed these waters. She withdrew her head into the cabin and closed the hatch.

Alone on the bunk, her arms clasped around her knees she waited, her hearing finely tuned for any sound from the men, or change of tempo in the boat.

Hannah felt it before she heard it. A different vibration, one not belonging to the craft she was in. The tremor grew more noticeable until it manifested itself into the throb of heavy engines nearby. Alarmed, she peered out of the window and caught her breath. The ship she'd seen earlier was passing within a few hundred metres of her nose. It appeared enormous and much too close for comfort. Its huge, slab sided hull towered above her. The ship's name, originally painted white, now barely legible in the rusty streaks, spelled MONIKER V. The name of the ship she'd seen on the schedule in Lennie's drawer.

It passed by and as the stern came into view she could see a seaman low in the scuppers holding a bucket. He lifted it and chucked the contents overboard. Seagulls following the ship swooped with raucous cries on what looked like kitchen waste.

The ship rumbled on, heading for Botany Bay, and disappeared from her restricted view. The launch tossed around in its wake. She grabbed a handhold above her head. Although barely perceptible, Hannah felt their forward motion increase. Slowly they headed for the patch of gulls and the rapidly dispersing jetsam.

The sound of a creak from above startled her. Someone was walking on the deck. She drew back from the window. Fear knocked at her throat again. Quickly she slipped the bolt across the hatch, in case he should take it into his head to look in on her. A pair of Reeboks over grey woollen socks blotted out the light from the window. She watched and they moved on. Cautiously she peered after them. She could see bare legs, tanned and muscular. Golden hairs glinted in the low sun. Jed.

Hard against the side of the cabin, she peered through the narrow window to see what he was doing. She could see him only from the waist down. He held a boathook and, leaning out over the guardrails, he probed around as though gaffing a fish. He pulled back and lifted. On the end of his boathook, he'd picked up a small buoy, with a float and a marker flag, similar to the ones she'd seen in Betty's shed. He pulled it inboard along with metres of rope until three large plastic containers came aboard. He stooped, grabbed them all in his arms and stumbled along the deck back to the cockpit.

So, that's the way they did it. Her ears strained to catch any sound the men might make. Once they had hidden their haul away, it would be her turn next. There was no way they would let her go. The stakes were much too high.

Hannah looked towards the shore. It appeared impossibly far away. Rays of sunlight flashed off the hulls of other fishing craft nearer the beaches. Maybe one of them might see her swimming and pick her up. Failing that, a small rocky islet now lay between her and the nearest landfall. They didn't appear to be any nearer the headland she'd had her eye on. The sea was her only option. Once they came to get her, they'd throw her overboard, probably tied up in the sail-bag again. She needed no further incentive.

Before she could move, the engine note changed once more. Their speed picked up, they were heading northeast, away from the shore, away from prying eyes. Quickly, Hannah pushed back the hatch cover, stood on the bunk and hauled herself through the opening. Invisible from the cockpit and the bridge, her biggest danger would come the moment she left the boat, when they might see her jump, or hear the splash.

She lowered the hatch behind her and belly crawled towards the gunnels. Spray from the bow wave washed her face. At the guardrail she didn't hesitate, but launched herself, head first between the chromium bars and into the sea. Barely conscious of the cold, she swam away rapidly to avoid being caught in the churning propeller.

From this level, she could no longer see the shore. The sun, gaining strength by the minute, hung brightly in the sky on her left. It blinded her to everything on that side, but was good for orientation. She had to keep the sun behind her.

Waves, thankfully small, buffeted her; salt water stung her eyes and the back of her nose. She had covered a fair distance when she chanced a look over her shoulder; the launch was still heading away from her. Easing up for a moment, she trod water trying to dislodge her heavy shoes toeing and heeling them until they fell away.

The sea felt clean and cold to her skin. It washed the sweat from her body and the blood from her arms. Blood. Sharks. Hadn't they caught a giant white pointer here only last week? She gulped and swallowed water. Her head swivelled around, eyes searching for a telltale fin. With images of scissoring teeth biting at her heels, she raced again for the invisible shore.

Her fast pace tired her quickly. Forget the shark; go for a

slower energy-conserving swim. The next time she looked behind, she moaned in fright. The launch had turned and was heading back. She caught a flash of light from the deck, binoculars. An arm pointed and the launch lined up on her position. She swam for her life.

Seconds later, she turned her head. No one heard her cries as the launch came roaring in, its bow wave either side higher even than its decks. Mesmerized, she stared at approaching death. She forgot to swim. Cold water closed in over her head. She took a breath too late, gasped, choked, and sank into the blue green world of muted sound. Bubbles raced past her eyes heading for the surface.

Her chest tightened as she ran out of air. Survival instincts returned, she thrashed her arms and kicked out her legs. Her head broke through into daylight, right in the path of the oncoming launch.

Adrenaline pumped and time fragmented. In detail, she saw the mass of white water, with an array of tiny rainbow arches each side of the knife-edged bow as it sliced towards her face. She hurled herself to one side and struck out at an angle. A great shadow fell across her. From the eastward side, directly out of the glaring sun, loomed a huge, black shape. Another boat. Another threat. Nowhere to go.

Hannah floundered in her terror. Which way to turn? Jed's launch slewed away to avoid a collision with the second vessel, white water boiling in its wake. Turbulent wash picked Hannah up and swept her down the side of his launch. She raised her arms to fend it off, and as the boat bent away, she smashed into the turning corner of its stern. And her watery world turned black.

* * *

227

30

Voices called her name. Beneath her body lay a solid deck. She opened her eyes and stared into a pale blue sky criss-crossed with cables and black antennae. Two dark heads leaned over and blocked her view.

Someone rolled her on her side as she vomited seawater and lay choking, gasping for breath. Hands held her shoulders. Voices encouraged her on. Her stomach heaved, her throat burned, but she was alive.

One of the men beside her wore a diver's black wetsuit, the other a sopping wet tracksuit. She stared from one face to the other. "Mac... Doug..." never had their crinkled grins been so welcome. "What kept you?"

"She's back! How're you feeling?" Mac shouted at her as though she were deaf.

"Godawful. How did I get here?" She struggled to get up. Mac and Doug moved back. An officer in a bright white shirt, and a halo of golden hair, appeared at her side.

"Take it easy, now," she said, "you've been concussed. My name is Samantha, Sam. I double up as the first-aid officer. Where do you hurt?"

"Everywhere! No, I don't know, I just ache all over."

"Okay. Let me look at you. You've taken a bit of a battering. I'm just checking for broken bones." Sam ran her hands lightly over Hannah's legs and up her arms.

"Ouch!" Hannah looked down at her purple arms. "Ooooh! That looks messy."

"Can you move your hands?" Hannah wiggled her fingers and wrists. "Looks nasty, but doesn't look like anything's broken. Okay. We'll get you checked over by the doctor when we get back to base. You were lucky."

Not that again. "You reckon?" She sat up and put a hand to her head to ward off the dizziness. "It's all right, I'm okay." She waved the officer's hand away.

"I'll see if I can rustle up some dry clothes," Sam said.

"Come on then, let's get you below and warmed up." Both Mac and Doug helped haul her to her feet.

"It's all right, I can walk. I'm a big girl now." They ignored her protests.

Someone on the deck shouted. He held his arm out, his finger pointing. "Gottem! Heading north."

Doug let go of her, and raised his hand in a wave. "Okay Han, see you later. Mac'll look after you. We'll get the buggers." The helmsman turned the wheel and set a new course. Below their feet, the engines roared as the police launch heeled around and raced after the escaping boat.

Down below the first-aid officer gave Hannah a shirt and a pair of overlarge dungarees, and pointed forward. "There're a couple of cabins you can change in. Do you need help getting out of those wet things?"

Hannah shook her head. "If I do, I'll yell."

Shaking with the cold Hannah struggled out of her wet clothes and into the dry in the quickest possible time. When she returned to the main cabin, she saw Mac had changed too, and had a thermal blanket around his shoulders. Sam draped another over hers.

"Here you are, wrap that around you. Hot drinks coming up."

Hannah slumped onto a bunk and drew her legs in under her. She pulled the blanket tightly under her chin and tried to take an inventory of how she truly felt. Her arms hurt like hell; they had taken the brunt of her collision with Jed's boat. Her breathing felt ragged; her whole body shook as though wired, but other than that, she was all in one piece.

Sam offered her a cup of coffee that she'd poured from a

flask "Can you hold this?" she asked, looking doubtful. Mac's hand shot out, he took it and sat on the bunk beside Hannah.

"Come on, drink this. You need to get warm."

The smell of the coffee reached Hannah, and the empty folds of her stomach growled in anticipation. Mac tested the coffee for temperature then put the cup to her lips.

"Let me do it. Mm, nectar." Sam waited to see how Hannah was managing, then handed Mac a cup for himself. Sam left them to it and Hannah glanced around, her eyes taking in the very expensive, state-of-the-art police launch.

"How did you get involved?" she asked Mac.

"We'd been looking for you for hours. When the water police became involved, Doug called me out to identify Jed's boat. God, you were lucky the wash threw you away from the propeller not into it."

Hannah's thermal blanket was doing its job and her shivers decreased. "Yes, but how did the police know I was in Jed's boat?"

"Steele had learnt about the rendezvous and the imminent pick-up of a drugs haul. They wanted to witness the pick-up, and arrest those responsible while they still had the evidence on board. There was an outside chance you were on it, according to Lennie. They tailed Jed's boat down the river in the dark, running without lights. They stayed a fair distance away and used night glasses to watch. Someone said the boat caught a rope or something around her screw. One of the blokes had to go overboard to cut it away."

Hannah nodded. The memory of what she was doing at the time still raw.

"But once the sun came up, how come they didn't see you?"

"We blended into the shadow of the shoreline. When it got light enough, we stayed on his sunward side."

"It worked. You frightened the daylights out of me when you appeared out of the sun!"

"I spotted you going over the side. Then just this head bobbing in the water. The two guys hadn't seen you go at that stage. They were still heading away at a rate of knots. Doug got the Zodiac ready and was about to go and pick you up when we saw their boat turn back. They were still nearer to you than we were. So we headed straight at him and tried to intercept him. He ignored us and only turned away at the last second."

"Well, by then it was too late to use the Zodiac, me and Doug, we dived in together."

A shout rang out from the bridge. "She's going about. Heading west. Making for South Coogee!"

"Here comes the cavalry!" Raucous laughter followed this announcement as the police launch changed direction.

"What's going on?" Hannah asked Sam, who had looked in on them.

"Customs have joined the chase. They're heading the perps off, turning them inshore."

Mac waved his empty cup at Sam "Thanks, Sam. Gotta see this. Thanks." He turned and climbed the steps out of the companionway. Hannah followed Mac up the steps and peered around under his arm. He moved to let her out. The air struck chill after the warm cabin. Mac gently curled an arm around her.

They were much closer to the shore than Hannah had seen before. The headland she'd had her eye on, when on Jed's boat, was far away to her left, a few fishing boats dotted the seascape, and she could see waves breaking along the distant beaches and around the rocky islet in the bay. Jed's boat, in a spray of white water, roared in full flight ahead of them. The shivers returned and wracked her body. She cuddled into Mac for warmth. He squeezed her gently until she winced from her bruises.

"You ought to go back in."

"No. I want to see."

Coming from the southeast, the police launch gained on the runaway boat. From the north the customs launch, bow wave creaming each side, formed the second side of the pincer. Voices from the bridge relayed their relative position on the radio. Overhead, a police helicopter, blades whacking the air, homed in on the scene.

The officers watched, their faces growing grave with concern, as both the police and customs converged on Jed's powerful motor launch. Their earlier hilarity suspended as the fleeing boat headed towards the small rocky island.

"They're going to hit!" The man on the bow shouted. At the last possible moment, two figures leapt away from the boat. One each side, seconds before it crashed head-on into rock and burst into flames. A secondary explosion, as the gas bottle blew, forced fragments of boat high into the air and dispersed them in a wide margin around the rocky sea. A sheet of fire engulfed the two bobbing heads in the water.

The police launch juddered into reverse gear and slowed its approach. Doug and his co-diver Rusty lowered the inflatable and scrambled aboard. The fire on the sea withdrew, and concentrated on the wrecked vessel burning on the tiny islet. Rusty eased the Zodiac around the oily water to the nearest head. Doug grabbed hold of the man, and pulled him to the side. Between them, they heaved the body into the boat, and then moved away through the debris to the next man.

As the Zodiac returned to the launch a thumbs-up signal from Doug told them the men were still alive. Hands leaned over the side to help lift them aboard and place them in canvas cradles. Hannah, shaking with shock, as well as cold, watched as Sam covered the men with blankets. Jed's blond hair had vanished, scorched from his head, his face blackened, raw and bleeding. Razor in similar condition, moaned in pain as they carried him below.

Doug stamped his feet on the deck. "Shit, shit, shit! That's the evidence gone up in flames," he roared at Mac. "After all that bloody work!"

Hannah held her blanket close barely able to stop the chatter of her teeth. "Doug, stop, listen. They could've dropped it overboard before they jumped. If it's still in its container, it could survive the fire under water. Look for a small red buoy with a flag on top. The stuff's in plastic bottles on the end of the rope. Maybe they intended to swim for the beach, and come back for it later."

Doug relayed the message to the man on the radio. He turned back to Hannah. "Thanks Han. We've informed Customs. They'll finish up here. We're heading for base to get those two hospitalised for their burns."

*

The police launch sped up the river heading for home. Hannah sat on the top step of the companionway, on the inside, where she was sheltered from the wind. She could see Mac, Rusty and Doug grouped in the cockpit. Sam, in her role as first-aid officer had suggested she take a bunk and rest awhile.

"Thanks, but I'd rather stay here. I want to be part of whatever is going on, plenty of time to sleep later." Sam nodded, left Hannah and disappeared forward to monitor the two wounded men.

Hannah looked out on the golden day; the pale blue sky, the dark water; the sparkling whiteness of their bow wave; all the bright colours of the river coming to life, its ferryboats, water taxis and the early starts of sailing holidaymakers. Sated with a sense of well being and unable to take in any more, she clasped her head with both hands to stop it from bursting.

It took a conscious effort to pull her mind back to sensibility. She glanced around the launch. Mac, Doug and Rusty were still in the same spot, the rest of the crew were busy about their business. No one was taking any notice of her. She looked below for signs of Sam. She saw her come away from Jed's area and move forward, presumably to check on Razor.

Quietly, Hannah backed down the steps and made her way forward to the place where Jed lay. She entered the tiny cabin and looked down on his blackened face, his arms and upper body wrapped in a sheet. His bare feet protruded from the blanket. With no one there to guard him, they'd cuffed his unburned ankles. He must have sensed her presence, for he opened his eyes. Slits that glittered in red flesh; the lashes had gone, leaving his eyes naked and apprehensive as he recognised his visitor.

Here lay one of the perpetrators who had caused her so much grief over the last five months. Where was the hatred she ought to feel? The magnitude of it all suddenly eluded her. Simon's death was not down to them. She'd come through everything they'd thrown at her, but he, the once good-looking Jed, would bear the scars of his work for the rest of his life. Revenge had never been in her mind, only justice. All she wanted now was to hear him admit his guilt.

"I want some answers," she said.

"Why would I talk to you?"

"I could say, because I'll twist your burnt ear off, if you don't."

"But you wouldn't, would you?" He sounded sure. She was not so sure.

"Why did you kill Vicky?"

Jed moved to shrug his shoulders, but winced instead. He worked his mouth around as though lubricating his tongue in order to speak again. "She asked for it. All promises – no pay-off."

"So, you raped and killed her?"

"Billy was last on top. He killed her, not me!"

Hannah stared down at him, an empty feeling in her gut. "What do you mean, *last on top*? Billy *raped* her?" her voice louder than she intended.

"Yeah. He saw me. Had to give him a go. Told him, make a real man of him. Always wanted that, Billy did, to be a real man." He stopped as though gathering more strength. "She was gonna scream, had to shut her up. But she was still with it when I finished with her."

His white uneven teeth gleamed in his black, oil-fired face. Even through his pain, she could see he was enjoying the memory. He twisted his burnt lips in a parody of a smile.

"After Billy, she didn't move. Told him he'd killed her. Thought that'd keep him quiet. Mighta done too if you hadn't interfered."

Hannah felt a pain under her heart. Billy's conscience had the better of him. He wanted to talk. She could see it now. Razor had understood Billy's loose babblings, and had taken him into his back room. His was the phone call that took Jed away from the sailing club's party night, and together they had dealt with Billy. Jed's warped sense of humour had been the cause of Billy hanging from the yardarm like his grandfather, instead of Razor's preferred method of disposal at sea, the fate they had intended for her.

Jed was in Razor's pay over the drug smuggling. If the law caught up with Jed over the murder of Vicky, who knew what other avenues the investigations would have opened. In protecting Jed, Razor was protecting his own. Just like Morgan, who, in burying Vicky thought he was protecting his nephew. How Jed must have laughed up his sleeve when he realised what Morgan Draper had done.

She remained silent for a long moment, hearing his laboured breathing above the rush of sea against the hull.

"What had I done to you and that animal that raped me? Had I asked for it, too?"

"You got nothing on me for that one." His face twisted into a leer.

"On the contrary, you pissed your DNA all over me. It's safely on the database waiting for a match. Once they've finished processing the Draper's Wharf samples, they'll have you."

"Yeah? Why the big deal? It was only a game!"

Before her clenched fist could smash into his raw, bleeding face, Hannah turned her back on Jed and stumbled out of the stifling cabin, her gorge rising.

Only a game!

* * *

Epilogue

The fishing smack rested snugly in her cradle like a dowager duchess in a rocking chair. The black hull looked patchy where Mac had sanded the paint off, but to Hannah she looked solid and workmanlike. "It's beautiful, Mac. I didn't imagine anything as big as this," she said.

"She needs a complete re-paint, of course. So far, I've gutted and cleaned it out. I'm now in the process of rebuilding the inside to my own specifications. You want to see?" His dark eyes, fired with enthusiasm, delighted her.

"Love to."

Mac pulled at a rope, eased a ladder down, and climbed it. Hannah followed and stood in the cockpit, looking around. He pulled the tarp away from the top of the cabin.

"This little lady's going to change my life. Get me out of the pub and back into the water," he said. "It's still messy inside, but at least it's under construction now." He pointed out what he had done and what he was going to do.

Hannah nodded approval. "All timber, I like it. Has more character than the modern fibreglass boats, like..." had it only been two days since she'd leapt off Jed's boat?

They'd kept her in hospital overnight for observation. Apparently, Sam had found her collapsed on the floor in the heads her arms around the toilet bowl. Although she couldn't remember how she'd got there, she did remember every word Jed had spoken and still shivered at his callous words.

She'd had a debriefing with Doug when he collected her

from the hospital. He was pleased with the outcome. Customs had found the evidence just as she'd said. The villains had dropped it overboard before crashing their boat. Their intention had been to swim ashore and leg it away from the pursuing launches. They hadn't planned on the gas bottles exploding. Lennie had turned super-grass. He denied any part in killing Vicky. Reckons that he and Jed had planned to teach her a lesson, find out who the new man was, that's all. Jed went over the top. Zack now released, was holed up in The Harbour Lights with a marriage to mend. Izzy Foster who had only recently joined Razor's gang, intended to use his service station as a collection and distribution point for certain reps he knew. So far, they had no evidence to tie Morgan Draper either to the disposal of Vicky's body, or the drug scene. But once Jed and Razor were well enough for interrogation, who knows what might come out.

"I suppose you'll be off back to the city now, back to the cop shop," Mac's voice broke into her reverie. He said it without rancour. She looked up at him.

"Forgiven me?"

"Nothing to forgive. I'm the drongo. I should've realised just listening to you and Doug talking. I just hope this isn't the last we'll see of you."

She heard a catch in his voice. "Next weekend I'm going to see my mum. I've some catching up to do there. But, after that, yes, I'd like to keep in touch."

"Doug says your boss is happy enough with the result even though it didn't go to plan." Mac put an arm around her shoulders. He pulled her close, very gently, aware her bruises hadn't yet healed. His lips felt warm as they met hers. She moulded her body against his and felt him stir. She savoured the moment, wanting to parcel it up and take it home. They ran out of breath and broke apart in laughter.

He was reluctant to let her go. "Hey, what's this?"

Hannah fingered the patch on her arm "Insurance. Trapped in Jed's forecabin, I discovered that the world was a great a

237

place to live, and I wasn't ready to leave it yet. I promised my dad once more, that if ever I got out of it, I'd never touch another smoke as long as I lived. And this is going to help me do it."

She took Mac's hand back in hers, held it, and turned her attention back to his boat. She nodded towards half built living quarters. "How many will she sleep?"

"Eight, that'll mean after me and my certificated diver I can, theoretically, take six paying passengers out at any one time. More than enough."

"So, when do you plan to start?"

"Probably in six months or so, say at the beginning of the summer season."

"You have to cater for all those people? What are going do, take Mrs Bates along?"

"You're joking!" He looked at her with a glint in his eye. "Are you angling for another job by any chance?"

She smiled. "Who knows, in six months time I might be fed up with city life and longing for the wide-open spaces and the roaring seas once more. Why, you offering me another job?"

"It'll be hard graft and little money."

She raised her eyebrows.

"Living on the boat. Cramped quarters, wet clothes, smell of rubber, stinky feet, long, boring hours sitting on deck with me waiting for the divers to come back ..."

"Sounds wonderful."

The End

Acknowledgements

My thanks go to crime writer Felicity Young, Dr. Patricia O'Neill, and Christine Nagel from the writing group for their continued support. To my on-line reviewers in the Internet Writing Workshop, all who over the years have helped to hone my work.

Thanks also to my husband, Bill, for putting up with late dinners and distracted airs when I'm deep in the middle of a plot. Special thanks to Pauline Woolley for the times she spent for her early morning/evening dashes off on her bicycle to capture the moon for the front cover photograph.

~

Other books by Carole Sutton
Ferryman

Enjoy a roller coaster ride. Angela goes missing and Steven, on flawed evidence, is jailed for manslaughter. When two years later her body turns up only one week dead, DI Grimstone has to re-evaluate his handling of the case. Steven Pengelly is released, and teams up with Veryan, a woman whose sister is also missing. Determined to find the truth, Steven and DI Grimstone's parallel investigations converge towards the same destination until the old enemies are forced to work together in an explosive finale.

Published by YouWriteOn.com

December 2008

Todd Fonseca – Minneapolis - from Goodreads TMBOA says:

Ferryman pulses with action, intrigue, and mystery ... I found myself turning the pages at a rapid pace ... Ferryman is one of this years favorites for me.

Barbara Galvin – Toughcritic - San Francisco

The sailing scenes are utterly convincing; the characters interesting company

Dee Marie – author of Sons of Avalon

If you are a lover of murder mysteries, sailing, and superb suspenseful storytelling ... Ferryman is a must-read!

And the Devil Laughed

And the Devil Laughed